PRAISE FOR CARISSA ANN LYNCH

"Wickedly fun and highly addictive! Lynch delivers a thrilling locked-room mystery, loaded with gloomy atmosphere, scandalous characters, and twists you won't see coming. *The Traitors* is a delicious read with all the elements of a perfect whodunit!"

—Jeneva Rose, #1 *New York Times* bestselling author of *The Perfect Marriage*

"Carissa Lynch's *My Sister Is Missing* is the best kind of thriller. It peels back the layers of our everyday world and shows us the frightening truth beneath the surface. This is an unnerving, creepy, hair-raising novel, one that will have readers sleeping with one eye open and carefully watching their backs."

—David Bell, *New York Times* bestselling author of *Layover*

"*Like, Follow, Kill* is absolutely chilling, as much a journey through the maze of a tortured mind as it is down dark and lonely roads. One word of advice when reading this book—trust no one."

—Wendy Heard, author of *Hunting Annabelle* and host of the *Unlikeable Female Characters* podcast

"This author is one whose words seem to flow so effortlessly. I never had any trouble focusing, which is saying a lot. I loved this book!"

—Kiersten Modglin, million-copy bestselling author of *The Arrangement*

"Disturbing, chilling, and featuring a damaged, obsessed heroine, *Like, Follow, Kill* delves into the darkest side of social media and its influence on vulnerable people. It was hard to step away from this fast-paced read because I was desperate to uncover all the twists and turns, which lead to a shocking ending."

—Samantha M. Bailey, #1 international bestselling author of *Woman on the Edge*

"A gripping mystery . . . the tension builds to a nerve-racking ending."

—Sue Fortin, #1 bestselling author of *The Girl Who Lied*

"Lynch explores themes of revenge, classism, and domestic violence. Readers will not see the twists coming in this thriller perfect for fans of Ruth Ware, Lucy Foley, and Shari Lapena."

—*Booklist*

DEAD GIRLS TELL NO TALES

OTHER TITLES BY CARISSA ANN LYNCH

Stand-Alones

My Sister Is Missing

Without a Trace

Like, Follow, Kill

The One Night Stand

She Lied She Died

Whisper Island

The Secrets of Cedar Farm

The Bachelorette Party

The Summer She Disappeared

The Traitors

This Is Not About Love

Searching For Sullivan

Series

Flocksdale Files

Have You Seen This Girl

House of the Lost Girls

Carnival of Dead Girls

Horror High Series

Cheerleading Can Be Murder

Cutting Up The Competition

Killer Moves

Short Stories

"Becoming a Cat Person" (Chicken Soup for the Soul: What I Learned from My Cat)

"Fear of Boys" (Fear of Clowns: A Horror Anthology)

"Loves Me Not" (Twist Me: A Dark Romance Anthology)

"Homecoming" (Shattered Time: An Anthology)

"Caller Number Nine" (Things Only the Darkness Knows: An Anthology)

"Ricochet" (13: An Anthology of Horror and Dark Fiction)

"See You on the Flip Side" (13 Déjà Vu: An Anthology of Horror and Dark Fiction)

DEAD GIRLS TELL NO TALES

CARISSA ANN LYNCH

THOMAS & MERCER

Published by Thomas & Mercer, Seattle

www.apub.com

EU product safety contact:
Amazon Media EU S. à r.l.
38, avenue John F. Kennedy, L-1855 Luxembourg
amazonpublishing-gpsr@amazon.com

ISBN-13: 9781662538292 (paperback)
ISBN-13: 9781662538308 (digital)

Cover design by Emily Mahar
Cover image: © Igor Ustynskyy / Getty

Printed in the United States of America

This book is dedicated to all the lonely girls with their heads up in the clouds and to the other versions of this story that died a slow and painful death.

All the world's a stage,
And all the men and women, merely players;
They have their exits and their entrances,
And one man in his time plays many parts,
His acts being seven ages. At first the infant,
Mewling and puking in the nurse's arms;
Then the whining schoolboy with his satchel
And shining morning face, creeping like snail
Unwillingly to school. And then the lover,
Sighing like furnace, with a woeful ballad
Made to his mistress' eyebrow. Then a soldier,
Full of strange oaths and bearded like the pard,
Jealous in honour, sudden and quick in quarrel,
Seeking the bubble reputation
Even in the cannon's mouth. And then the justice,
In fair round belly with good capon lined,
With eyes severe and beard of formal cut,
Full of wise saws and modern instances;
And so he plays his part. The sixth age shifts
Into the lean and slippered pantaloon,
With spectacles on nose and pouch on side,
His youthful hose, well saved, a world too wide
For his shrunk shank, and his big manly voice,
Turning again toward childish treble, pipes
And whistles in his sound. Last scene of all,
That ends this strange eventful history,
Is second childishness and mere oblivion,
Sans teeth, sans eyes, sans taste, sans everything.
—*As You Like It*, Act II, Scene VII. Written by
William Shakespeare, spoken by Jacques

Act One

She's Out of This World

Chapter One

I wake up in a town called Star Creek.

I wake up in a forest called Fawn.

I go to sleep on a U-boat, seeking asylum from some yet-to-be-named war.

Then I wake up in the future, fighting a new brand of extraterrestrials.

I administer war paint; pure bravery is my weapon of choice.

I ride on the back of a prehistoric whale, clutching its rubbery skin, holding on by my teeth and nails.

Places, towns, worlds . . . that exist only on paper. They were built from the ground up, engineered by the mind. Cultivated by their own characters.

This all sounds silly, I know. But this is my life—a made-up town on Monday. A haunted village on Tuesday. By Friday, I'm on Narcel, a dry planet unable to sustain human life—except for mine, of course.

The life of a writer . . . It's strange, to say the least. It's a life of boredom, but for someone who hasn't left the house in days, I consider myself well traveled.

That *was* my life, I should say. When I used to write science fiction and when I used to do it well.

I used to wake up in Bangladesh—not the real Bangladesh, but the better, made-up version. My characters were freedom fighters, changing all that was wrong with the world.

But now my mornings are earthly, and painfully mundane. It's Wednesday.

Wednesdays equal dinner with my overly critical mother.

"You look like shit," she tells me. Compared to her, with her freshly cut bleached-blond bob and ironed slacks, I probably do—all greasy, unwashed black hair and loose-fitting pajama pants.

"I'm writing a book on LSD, and I figured I should experiment. Haven't slept for weeks . . ."

Her lips part, then curl up on the ends. She narrows her eyes, and one side of her jaw flexes. I study the features so I can write about them later—a pained look, with a tinge of anger and a whole lot of disappointment.

Mental note: This is what disapproval looks like.

"Mom, I'm kidding. Well, not about the sleeping part. Only the LSD . . . Nobody takes that drug anymore."

"I swear, Adrianna . . . I think you enjoy causing people concern. You should get a job with normal hours, one that allows you to sleep at night and work during the day. To earn some money." My mother points her pitchfork at me. It's loaded with bloodred noodles, and I can't help thinking about a new book creature I could create, using her as inspiration.

A normal job . . .

I haven't had one of those in a while, and nothing has ever sounded so terrible.

I fill my mouth with bloody noodles, nodding along as she mentions a few places in town that she knows are hiring. I've already submitted more than two dozen job applications on Indeed, but I don't bother sharing. What's the point? No one is interested in hiring a college dropout. Either I'm underqualified because I didn't graduate or the mention of college on my résumé makes them think I'm unwilling to flip burgers and scrub pans.

I'm tired of stressing over jobs—more specifically, my failure to find one. So I keep chewing and nodding, all the while pretending to listen but feeling a general sense of numbness that has become commonplace for Wednesday-night dinners with Mom.

I've learned that nodding can save me from a whole lot of lectures.

Mental note: This is what placating feels like.

After I escape the sci-fi-horror movie loosely titled *My Mother*, I return to my apartment and collapse into bed. Out of sheer habit, I sign into Facebook.

Impulsively, I switch my status to "grieving" and write: Some of my friends died.

I'll leave it at that—just enough to stay vague while keeping their interest piqued.

The people on my friends list are nice and well intentioned. I imagine them lining my post with strings of question marks, well-wishes, thoughts, and prayers. If they only knew the truth . . . that I'm grieving the deaths of my imaginary characters. The death of my career.

In a way, it feels like the death of *me*—a version of me that I actually sort of liked.

My characters are real, but they're also not real.

Lately, I've started to feel like they're all dead—like need-to-have-a-funeral-service type of dead. I haven't been able to write in months. I miss the colony I started building on Planet Narcel. It's probably been nuked by its rival, Darcy, by now.

I hit the backspace key, remove the dopey "grieving" emoji, cancel the post, and sign out of Facebook. I don't want to alarm anyone by making them think I'm unstable or unhinged or that, God forbid, someone actually died. Plus, if I posted something like that, my mother would never let me hear the end of it.

Chapter Two

"Read the smallest line you can make out," the optometrist tells me.

I squint through the space-goggle machine that covers my eyes and nose. These goggles are cooler than the ones I wear on Planet Narcel.

"*E*," I mutter, disgusted.

The doctor makes a *tsk-tsk* sound, then writes me a prescription for glasses.

"Wear these all the time." His voice has a gravelly sound to it, his mouth set in a straight line. I study his features so I can write about them later. This is what you call a *grave expression.*

And *this* is just another mental note, for when I get back to writing.

If I get back to writing.

The thick black glasses leave chafe marks on the bridge of my nose, but I leave them on, heeding the doctor's advice, and spend the entire drive home *thinking* about writing.

But even with my newfound eyes, my mind turns into a blank slate as soon as I get home and plant myself in front of my computer. *Tabula rasa.*

Blank slates used to be a good thing. A breeding ground of sorts; a place where anything could happen. Where idea babies were born . . .

But now the blankness breeds more blankness, and I sit in the dark, scrolling through more job listings. The spaghetti monster was right all along. I need a job. Not only for the money, but also for the inspiration.

Inspiration. Devastation. Anything to cling to . . .

There was a time when I used to feel proud of my writing accomplishments. Ten published novels amounted to an entire bookshelf lined with extra copies of each book, including special and foreign editions. In the beginning of my career, there were even a few awards . . . but now those shiny glass plaques stay covered in dust. Forgotten—just like the author who wrote them.

It's not that no one will publish my stories . . . in fact, I'm still under contract for two more books. The problem isn't them; it's me. They can't publish my stories if I don't write them. And if they don't publish my nonexistent stories, then I can't get paid. Worse than not paid—I'll have to pay back the advance money they gave me. The same money I already used to pay up front for a year's worth of rent . . .

Chapter Three

I'm not in Bali or a creepy circus in Loon. Planet Narcel is a dusty field of nothing, courtesy of Planet Darcy—I don't know this for certain, but I have a hunch that I'm right.

The day begins with a text from my mother—Maybe you should get a writing coach. Or what about returning to college?

College. I can't believe she would even *go* there. She knows I hate it when she brings it up.

It's been six years since I pulled out of campus parking and officially "dropped out" of college. My mother thinks the decision was voluntary, and in a way, it sort of was. I volunteered not to follow through on the performance-improvement plan they created and demanded I complete. I *chose* to let them discharge me.

I thought I didn't need it then, that pointless degree. Who needs a degree when you're writing every day and your books are selling? Not me.

Not me.

If I say it enough, maybe I'll start to believe it.

◆ ◆ ◆

The nut-and-fudge shoppe on Monroe Street—a real street, by the way—is hiring cashiers and "nut scoopers." I could make a joke here, but why bother? I have three-quarters of a college degree under my belt and ten published novels that no one reads anymore, and even if they did, that wouldn't impress the owner of a nut-and-fudge shoppe (yes, she spells it the fancy, archaic way), whose name is ironically Candy.

Candy found my résumé on Indeed. She also has the puffiest lips I've ever seen, possibly created by lip injections, and when writers talk about chiseled cheeks, she's the prototype. You could open a can of corn with one of her cheekbones. At least she has a "marketable skill," unlike yours truly.

But it turns out Candy is my new best friend. She offers me minimum wage but agrees to pay me "under the table."

"Works for me," I tell her. Anything to dick over Uncle Sam really gives me a boner.

"You're older than most of the girls I hire," she warns.

I open my mouth to tell her that I'm not even thirty-five yet, but then I remember I'm thirty-eight. Thirty-eight and unemployed. Without useful, cutting-edge cheekbones.

I need this job, and I need her to like me.

"Thank you for this opportunity. When do I start?"

She tosses me a dirty apron that has certainly seen better days and tells me that I start tomorrow.

Every square inch of the shoppe is loaded with cases of candy, fudge, and—of course—nuts. The scoops in the trays are huge, bigger than my head. As I look around the old-timey store, I suddenly feel inspired by the dusty old smell of nuts and the alien-like features of my new boss's face. She and the spaghetti monster would be perfect rivals.

I leave the shoppe before Candy can change her mind, eager to get back to my shitty apartment and try to write a few lines.

Minimum wage sucks but so does being a freelance writer who can't write anything good these days. At least I won't have to make up lies to earn money from Candy. I'll show up to work at the shoppe, plaster a smile on my face, and collect my illegal cash at the end of the week.

At home, I kick off my shoes and head for the bedroom. The sweet and salty smell of the shoppe fills my every thought; I need to write about it.

I wait for the computer to load, tapping my chewed-up, now slightly bleeding nails on the desk. A blank screen pops up.

My hands hover over the keyboard as I stare at the bright white page. I'm pumped, electricity ready to explode from my fingertips . . . *inspired inspired inspired . . .*

Wasn't I feeling inspired?

But once again, I'm shooting blanks.

Chapter Four

My waterbed used to feel like the stormy black waters of the Whispering Sea, but now it just feels like an outdated waterbed.

Freshly showered and draped in my new apron with my hair in a don't-care bun, I can almost pretend that this isn't me. I'm not a middle-aged cashier who got kicked out of college and wrote a bunch of shitty novels. No, I'm a beguiler, masquerading as an old-timey shopgirl. My real purpose in life is to gather intel from my top-secret customers, wearing a dirty old apron and a big smile on my face all the while. Saving the world, one scoop at a time.

After that moment of inspiration passes, I head to work, reporting in for my first day at Candy's. I'm five minutes early.

I don't see Candy, but there's a young girl working at the counter, and she lifts her head at me in some youthful display of acknowledgment. *See? You exist, Adrianna McMahon. It doesn't feel like it, but you do—someone actually sees you today.*

The girl is wearing an apron that's cleaner than mine, and it looks like she knows what's she doing. Have I already been replaced? Is it legal to fire someone before they even start? But then again, maybe so, since I'm a ghost on paper, collecting pennies directly from Candy herself and leaving no paper trail.

See? I really am like a shopgirl-spy.

I wander over to the cases of fudge. Fingerprints are smeared on the glass.

The girl motions for me to come around past the register, through a swinging wooden door that separates the customers from the help. She leads me to the backside of the display cases, where you can access the food. My stomach rumbles noisily.

"Hi, I'm Adrianna. I'm new here," I say, following her to a row of shelves in the corner that house long plastic containers of—shockingly—more nuts.

"I'm Rebel," she says, popping gum in her mouth. She looks like a twelve-year-old, but I know she must be at least sixteen if she's working here. After all, that's the law in this state. But, then again, so is paying your taxes.

"I'm seventeen," she adds, putting an end to the mystery.

She scrunches up her nose at my apron and holds up one finger. Then she gets down on the floor by one end of the fudge display, reaches into a small wooden cabinet that's practically hidden underneath the case, and pulls out a fresh, clean white one.

"Thank you." I switch out my apron with the new one and follow her around the shoppe.

"There's the cash register," Rebel says dully. "There's the sink for washing scoops and the scales for weighing orders. There's a price guide over there"—she points—"so you don't forget the price of things. Oh, and never go in the kitchen." She motions at a big silver door on the back wall. It's closed and appears to have a lock on it.

"We sell the treats; we don't make them. That's Candy's job, okay? And that's where she works. Back there, alone. I'm sure she probably told you this already. That's where she does her magic." Rebel pauses and rolls her eyes. "She's exactly like Willy Wonka—doesn't let people inside. Got it?"

I fight the urge to correct her. He *did* let them in, eventually. Right before he tricked them to their gruesome deaths, with the exception of one golden child.

Rebel's watching me now, a curious expression on her face. Her lips are pursed, creating the shape of a tiny little Christmas bow. Her hair is white blond and greasy, and it doesn't take long to realize she smells a little too. Not like a sweaty-teen-spirit sort of smell, but the needs-a-bath-really-bad variety of odors.

My lesson isn't over yet. Rebel walks me through the steps for measuring and bagging the merchandise, and then she teaches me how to tie one of Candy's signature pink-and-black bows around the top of each bag.

I listen and nod along, all the while holding my breath.

Despite the body odor, Rebel is a pretty girl. She has long curly lashes and a few freckles. Her teeth are berry blue, courtesy of the raspberry slushie she keeps sucking on behind the register.

For the next six hours, I wipe counters, tie bags, and scoop nuts for customers. I ruin a dozen or so bows and stand behind Rebel (still holding my breath) so I can learn how to run the cash register.

Business at the shoppe is slow but steady, customers trickling in a few times per hour. Candy never makes an appearance.

Just when it's time for my shift to end, Rebel turns to me abruptly and says, "You're that writer, aren't ya." Just like that . . . like she doesn't even need an answer.

I mutter something ridiculously childish like, "I don't know who you're talking about . . ." Then I say my goodbyes for the day and run for the door.

Chapter Five

The next morning, someone knocks so hard on the door of my first-floor apartment that I worry the building's on fire.

When I look through the peephole, I'm mortified. It's Rebel, the stinky girl from work.

"I need to ask a favor," she says as soon as I open the door. It's pretty sad when the first thought I have is *Does she want to use my shower? Or borrow some deodorant before work?*

Despite my better judgment, I let her inside my apartment.

"What can I do for you?" What I really mean is *Why the hell is she in my apartment? And how does she know where I live?*

"I rode my bike here," Rebel says, which doesn't answer my real or imagined questions. She points toward the side of my apartment building.

Rebel plops down on my shabby, worn pleather sofa, and it's only now that I notice what's in her hands—a thick spiral notebook with a purple cover.

Somehow, I already know what's coming.

She presses the notebook to her chest and looks around my living room nervously.

I wait for her to explain.

Finally, she says, "I have a writing project for school. Well, that's not true. It's not a required assignment . . . It's a contest." She blurts out the words as fast as she can, like they're poison pellets in her mouth. "There's money involved. Nearly two hundred dollars."

I think she's trying to impress me. Frankly, $200 is pretty impressive these days.

"That sounds fun, Rebel. I'm not sure how I can help, though."

"Well, I've read your books. Not all of them. Some aren't very good. Wait, that was rude. Sorry." Rebel tucks her hair behind her ears, again and again. It seems like a nervous tic.

"Anyway," she continues, "I was thinking that if you could just help me with the contest, then I could split the prize money with you."

"Oh." The sofa is too small for both of us, so I half sit, half lean on the water-stained coffee table beside it. Letting down a child will probably feel awkward, and frankly it's a new experience for me. I didn't grow up with siblings, so there aren't any chubby-faced nieces or nephews to practice on when it comes to dishing out disappointment.

I feel bad, but there's no way I'm helping this kid with her writing. I can't even help myself these days, with writing or anything else.

"Writing is less of a skill, and more like a feeling . . . Maybe what you're thinking of is an editor. I'm not very good at editing stuff. There are people you can pay to help you. Or there are beta readers . . ."

Rebel pouts, staring down at the floor. Her white-blond hair slips over her face like a sad, creepy curtain, and I'm filled with guilt.

I struggle to come up with the right words, but then my voice turns serious. I've turned into the optometrist, feigning his "grave expression."

"Listen, Rebel. It's important to separate facts from fiction. You don't want to get stuck in a fantasy world . . . because when you return, real life is the pits. Are you sure you want to be a writer? It's not all that great, sometimes . . ."

Rebel peeks at me through the hair curtain and grins. "You're pretty weird, you know that?"

I nod. Yes, I do know that.

"I never said I wanted to be a writer anyway, just that I have a story to tell. Don't you think there's a difference?" she rambles. "I need a little help with it, and I want to win this contest. There's a lot at stake here, and I could use your guidance. You can be, like, my writing teacher . . ."

"I see." I want to tell her no again, but I can't bring myself to do it. I'm not an editor or a teacher. I'm not even a decent low-wage nut-scooper. But I am familiar (many mental notes) with what desperation looks like. And Rebel stinks of it—quite literally.

So . . . that's how it starts. I agree to teach someone how to be a better version of me, which seems like a pretty doable task considering my current trajectory.

"Okay. Leave it here and I'll take a look." I reach for the notebook in her hands, but Rebel springs to her feet and heads for the door, still gripping the pages.

"Not yet. I'll let you know when it's ready," she says mysteriously. "I'll be back tomorrow."

It sounds less like a request and more like a warning. I don't want to see anyone tomorrow; it's my day off.

But she's gone before I can say no.

Chapter Six

"Is wearing pajamas part of the writing process?" Rebel asks on our third day of "writing."

"These are leggings. Don't be an asshole."

Rebel is sitting at my kitchen table, legs twisty and bent, like a human pretzel. She has a knack for chewing the shit out of pencil erasers. Another one of her weird tics.

Loose pages are scattered all over the table. Rebel pushes them aside and yawns. She's bored, and she's not the only one.

The writing prompts I downloaded from the internet are cringy and mostly unhelpful. I googled *writing exercises for beginners* and printed off the first few activities I could find.

What I'd really like to do is talk about Rebel's pages, but that would involve her actually forking over that notebook of hers.

This whole thing seems like a big mistake. Yet I've enjoyed Rebel's company over the past few days, which is an embarrassing truth to admit. Even more embarrassing is the fact that I like feeling smart and competent as I talk about writing. She doesn't know that I'm a college dropout or that I've lost what little writing spark I had to begin with. She doesn't know that most people in my life—and there are too few to warrant counting—consider me to be irresponsible and lazy. She doesn't know that if I don't start writing soon, I'll not only lose my apartment; I'll also owe a lot of money for not following through on my book contract.

But it's starting to seem redundant, all of it. Like a worn-out plot device. What is she even doing here, really?

Worst of all, we haven't made any real progress, and she still isn't ready to show me what she's working on. How can I help with a story if I don't even know what it's about?

We kicked off day one of our "writing project" with a series of questions: What do you like to read? What have you written? What topics interest you? What are you passionate about? Why do you feel like you're the right person to tell this story? (Please insert: What the fuck is the story about?)

Rebel seems more interested in asking about my writing process and ragging on my pajama pants than she does actually discussing herself or the story she wants to write. The deadline for the contest is coming up (insert: When the fuck is it due, Rebel?), and I'm not even sure if there's a theme for it.

I'm starting to wonder if the contest is as real as my make-believe book friends, and if the notebook she's carrying is actually filled with blank pages.

"Did you change your name when you published your first story?" Rebel asks. More questions. She is, apparently, an endless series of questions jumbled together in the form of a girl.

"No. Adrianna McMahon is my real name. What about you? Rebel is a cool first name. There must be a story behind that."

"I don't want to tell the story of my name, mostly because there isn't one." Rebel lifts her arms over her head and arches her back, stretching out like a cat.

She's a nervous, restless girl, which reminds me of myself.

Unable to sit still in a world where there's nowhere to go.

Memories of doctor visits as a child flood my brain, and I'm flipping through pages of my young life like it's a photo album—my mother, Sarah (a.k.a.: Spaghetti Monster), asking the doctor to prescribe Ritalin; the doctor finally relenting; me flushing said pills down the toilet because they made me feel sick; then shoving my fingers down the back of my throat to puke them up when she found out and made me swallow.

Me getting kicked out of school for absences and promiscuity—not college, but the period that came before that. I went to what used to be called an "alternative" high school, for girls who couldn't cut it in a normal classroom.

"It's a nickname, obviously. I gave it to myself since my mom insisted on naming me something boring," Rebel says, relenting.

I wait for her to tell me what her boring real name is, but she doesn't.

"Aren't you worried someone might recognize themselves in your stories . . . if you don't hide your identity?" she asks, shifting topics again. She walks over to my refrigerator, opening and closing the door. Something inside the fridge stinks, and it floats up my nostrils, but I have no idea what it is. The smell has been worsening by the day . . .

"What do you mean by that?" I prod.

"Well, if everyone knows your real name, then they'll recognize who you're writing about in your stories, won't they?"

I flip through my stories in my head, mental fingers brushing over dusty spines . . .

Then I say, "All writers use inspiration from their daily lives and interests . . . but if you're writing fiction, Rebel, then you shouldn't be writing about real people or using their real names. Wait. Are you telling me that your project is a nonfiction piece?"

For a moment, I feel like I have my first real clue—is she drafting a true story?

Please don't tell me it's a memoir, I think, cringing internally.

Rebel shakes her head noncommittally, and then she shrugs her backpack onto her shoulders and slips on her shoes. She's halfway to the front door of my apartment before I can stop her.

"This place isn't very inspiring, you know that?" She flings open the front door and squints out at the sun. We both look out at the half-empty parking lot.

At this time of day, there are few cars around, since most people in my apartment complex—and the world—wake up in the mornings and go to work. The complex itself is a mix of occupants: some low-income and government-assisted renters; some singles and not-yet-divorced couples; a few single parents; and other mid-grade losers like me. The building is drab and industrial, almost like a low-security prison. I rented the apartment sight unseen when I left college, paying my security deposit with my Cash App. There aren't many rental options around here—it was here, the trailer park, or moving back in with my mom. I chose here, certain that I would be too busy writing to care about the crappy conditions.

I dreamed of moving away from my mother's house. Away from Hornsey. Away from the ghosts of my past. But when I got to college in Bloomington, I wasn't at all prepared for the other side of that dream. The actual work involved in earning the degree.

Living on campus was loud and expensive. Most of all, it was lonely. I didn't fit in with the other students or my roommates, and I couldn't keep up with the workload. I found my classes to be tedious and boring; classical literature was a snooze fest, and the assignments left very little room for creativity. When I tried to put my own spin on writing assignments, I was met with ridicule and disdain by my professors and classmates. Most of my classmates wanted to be journalists or fancy Kerouac types—I just wanted to write a story that kept my readers up turning pages all night and that kept my own demons at bay. By the second semester, I'd stopped attending classes altogether—instead, I was holed up in my dorm room, writing my own stuff. Although I flunked out of college, I earned my first publishing deal by skipping classes.

Unfortunately, writing stories instead of turning in assigned essays didn't help me pass and after the three mostly failed semesters, I had to make a choice—retake (and repay) for all my classes, or leave with my head hung in shame . . .

Hornsey isn't a great town, but neither was Bloomington or any other town I've been to so far . . .

I'm not sure if Rebel's comment is referring to the town or my shitty apartment as uninspiring, but both apply.

"No, not at all," I admit.

For the first time, I wonder if that's why I am what I am—a creator of worlds that are infinitely better, or at least more interesting, than this one.

Her bike is nowhere to be found in the parking lot, and I'm just about to ask her if she needs a ride home when she says, "Did you make all A's in English?"

Rebel's questions are exhausting, especially this one. The last thing I want to think about is high school English. Or the subsequent writing classes I took (and failed) in college.

I have this vague memory of standing up to read a zine I created in elemental composition. It was a story about a "nuthouse" with a secret portal that led to sanity. When I finished reading, nobody said a word. But those side-eyes my classmates were giving each other were the only feedback I needed.

Mental note: That is what humiliation looks like.

I cringe at the memory of English classes—at all levels of my (mostly unsuccessful) education.

"No, I didn't make A's. Far from it. What about you? How are your grades?" I don't want to sound like my mother, with her motivational interviewing and critical questions, but Rebel seems a little troubled, like there's more on her mind than just writing and grades. There's something she's not telling me, and I haven't quite figured her out yet.

But I will. Writers always do. We're good at studying people and making up stories about them, usually laced with a whole lot of truth.

What is Rebel's truth?

As she clutches the straps of her backpack, leaning back on her heels restlessly, it occurs to me for the first time that I haven't seen her with a cell phone, not at the shoppe or when she comes here either. Not being glued to a cell phone seems unusual for someone her age. Or anyone of any age, these days.

She hasn't mentioned any friends or hobbies. No interests, besides this mysterious writing contest at school, and I don't even know if she's really interested in that either. She seems to have something else on her mind.

"My grades are okay," she says finally. "I like science and math, but some of the other classes at New Day are awful."

My back stiffens at the mention of ND High, or "New Day" as it's formally called, and an eerie chill runs from the top of my head down to the tips of my toes.

Mental note: This is what dread feels like.

I haven't thought about ND High School in a long time. It had never once occurred to me that Rebel might attend there—most kids around here go to Boulder Creek, the regular public school.

"What's so awful about New Day?"

I watch the way Rebel's face changes as she mulls over my question—it's almost like I can see her own mental pages turning in her head . . . Maybe she has her own book of memories to flip through. Or maybe I'm just projecting my own childhood issues onto this strange girl I barely know . . . which feels quite unfair.

"It's not the school that's the problem. It's this whole damn town," she says.

We stare at each other, facing off on my front stoop. Unblinking.

For a moment, I have a weird flash of inspiration—I could write a time-travel story, in which Rebel's my past and I'm her future . . . writing is the portal we use to travel, switching bodies between the pages.

"See you at work tonight," Rebel says abruptly. She vanishes around the corner of my apartment building in an instant, almost like she's a phantom I created in my own head.

Chapter Seven

I wake up in Loon, where creepy clowns chase me through a maze of broken mirrors. High-pitched giggles echo through the dark.

As I run from them, I'm laughing too, full of delight, shouting over my shoulder as I weave my way through the maze, "I missed you guys. Where you been?"

My own giggles are so loud that I wake myself up from a heavy sleep, rocking side to side in my low-on-water waterbed that's starting to hurt the hell out of my thirty-eight-year-old back.

Half asleep, I'm still thinking of Loon as I pour myself a bowl of cereal. The frosty flakes are, somehow, both stale and chewy in my mouth at the same time.

I'm off from work today, but it's my first real payday, and since the payments are under the table, I have to go pick mine up in person at the shoppe.

But before I can leave, someone's banging on the other side of my door. Rebel isn't supposed to come over today. She's scheduled to work at the shoppe, and I told her that we would get together next week—*after* she shows me her pages so I have something to work with.

This is me trying to set boundaries with her, but she doesn't seem to mind stepping all over them. For example, why the hell is she here today, when I told her not to come?

But when I unlock and open the front door, I'm shocked to find that it isn't Rebel. I frown at the clown on my doorstep. Clowns aren't welcome either.

Though this is not a clown from Loon, just a busty woman in very high heels, with very heavily applied makeup.

"Hello, can I help you?"

"I'm Michelle James." She says it with a long *e* sound instead of an *i*, and she says it slow, like she thinks I won't understand, or like the words taste like shit in her mouth.

Mental note: This is what anger looks like.

Scratch that—this is more than anger. M-ee-Chelle looks like a word on the tip of my tongue. *Venomous.*

"I'm Jane's mother. Or you might know her as Rebel," she says, pushing her way inside.

"Oh." I stumble back, confused by the fact that this creature is Rebel's mother—they look nothing alike—and that she's here in the first place. How the heck does she know who I am or where I live?

Michelle looks around my living room, turns up her lip at my tattered brown sofa, and sneers at the stain on my carpet—a coffee spill from last year, no less.

"How can I help you, M-ee-Chelle?" I say, crossing my arms over my chest and watching as she searches the kitchen and then the dining area. What is she looking for?

Anger brews deep inside me, bubbling beneath my skin. She had no right to come here or bust her way inside. She should be grateful—I've been trying to help her daughter; it's not like I'm some sort of criminal who kidnaps children.

That's when I realize it's not *what* she's looking for—it's *who*. She must have come here looking for Rebel.

"She's not here. I think she's working at the shoppe today," I say.

Michelle stops looking around, and, finally, those creep-show, spidery eyes focus on me. "Jane came home yesterday with grape jelly under her nails and a notebook full of blabber, so, naturally, I asked her where she'd been all day. On Sundays, we go to church. We don't hang out with strangers who play around with their condiments."

The jelly. Another silly suggestion that I found online, but at least it involved an activity that I found useful in the creative process. And the gooey mess was entertaining for Rebel.

I'd tried it out myself last night, hoping I could use some of the same "teaching" tools for Rebel on myself to help with my own writing. Needless to say, it didn't work for either of us.

"You said your daughter's name is Jane?"

Michelle groans. "Rebel is what she likes to call herself these days so she can feel cool. My daughter's name is Jane, and you're some weird stranger I don't know."

I clear my throat. "I'm Adrianna."

"Aren't you a little old to be hanging out with teenagers, Adrianna?" The way she enunciates the syllables makes me want to change it. Maybe Rebel was onto something.

Jane James. Rebel's right—M-ee-Chelle picked a boring first name.

I sigh and adjust the belt on my robe. Michelle's not exactly wrong either, though. I *am* too old to hang out with teenagers, but I thought I was *teaching* her something.

I thought I was doing something good for somebody else, for once in my life . . .

"Look, I'm sorry about the jelly. I hope it didn't stain her clothes. It's a method of teaching I wanted to try out. The idea is that if she can practice describing things by feel instead of sight . . ."

Michelle narrows her eyes at me, like she knows I'm some sort of creep. I might be a creep, but I'm not *that* kind. But I guess there's no way Michelle could have known that, and Rebel is only seventeen . . .

Thoughts of my own teenage years rush in. I had a job like Rebel. But I also had a car and a few friends, too, by the time I was her age. My mother was overbearing and critical about certain things, but she didn't chase down every adult who spent time with me . . .

Looking back, maybe she should have.

Maybe Rebel's mother is the sane one here; maybe she's on the right side of the nuthouse portal and I'm on the wrong one. As usual.

"I think Rebel—I mean, Jane . . . I think Jane wants to be a writer, like me," I explain.

Michelle looks me up and down, jaw clicking. "I think she should aim for better," she says. Her eyes have shifted to the coffee stains on my robe.

What can I say, M-ee-Chelle? My life is full of stains, and the ones caused by coffee are the least of my concern.

"Okay, I won't let her come over anymore. Sorry for the misunderstanding," I say, and I mean it. Rebel/Jane is her daughter, and how she feels about her daughter's career choices is not my business. None of this is.

It's not my place to decide who her daughter can, and cannot, talk to. I probably should have asked to make sure she had her mom's permission before I let her come inside.

"Damn right you won't, loser," Michelle says. She drags out the word *loser* like she's watched the movie *Mean Girls* a thousand times, then tosses her head back and laughs at her own insult.

These aren't the sort of clown giggles that give me a thrill.

Screw being nice. I hate this lady. And I don't feel bad for helping Rebel.

Done with platitudes, I watch her exit, and then I slam the door in her ridiculous drawn-up face and lock it. When I reach up to touch my own face, I'm shocked to find it covered in tears.

Mental note: This is what humiliation feels like. Again.

Chapter Eight

"Write," I say, pointing at Rebel even though she's not looking at me. She's in a chair behind the nut counter, hunched over that notebook of hers.

I'm working, but I'm not working. What I'm really doing is pretending to manage the register by myself while Rebel stares at her mystery pages, but I can't stop pressing the wrong buttons and undercharging customers without her teenage guidance.

She's reading through the pages instead of writing. Does this mean she's almost done with it? Doing a final proofread?

Rebel's mother's, M-ee-Chelle, doesn't want her daughter spending time at my apartment anymore, but she can't make me quit my job. I need the money—and while I'm here at work with Rebel, I might as well help with the writing project if she still wants me to.

Rebel groans in frustration, head bent over the page. She's stuck on something, chewing that eraser of hers. Little pink flecks of eraser dust decorate her chin.

"Want me to take a look?" I transfer a sugary smear of fudge from my hand to my pants and try to peek over her shoulder to see what the problem is.

"Not yet!" She covers up the page with her hands so I can't see.

I step back in surrender and mutter "Sorry" under my breath.

A group of teenagers enters the store, peeking through the glass cases and stealing glances at Rebel. She's disinterested in other teenagers when they come in the shoppe, and I can't help wondering if she has any friends at school, or church.

For me, attending an all-girl high school made me more interested in seeing people outside of my normal school setting, at least back then. There was a yearning inside me to make connections with others, especially boys—even if those connections were unhealthy.

After work, I stock up on a few groceries from Dollar General. Eggs and cereal. Meats and cheese. The cheapest loaf of bread money can buy. Tonight is mandatory dinner night with my mother; we're probably having spaghetti again.

For the first time in a long time, I consider skipping.

Would it be so bad if I joined a dating site or called one of my friends from college to go out to dinner tonight? I can't stop thinking about that nasty look on Michelle's face when she called me a loser and how I kind of agreed with her assessment.

Even if I do enjoy the company of my characters more than real people, I don't want to be friendless and alone for the rest of my life. Plus, lately, the characters show up in my head only when I don't want them to—interrupting my sleep or making me laugh in public at inappropriate times.

By the time I make it home and the groceries are stored away, I've changed my mind about socializing tonight. I don't want to see old friends or my mother. My body is tired from work and from worrying about the Rebel situation, and all I really want to do is lie on the couch and read. I shoot off a text to Mom, writing that I'm sick and can't make it, before I can change my mind.

I settle on the couch with a book I've read at least five times—a repeat mystery that never fails to leave me feeling satisfied, unlike my life.

My eyes are drooping with exhaustion when I hear a shuffling noise that's coming from outside.

"Jesus!" I drop the book from my lap and stare out my living room window, confused and a little shaken. A moon-white face peers back at me through the curtains. For a moment, my heart stops—it's like looking at my own reflection, or worse, a ghost.

But it's not me—the young, troubled-teen version of me—it's Rebel. And she looks haunted.

Was she watching me through the window while I slept on the couch?

Groaning, I get up and open the door. I stick my head through it; there's no way I'm letting her in without her mother's permission.

"Why the hell are you standing outside my window like that? You look like a ghoul! And you're not supposed to be here. Your mother said . . ." My anger evaporates as I get a good look at her face.

Rebel's wearing makeup, which is unusual. Her eyes are coated in dark shadows and mascara, with a thick layer of bright white concealer that doesn't quite match her skin tone. It's caked on so heavily, I'm tempted to reach out and scratch the surface.

"Did Michelle do that to you?" I'm not talking about the makeup.

The makeup isn't the tragedy here; it's the blue and bulgy bruise on her left cheek that the makeup is trying, but failing miserably, to conceal.

"Tell me what happened," I say, motioning her to come inside. Michelle be damned. Rebel is a pain, but she's grown on me—I care about this girl.

"Come in," I insist. But she stands there in the doorway, unmoving.

"Don't worry about the bruise. There was an incident at school after work," she says, tenderly touching the bruise on her cheek. "Volleyball. Took an elbow to the face." She sighs.

Do I believe her? Maybe. Memories flash—me getting slammed in the face and gut by kickballs every Wednesday. I can still feel the pain. *Oof.*

"I do have a story to share, though. I'm not going to tell you because I can do better than that. You said that writers should 'show, don't tell,' remember?" Suddenly, she's thrusting her secret notebook into my hands.

"Thanks for this, but I need to know what's going on first. Are you sure someone didn't hurt you, Rebel?"

She points at the book in my hands, spins around, and disappears on foot, zigzagging around cars in the parking lot, as though she's in a big damn hurry.

Should I chase her? Should I call the police?

My eyes search for her in the dark lot, but my vision is skewed—I took my glasses off so I could see up close while reading, and everything at a distance looks fuzzy, like an out-of-focus photograph.

I know I'm supposed to do something at this moment, but how can I help Rebel if I don't even know if something's wrong?

It's a gut feeling, and let's face it, my judgment is off, sometimes, and I'm not always known for making great decisions, at Rebel's age or my own.

I stare down at the notebook in my hands. The pages feel unusually heavy.

Does this book have the answers I'm looking for inside it?

Before

"The door is painted red. Not candy-apple or dark-brick red, not the brownish shade of old blood. I'm talking about red *red. Red like the anger that brought me here. Bright and intense, it burns from within. It sets my skin on fire. Hell, maybe it could catch this whole building on fire. Perhaps that same shade of anger is what fills everyone when they are forced to enter that bright-red door."*

I cleared my throat and stared at my words on the page, cheeks burning their own painful shade of red, the color of deep embarrassment. The classroom was unbearably quiet, and suddenly, I regretted volunteering to read the first paragraph of my story. What was that overused cliché? *So quiet, I could hear a pin drop.*

"Wow. That's an intense opening. What does everyone else think?" the teacher said.

I looked up at him, filled with gratitude. But his eyes were elsewhere, moving through the rows of my classmates, urging them for some sort of response too.

Finally, my best friend's hand shot up from the seat beside me. When your bestie gets ready to comment on your writing in a classroom full of troubled girls, you should probably feel relieved—but no, not me. Because when it comes to writing, she's as competitive as they come.

"I don't know," she said shooting an apologetic glance in my direction. "It seems a little pretentious, don't you think?"

"You probably can't even spell *pretentious*," someone muttered from the back of the room.

I glanced over my shoulder, unsure who the heckler was but grateful toward them. Lately, it seemed like my "friends" were working overtime to drag me down, including the one who was supposed to be my closest companion.

If she heard the voice in the back, she chose to ignore it.

She continued with her analysis: "It just seems a little showy for describing something as mundane as a red door, you know? I mean, who cares about the color of a door? Is that relevant to the story? And we don't even know who's speaking in the first paragraph, so why would we care about their anger?"

Heat rushed back to my cheeks. Maybe she had a point. It was only a thousand-word short story. Spending so much time on flowery descriptions in the beginning *was* a little pretentious . . .

I squeezed my eyes shut, wishing I were anywhere but here—in this muggy classroom, filled with too much estrogen and drama . . . a room full of pissed-off girls, all of whom found our way here because we messed up and got thrown out of public school.

What was the point of being a good writer, anyway? It was not like anyone was going to hire me after high school, with my shitty alternative diploma from New Day . . .

But when I opened my eyes, my teacher was standing right in front of my desk. He tapped the words that were written on my page and smiled. "I disagree. I don't think it's pretentious at all. In fact, I think it's beautiful. And who cares who the writer is? I bet every single girl in this classroom has experienced anger or even red-hot rage. Wouldn't you all agree?" A murmur of yeses rolled through the classroom, and I could feel my best friend's eyes on the side of my face, burning a hole in my cheek.

Our teacher was right, though . . . Rage was something I was deeply familiar with—both on and off the page.

Act Two

She's Sleeping with the Fishes

Chapter Nine

Forget about writing. Forget about anything that ever seemed important.

Rebel's been missing from work for four days.

I bang on the door of a dilapidated trailer on Cherry Street, like an overzealous salesman. According to Google, there is only one Michelle James in the town of Hornsey, so this has to be where Rebel lives with her mother.

As much as I wish Cherry Street wasn't a real place, it is. This is the "bad side" of town if there ever was a bad side in Hornsey. There aren't many good sides to choose from around here, in this sad little Podunk town.

I peek in the windows of Rebel's mother's trailer. Now I've gone from salesman to full-blown creep. Peeping Tom Extraordinaire—let me add that to my list of marketable skills on my next résumé.

Nothing stirs inside the trailer and nobody answers the door.

I contemplate breaking out one of the windows with my fist or a nearby rock—that's what my characters would do.

But instead, I kick the door once for good measure, more out of frustration than an actual attempt to get inside, and then I get in my car and drive away. I have to work at six o'clock, and there's no one there to fill in for me, especially now that Rebel hasn't been coming in for her scheduled shifts.

She is not your responsibility. This is none of your business. You're not some Nancy Drew heroine whose job it is to save some girl you barely know . . . Who cares if she doesn't come to work? Not your problem!

And maybe if I say it enough times, I'll actually start to believe it.

Chapter Ten

Everything in the nut shoppe has Rebel's stamp on it. Her scraps of scribbles in the wastepaper basket. A drawer full of ponytail holders, broken pieces of blond hair twisted around the elastic.

My job is much harder without her here, and I find myself moving around the store as though in a trance, my thoughts in pieces.

A surprise visit from Candy shakes me out of it. I try to hide the evidence of my incompetence by quickly sweeping up a pile of pistachios and cashews off the floor, kicking them under a glass case with my foot just as the kitchen door slams open. Candy comes barreling through it, wearing a long brown apron and a mask that covers her mouth and nose. She looks less like Wonka in this moment and more like Leatherface, preparing to snatch me up from where I'm hiding behind the counter and hang me on a metal meat hook to rot.

"Where's the other girl? I'm paying two people to work this shift, not one!"

"Rebel? I haven't seen her. I figured she had called in sick or something . . ." Not really—I had already checked the caller ID on the store phone several times; there were no incoming calls from anyone who appeared to be Rebel.

Candy taps the screen of her iPhone with a long red acrylic nail.

"Are you calling her to make sure she's okay?" I say, feeling hopeful.

I don't know Rebel's phone number, and there aren't any numbers for her listed on any of the paperwork I've come across while snooping instead of sweeping these last few days.

Candy looks at my face as though I've grown fangs. "No, I'm not calling her. Anyone who no-call no-shows is automatically fired anyway. Who cares where she is? Probably off with her friends, goofing off the way teen girls do. I'll call around and find a replacement for her, but until then, you're on your own in the evenings, and if you want to keep collecting your pay, then I'll need you to cover her shifts on your days off until that happens."

When she leaves, I stare at the dusty cases of fudge. There are traces of Rebel's fingerprints all over the glass.

Despite Rebel's age, general smart-ass-ness, and annoying inquisitiveness, she is a good worker who always seemed to show up on time. Candy mentioned that she was probably off somewhere with her friends, but as far as I know, Rebel doesn't have any. And middle-aged failing writers don't count.

◆ ◆ ◆

There are a lot of places I consider going after I leave work: the police station, the school . . . But what would I even say? I barely know Rebel, and her mother clearly doesn't want her to visit me for writing advice or anything else either. It's possible that her mom made her find a different job to keep her away from me.

But that bruise on her cheek . . . that's the part I can't move on from.

At the four-way stop on Dixie, I consider making a left and driving back over to Cherry Street to see if she's home this time.

But I'm tired from work, and all I want to do is take a shower and go to bed. Attempting to write is hard enough on a normal day, but I can't think straight with Rebel missing, so there's no point in even trying to work tonight.

She's all I can think about.

As much as I'd like to return to Cherry Street, I know it's a bad idea. I don't want to show up over there and get arrested when her overzealous mother reports me to the cops for stalking.

I flip on my turn signal and make a right instead, heading up the hill to my apartment. Another bleak night ahead for me—a night of no writing, of having weird dreams, and of worrying about a girl I barely know. Sounds fun.

I'm not a huge fan of listening to the car radio, choosing to spend most of my time behind the wheel lost in fantasy worlds and swirling cyclones of anxious thoughts. But I turn up the dial anyway, as loud as I can stand it. I need to drown out my thoughts.

But there's no music playing. Instead, I'm just in time to hear the latest local news bulletin that's coming across the airwaves and invading my skull.

"Breaking news: A body's been found near Cooper's Canyon, about five miles east of Hornsey. It's unclear at this time who the body belongs to or the cause of death, but some local law enforcement is saying that they suspect foul play and that the body might belong to a child . . ."

The radio host is still talking, but I can't hear the words. My brain is stuck on that word: *child.* It rolls around inside my head, then tries to claw its way back out.

Rebel is technically a child, but would they call a teenage girl a child if they found her body?

I rub the bridge of my nose until it stings. There's no reason to think the body belongs to Rebel. She isn't even reported missing! Or is she? I truly have no idea what's been going on in world news, much less my local crime bulletins.

No one on the news has reported a girl missing, have they?

I press my foot down harder on the gas and turn the radio up, but the news has moved on to something else: "Breaking news. The Strawberry Festival set a new record this weekend with nearly two hundred attendees in a single day!"

I turn the radio off.

The body in the canyon has nothing to do with Rebel James. How could it?

But that word, *child*, comes floating back, and it haunts me.

Reported or not, there's only one missing child in Hornsey I can think of.

Chapter Eleven

My apartment is gloomy, a dusty film clinging to the air. I've never felt this *bleak* before. It's a feeling I can't quite describe, which makes me feel uneasy.

I fight the urge to turn the TV in the living room on, stumbling down the dark hallway instead, all the way to my bedroom. My eyes are immediately drawn to the one light source—my computer screen.

I must have turned the monitor on before I left for work.

Now that I'm home, I can do my own internet search and see what I can find out about what happened at Cooper's Canyon. It's not Rebel's body. It can't be, and the sooner I read the news and find out what actually happened, the sooner I'll know the truth.

And the only truth I will accept is that my coworker isn't dead.

Nervously, I sit down at the computer desk, slide my Magoo glasses back on my face, and edge up to the screen.

Something is wrong. Deeply wrong.

I lean back in my chair, staring at the screen in an odd mixture of joy, confusion, and horror. "What the hell?"

There's writing on my computer. Actual words this time. This should make me happy (words—yay!), but there's only one problem here: I didn't write this story.

Or whatever the hell this is . . .

> She only has two friends in this world. Her boat and the sea she rides on. The Whispering Sea truly earned its name. The ghosts of the people who used to live here whisper in the distance, so low she can barely hear them. They're urging her to turn back now, before it's too late. Go home, they're shouting!!
>
> But she can't go home, even if she wants to. The boat is full of holes, and her home is too far away. If she doesn't reach the shore soon, she'll sink. There are things waiting in the deep, dark water below . . . waiting to see if she makes it while silently rooting for her to fail.
>
> Turn back, the whispers tell her!!
>
> No, she says!! This is my voyage now, ghosts be damned!!!!

I read through the words again and again. I know, without a doubt, that I didn't write them or add those ridiculous exclamation points.

But if it wasn't me, then who did?

Has Rebel been inside my apartment? Is it possible that she's the one who wrote these words and left them on my computer for me to find?

I slump back in my computer chair, flabbergasted. If it was Rebel . . . how did she get in? And where the hell is she now?

An even scarier thought is forming: If it wasn't Rebel writing these weird sentences in the dark, then who was it?

Somebody has been here, invading my space while I was away at work.

Cautiously, I roam the halls of my apartment. I'm searching for Rebel's stamp—some clue that she's been here recently. I sniff the air. It smells of last night's pizza covered up with Febreze, not angsty Rebel BO.

I check the front door. I check the windows. I force myself to peek into the closets and rip the shower curtain aside.

There are no obvious signs that someone has been here, except those words.

Those words . . . what could they possibly mean?

I still haven't read Rebel's notebook. I've been too busy, working and worrying, and the first few pages I skimmed weren't very good. The main character had obviously been fashioned after Rebel herself.

I need to try reading it again. Maybe I can compare the writing style in the notebook to the writing style on my computer and figure out, once and for all, if it really was Rebel who broke into my apartment and left me this poorly written message.

But first, I look at the news. I'm not expecting much information yet; after all, the body was just found a few hours earlier. But my local news app is providing live coverage at the scene.

I hold my breath and press Play on the live video.

Two reporters, working hard to look stone faced, fill my screen. Their mouths are moving, but it sounds like their voices are underwater.

Everything around me is fading, growing smaller and smaller, as I zero in on the one image I can see clearly on the screen behind the talking heads.

Twisted metal, flashes of pink. Sparkles, maybe.

A child's bicycle mangled so badly that it's hard to determine the size of it before whatever form of destruction was inflicted upon it.

"The bicycle was found near the crime scene, less than twenty feet from where the body lay. The deceased was discovered by a photographer who was out hiking around the canyon, taking pictures of our local topography . . ."

I mute their voices and stare at the bike on my screen. Would Rebel really ride a pink bike with sparkles on it? It's totally not her style. But still . . . if it was her only way to get to and from work, then she just might.

Something terrible has happened to the owner of that bike. That much is certain.

If the bike looks this bad, I can't imagine what the body must look like . . .

Chapter Twelve

I'm standing at the shore of the Whispering Sea. A tiny boat, so far away, a pinprick in the darkness of night. Moonlight sparkles around the boat as it moves closer to the shore.

Desperately, I shout Rebel's name into the wind. My shout catches, dancing around the seashore, echoing back in my face.

As the contours of her face become clearer, I'm relieved to see that the bruises are gone. She looks almost . . . peaceful.

She's got one rotten oar in her hands, and she's struggling to reach the shoreline with it.

"Row faster! Don't turn back!" I shout.

But that's exactly what she does—turns around and looks at something in the water behind her.

"No!" I scream.

When she faces forward, her face has changed, morphed into something else—something twisted and bent, something unrecognizable.

Helplessly, I watch from the shore as she's sucked beneath the roaring black waters of the Whispering Sea, never to be seen again.

◆ ◆ ◆

I try to forget about the dream. But it lingers there, dancing at the edges of my memory. And I can't stop looking at those bizarre words left behind on my computer. The document is unsaved, so I'm afraid to touch it and risk losing . . . losing what, though? Evidence that she was here? Evidence that's she alive and well and not in some dirty canyon, mangled up like the handlebars of a child's bike?

Not only were the words written on my computer, but they were also specific to me, clearly referring to the Whispering Sea, which is an imaginary place I'd written about in my books.

But how could Rebel have known that . . . ? Unless she really did read my books, just like she said she did on that first day, when she came here looking for help.

I force myself to choke down a bowl of cereal, all the while refreshing my phone screen again and again, checking for updates.

Surely, if a child were missing, it would have been reported to the police. Why hasn't Michelle reported Rebel as missing?

Because she's not. She's at home right now, working on her writing project alone. Her reasons for leaving the job are unbeknownst to me. And frankly, none of it is my business. As long as she's safe and sound at home and not the one in that canyon, I can deal with never seeing her again.

Even if she were missing and Michelle reported it to the police, would it be covered heavily in the news? A troubled runaway doesn't slap the headlines, not like a dead one does.

But if Michelle were involved in something, something bad to do with Rebel—like *murder*, my brain is shouting at me—then she wouldn't have reported her daughter as missing. She would have covered it up.

But Rebel has to have a dad too, right? My own father was shitty and terrible, but I still have one. He exists. And out there somewhere, Rebel has a father too.

If her parents didn't report her missing, then surely, the school would have called authorities after five straight absences. Wouldn't they?

But that's the thing about ND High, though. The school is full of "troubled" teens. Kids unable to walk the line in public school and follow the rules. Kids with frequent truancy issues and other disciplinary problems. Would they notice if she were gone for five days?

The imagination of a writer is both a gift and a curse. Because my mind is going places it doesn't want to, down the slippery slope of fear and despair.

Besides being a bitch to me, Rebel's mother did nothing to indicate that she would hurt her own daughter, and Rebel explained the bruise—an incident that occurred at school while playing volleyball.

I check the news for updates. There are more articles posted today, but they are basically the same. Regurgitated versions of the same story. Dead child in the canyon. Mangled bike. Cause of death unknown, but some sources reporting that foul play is suspected.

I google the number for New Day High School, and before I can change my mind, I'm dialing . . .

Act Three

She's Worm Food

Chapter Thirteen

"New Day High School. How may I direct your call?"

New Day High School, where every day is a new day. A chance to start again and make better choices—the daily morning motto.

Thinking about those morning incantations makes me sick to my stomach.

I swallow the nervous spit in my throat and lower the register of my voice. "Front office, please."

"This *is* the front office. How may I direct your call?" the receptionist says, clearly irritated.

"This is Officer Shannon. Local PD, ma'am. I need some basic information on a student there: Rebel James. Real name's Jane James."

"What's this about?" she asks hesitantly.

I clear my throat and force out the words. "We're investigating a murder in the canyon, and we need to ask her a few questions. I would appreciate your cooperation."

There's silence on the other end of the line, and I squeeze my eyes shut, hoping she didn't hang up and decide to report me to the *real* local authorities.

"Are you still there? This is an important police matter. We are trying to get in touch with a student named Jane James who goes by the nickname Rebel." I'm channeling Shannon, the sexy, hard-ass cop who investigates paranormal clown sightings in Loon. She's determined to shut down those circus clowns, one by one, even if it's the last thing she ever does . . .

But I'm not Shannon. I'm just a pathetic writer pretending to be someone considerably cooler. And now I'm a bona fide creep, trying to gain information about an underage girl I barely know from my local high school.

I'm on the verge of hanging up when the receptionist finally responds. "Yes, of course. I'm still here, just looking . . . Jane's okay, isn't she? Do they know who . . . ?"

"I can't comment on that at this time."

In the background, I hear the unmistakable sound of fingers plucking keys. Boy, do I miss that sound. Now it's a stark reminder that a clock is ticking. Tick tock, tick tock. Time and money are running out, and if I don't get back to writing about my characters instead of impersonating them, then I'm going to lose everything—not just my apartment, but my readers too.

There's a part of me that wonders if I'm doing all of this to avoid writing—or thinking about not writing. Indulging myself as an amateur sleuth certainly won't help with my writer's block . . .

I'm right on the verge of hanging up, when the receptionist returns to the line.

"Here it is! Yes, that's what I thought . . . she's been absent since last Thursday."

If she wasn't at school on Thursday, after I saw her at my apartment on Wednesday evening, then she's been MIA for six days.

"Okay. Are those absences excused?"

"No. Unfortunately, we didn't receive a phone call or doctor's excuse. So the reason for the absence is unknown. Typically, we don't file reports with the state until the child has accumulated more than ten unexcused absences. It used to be five, but it changed after COVID," she explains.

"Thanks for that, ma'am. Can you verify the address on file for me?"

She reads it off and I write it down, even though I already have it. That run-down trailer on Cherry Street.

But then I hit the jackpot when she starts reading off a secondary address they keep on file too. This one belongs to a man named Ronnie James, and he lives in town, a few miles away from the shoppe.

I can only assume the secondary address belongs to Rebel's father.

If Rebel's not with Michelle, then maybe she's with her dad. But that still doesn't explain the unexcused school days or the no-shows at work. I haven't known Rebel for long, but this doesn't add up—she doesn't seem like the kind of kid who just ditches her obligations. And Michelle doesn't strike me as the kind of mother who wouldn't know where her daughter is or report the absences properly to the school.

In the very least, Ronnie James might know where his daughter is and, ultimately, be able to put some of my own fears to rest. But first, I need to talk to him.

It's worth a shot, and now I know where to find him, courtesy of Officer Shannon's relentless bravado.

Chapter Fourteen

Carmella Street is eerily quiet, one lone streetlamp casting an orange smoky glow over the cracker-style houses that line it. The two-story house at the end of the road looks old but well kept—at least, it does until I move closer and put my glasses on.

Shingles are missing. Blankets cover some of the windows and doors. The siding could use a good pressure washing, and it doesn't look like anyone's cut the grass in months.

For a moment, I wonder if Ronnie James still lives here, but then a light pops on in an upstairs window, and I can see that somebody's home.

There's a flash of movement behind the glass. Is it her? Is it possible that Rebel is simply here instead, visiting with her dad and in possession of the perfect teenage excuse for missing both school and work for nearly a week?

I stare at the poorly lit window and the darker windows on either side of it, but nothing moves again. If there was someone looking out the window before, they're gone now.

I take a few uneven steps through the overgrown grass, debating my next move.

Michelle clearly asked me to stay away from her daughter, but I don't know her father, Ronnie. Hopefully, he doesn't know of me, either, or else Michelle will be banging down my door in no time, calling me a loser again, or worse.

I imagine M-ee-Chelle, with those long acrylic nails, clawing at my face. That woman could rip me to shreds.

Rebel's father could be perfectly normal. That's what I'm hoping for.

I try to remind myself that me coming here is normal too. After all, what could be more normal than wanting to check on my coworker and writing mentee to make sure she's safe, especially considering the recent death that happened near the canyon?

The grass in the yard is ankle deep and probably swarming with copperheads and wolf spiders. But when you grow up in the southern regions of Indiana like me, you get used to critters—even the creepy-crawly ones that move around sightlessly in the dark.

There are no exterior lights on the property, just a slash of moonlight to guide me, and the dull glow from the streetlights and one interior light in the window.

There are no cars in sight either, but the gravel is dusty and worn down, as though someone drives on it every day.

No bikes, either, I note.

An image of that mangled bike from the news flashes through my brain again.

Not Rebel. Not Rebel. Not Rebel.

A cool breeze lifts the hair from my neck, sending a shudder down my spine. Despite being alone out here, I can't shake off the sensation of being watched.

I spin around in a circle, looking at the wild stretch of grass and the thick tree line beyond it. Branches sway, limbs whispering in the dark as goose bumps sprout on my bare arms. What if there's someone out there, right now, hiding in those trees, watching and waiting?

But that's ridiculous, of course. Why, and who, would be watching me? I'm the least interesting person I know, and as soon as I know Rebel's safe and sound, I can get back to my boring life of being a writer who can't write.

My mind drifts back to those words on my computer. The Whispering Sea . . .

Turning away from the trees, I glance back at the house, eyes slowly moving up to the creepy old windows again. If not for the light inside, I might have thought the house was abandoned. But there is electricity inside, at least.

Moonlight illuminates the east side of the house, revealing a narrow stone pathway that leads to two outbuildings with corrugated iron roofs near the back tree line of the property.

I debate knocking, following the stone path, or better yet—*leaving*—but those plans are interrupted by the undeniable roar of an engine in the distance, coming closer. I stand, frozen in place in front of the old house, as a run-down gray truck with the loudest motor I've ever heard comes whipping up the road and turns right into the gravel driveway.

I hold my breath as the driver of the truck puts it in park and stares straight at me through the windshield, wide eyed and confused.

The engine cuts, and then a man gets out and comes walking toward me. I take a step back, deeper in the grass, unsure what to say or do.

The man is not much older than me—fortyish, maybe—and as he moves closer, I see that he isn't confused or angry; in fact, he's smiling, as though weird women creeping around his house isn't unusual at all.

"Hey, there!" he says, waving a hand full of truck keys.

He's tall and good-looking, with an intelligent smile, and he's wearing jeans and a T-shirt that look worn with dirt.

"Were we supposed to meet? Sorry, I must have forgot . . ." He stops right in front of me, grinning through perfect rows of straight white teeth and rubbing his hands through his messy white-blond hair.

"No. I . . . no, we weren't supposed to meet. Are you Ronnie?"

"Ronnie?" The man laughs and reaches into his right jean pocket, retrieving a packet of Marlboros. "Nah. I'm definitely not Ronnie," he says, cigarette clenched in his teeth. He lights the end and takes a long, smoky drag. He watches me, eyes thoughtful and evaluating.

Not-Ronnie looks me up and down—not in a disapproving way, but more like he wants to invite me inside and eat my body for dinner. My cheeks grow hot at the thought, burning like a fever.

Suddenly, I'm hyperaware of my own body—my stretchy, hidden-hole-in-the-crotch leggings, with a too-tight T-shirt and a flimsy, nipple-peek-through bra.

"You're not Ronnie?" I say, because I'm not sure what else there is to say as he checks me out.

"No. I'm Rocky. Ronnie's little brother. What would a pretty girl like you want to do with that shit-for-brains brother of mine?" When Rocky smiles, his eyes crinkle. I study them so I can write about them later.

Moments like these, I wish I were a romance writer. Oh, how I would love to slip into the skin of some attractive baddie with an attitude, a character who knows how to handle charming men like Rocky.

But, instead, I open and close my mouth like a guppy. Then, finally, I say, "I'm looking for Ronnie and his daughter, Rebel. She hasn't been at work in several days, and when I called the school, they said she's been absent from there too."

"You called the school looking for my niece?" Rocky's expression changes; his eyes narrow, and his head tilts to the side. I'm being reevaluated.

Mental note: This is what suspicion looks like.

But who could blame him, truly?

I'm not a baddie book heroine, not Nancy Drew or Sexy Lexi. I'm just a weirdo who calls the school of a seventeen-year-old girl asking questions, like a spooky stalker.

"Oh, I get it now," Rocky says, with a frown. "You must be her boss. Candy, right? She's told me some things about you. You don't look how I pictured you, though. You don't look . . ."

It's pretty sad when the first word that comes to mind to fit that blank is *competent*.

"Mean?" I offer instead, standing up a little straighter and putting a hand on my hip like Candy would do, when she goes full boss mode.

Rocky laughs. "Mean? No. I was going to say . . . older. And ugly. Like a bossy old shrew," he says, half chuckling, half coughing as he sucks on his cigarette again.

"You certainly aren't any of those things. I wouldn't mind having a boss that looks like you instead of the one I got," he says, with a wink. "Or used to have, I should say." He frowns, remembering something.

"Oh." Something burns deep in my lower belly. If I were a romance writer, I might label it desire. But instead, it feels like indigestion, and I just want to cut and run.

Rocky could be the lead in one of those stories my mother used to scowl at when we passed by them in the library aisles, the ones she labeled *bodice rippers*.

It's been nearly two years since I slept with a man—if that lackluster, one-night bar hookup even counts—and the fact that I'm picturing myself wearing a corset as Rocky rips at my "bodice" is humiliating to admit, even if it's just to myself.

"I don't have time for games," I say, pursing my lips like Candy would. "An employee of mine has gone missing, and there's no one to take her place. Do you know where she is or not?"

"Haven't seen Rebel this week," he says, blowing smoke rings like that hookah-smoking caterpillar in *Alice in Wonderland* in what I can only assume is an attempt to impress me. "Haven't seen her daddy neither. I'm living with my brother temporarily, helping him fix up this dump so he can resell it. But that asshole spends more time drinking than working or helping with the house. He's probably staying at one of his girlfriends' houses this week."

Unsure what to make of that, I ask, "And Rebel? Could she be staying at the girlfriend's house too?"

Rocky flicks the cigarette butt across the yard, and when he turns back to me, he no longer looks playful or cheery. "No, she's not. My brother pays very little attention to my niece, even when she's here visiting, which isn't as often as it should be. She lives with her mom most of the time. Ronnie gets her every other weekend, some holidays, and some summers. He's lucky he gets to see her at all, what with his drinking problems and all that."

"I'm sorry to hear that," I say, and I mean it. Michelle was no gem, but at least she seemed concerned about Rebel when she came to my house to confront me. If I had a daughter, I would probably do the same. Well, I wouldn't call random strangers losers. But I would want to know who my daughter was hanging out with, especially if it was an adult I didn't know.

"Rebel deserves better than the hand she's been dealt. Two shitty parents who spent most of their marriage fighting with each other instead of raising her. Ronnie and I grew up in a similar household, so I was hoping he might break that curse." Rocky shrugs.

I grew up with a flaky father and a self-absorbed mother who never got along. The similarities between me and Rebel are uncanny, I must admit. Which causes me to feel even more worried about her current whereabouts.

"Do you know where she might be? I'm only here out of concern as her boss," I say, voice softening.

"You said she hasn't been to work in a few days? That doesn't seem like her. I saw her about ten days ago when she came by to visit. She's seventeen now. Almost an adult. And I'm just the uncle. I don't keep track of everywhere she goes."

"Even school?" I say hesitantly.

"I had no idea she was missing school and work. Skipping class isn't all that unusual. She got in trouble for that before, and that's why she was transferred to New Day. But missing work? That's weird. She's been saving up for that Guzzi."

"Guzzi?" I know a lot of words in the English language, but *Guzzi* isn't one of them.

"A Guzzi is a motorbike. The one she has right now is pretty ratchet. I offered to help her practice driving so she can get a car, but she loves riding a bike. She just needs a better one. And that's why she took the job at your shoppe in the first place," Rocky explains.

A motorbike. Not a twisted-up, childlike pink bike like the one they found in the canyon. Thank God.

Relief floods through my body, and I let out a long, loud whoosh of breath, forgetting my audience. When I look at Rocky, he's watching me with a careful look. He isn't sure what to make of me.

"You're really worried about her, aren't you? She said you were a bitch, but you seem all right to me," he says.

I hold back a smile at that. Rebel wasn't wrong about Candy—she is a bitch. But I wonder how she would actually describe me if she did talk about me. I cringe, thinking about Rebel and her gut-blow comments about my attire and my boring-as-hell apartment, and decide that some things are best left unknown.

Rocky motions for me to follow him toward the house. It's a terrible idea—the kind of idea silly baddies have at the beginning of a love story that morphs into the horror variety.

But I'm no baddie.

So I put one foot in front of the other and follow Rebel's handsome uncle toward the dark house.

Chapter Fifteen

Rocky pauses on the poorly lit front porch, keys clutched in his hand.

"Damn porchlight needs to be my next priority," he mutters to himself, squinting in the dark as he tries to find the right key.

"I thought I saw someone moving around in that window upstairs," I say, engaging the flashlight app on my cell phone and holding it out for him to help.

"Could be Ronnie, I guess. But I'm pretty sure he's staying at his new girlfriend's place tonight. That's where he is most nights. Rebel has a key, but there's no way she would come here during the week. Her mom—have you met her yet?" Rocky sticks another key in the lock and this time finds success.

"Michelle? Yes, unfortunately, I have."

Rocky enters the house, flipping on light switches inside while I stand there on the precipice, unsure what to do, waiting. I could always turn back now, go home and try to write nonsense. Forget that I give a shit about a strange young girl I've known for barely a month. But at this point, it seems like I'm the only one who knows, or cares, that Rebel is missing . . .

Yellow light floods the front room, illuminating a large living room space filled with tall stacks of lumber, a roll of plastic tarps, and nearly a dozen cans of paint.

"Michelle doesn't care much about Rebel, but she does care about money, and since Ronnie is behind on child support, he isn't allowed to see her except during his scheduled times. Not that Ronnie's losing any sleep over that either . . . Truly, I think they should have stayed together. A match made in hell, those two. Why are you still standing out there?"

Cautiously, I step inside and enter the airy space. There's nowhere to sit.

Rocky dumps his keys on a stack of plywood and slides off his boots, one at time, keeping his eyes on me.

The living room / construction site opens into a mostly empty dining room with two chairs and a card table, and beyond that, there's a full kitchen that looks oddly normal and finished, considering the disarray around it.

A steep wooden staircase coils around like a snake in the middle of the construction, leading up to what I can only presume is the second floor. I'm just about to ask again about the possibility of Rebel being here despite it being a weekday when a furry golden retriever comes bounding down the steps, paws scratchy on the hard wood and tongue lolling out of its mouth, excitedly.

"There she is! My Sadie girl." Rocky kneels on the hardwood floor and opens his arms as the dog pounces off the last step with a *woof.* "Come here, Sadie."

But the slobbery dog bounds right past him and heads straight for me. Great.

"Oh. Oh, okay . . ." I brace myself as the dog jumps on me, placing her enormous front paws on the center of my chest and bopping me on the chin with her big wet nose.

"Well, hello to you too," I say, trying to keep my balance and hold back laughter at the same time.

Sadie sniffs me all over, including my hole-in-the-crotch leggings, and I try to gently ease her front end back down to the floor. I don't have much experience with dogs. My mother was a very no-pets-allowed kind of person, and as I grew older, I stopped fighting her rule and grew used to having an animal-free home. Even now, with my own apartment, getting a pet has never once crossed my mind, which fills me with a strange sort of sadness. Is this what regret feels like?

I stroke the top of the dog's head and run my hands over her floppy ears. Her breath smells like rotten milk and something fishy, but for some strange reason, I don't mind it.

Mom and I didn't have much growing up, especially after my dad left us, but what my mother did have, she treated like precious art—the fake leather sofa in the den was not for eating or drinking on; the towels in the bathroom were for "looks only" even though they were Target-brand and ugly anyway. And she was horrified when she saw people wearing clothes coated in pet hair. She really hated dogs.

"Get down now, Sadie. That's enough! I'm sorry. I know it's hard to tell, but she's still a puppy. I brought her with me when I moved in to help Ronnie, and she's not used to being around other people yet. We're working on her manners, obviously." Rocky gently tugs on the dog's collar.

I smile, wiping dog hair and slobber off the palms of my hands and onto the back of my leggings. She's awfully cute for such a stinky, slobbery beast.

Rocky whistles for Sadie to follow him into the kitchen. Nervous, I follow, too, reminding myself that I came here for one thing and one thing only—to find out information on Rebel's whereabouts. Her Uncle Rocky—as cute as he is, and the dog too—doesn't seem to have much information to offer. This whole trip feels like a waste of time.

The kitchen is sparse but clean, with newish-looking floor-to-ceiling cabinetry and appliances that still have plastic on the front, like they recently came from the showroom floor of an appliance store.

"This is the only finished room. As you can see, my brother and I don't do much cooking. Neither does Rebel when she's here on the weekends. I haven't touched the upstairs yet. We try to keep Rebel's room decent so it's clean for when she comes to stay. Michelle would throw a fit if we didn't."

I nod, shaking off thoughts of M-ee-Chelle. Trying to forget that day when she called me a loser. I can imagine her turning up her nose at this place, a house in disarray while under construction, in the same way she scoffed at my shabby apartment and clothes.

Rocky fills up a round metal bowl on the floor with kibble. We both watch and smile as Sadie scarfs it down noisily.

"I'll call Rebel and see what I can find out for you. It's been a week and a half since I last saw her. She should be coming to stay this Friday as scheduled, though. Hopefully, Ronnie will be back by then too. He's not Mr. Reliability. Some days I wonder if he's just letting the clock run out with Rebel, hoping to get rid of those child support payments he complains about so much."

There's a running theme here that I can't help noticing—there are too many people in Rebel's life who simply aren't paying attention. They don't keep track of where she is, too busy with their own lives and responsibilities.

Another frightening thought is emerging . . . Would Rebel's own father do something to hurt her in order to avoid paying child support? It's a horrible thought, but it wouldn't be the first time a man did something terrible to his own family in order to escape the responsibilities of fatherhood . . .

According to Rocky, Ronnie James was awfully busy these days with his new girlfriend . . . Is it possible that Rebel was getting in the way of him starting a new life?

As Rocky pecks away at his phone, I wander around the kitchen. There are no traces of Rebel here—or anyone. No proudly displayed photos tacked to the fridge door. No awards or A+ papers on the walls. But that makes sense, really, considering that the downstairs is a work in progress, according to Rocky.

"You said that you're staying here temporarily? How come you wanted to help? If you don't mind me asking . . ."

Rocky holds up one finger, and I wait, breathlessly, as he leaves a voice message for Rebel.

"No answer. Her phone's going straight to voicemail. But I'll send a text to her now and Ronnie too. Is it possible that Rebel found another job or there was a mix-up on the schedule?"

I shake my head. "I don't think so."

"And you asked why I'm here. Well, my brother and Rebel are the only family I got. I kicked alcohol a couple years ago, and I've been trying to make up for my past shitty ways ever since. But this time, Ronnie is the one running around making mistakes, and I'm like the older brother now. Lately, it seems like I'm the only responsible one, between the two of us."

"I'm sorry," I say, because I'm not sure what else there is to say. I've never had a sibling—it's just been me and Mom—but I can understand the drinking. My father did a lot of that in the early years leading up to his eventual departure from our lives.

"I thought it would be fun. Working on this old place together, flipping it. But it's mostly been me doing the fixing and Ronnie out running around, goofing off with his girlfriend and friends."

"What does Rebel think of that?" I ask, trying to slip inside her skin for a while and imagine how I would react in a similar situation. It's not easy for children to deal with divorce. New partners and stepparents . . . Just based on the fictional worlds I know, those things are always a playground for disaster when it comes to teenagers.

Rocky shrugs. "Rebel is different. She's totally focused on herself. Going to school and working. She's better than I was at her age. Better than her father too. She adores her father, but I think she's grown used to not having him around much. He doesn't bring his girlfriends around her too often, so that's good, I guess. Michelle, on the other hand . . . Well, let's just say that Rebel has had to deal with a few bad apples that Michelle brought around after her divorce from my brother."

Great. Not only does Rebel have to deal with a deadbeat dad, but it sounds like some of her mom's boyfriends are even worse. The list of potential suspects is growing in my mind, but I try to remind myself that I'm not even certain she's missing.

"You thought I was here for an appointment when you first saw me . . ." I say, remembering his initial reaction to seeing me in his driveway.

Rocky's cheeks flush red. "I've been dating, recently. Meeting some women online on that site. Tinder, ya know? Some of them are a little forceful if you know what I mean. I thought maybe you were one of the women I talked to on there, showing up at my house to demand an answer for why I ghosted your messages." Rocky laughs nervously, his cheeks growing redder.

"Ah. Well, I'm definitely not . . . one of those. I don't date," I say strangely, looking away because I feel so awkward. "Thanks for trying to reach Rebel for me. Will you please tell her I stopped by if you hear from her?"

Rocky tilts his head curiously. When he opens his mouth, I half expect him to ask me why I don't date, but instead he asks, "What did you say your name was, again?"

"Candy. When you talk to Rebel, please tell her that we miss her at the shoppe. And . . ." I try to think of something else, something authoritative the real Candy would say. "And if she isn't coming back, then she needs to let me know that and drop off her uniforms, apron, and key at the store."

Satisfied, I stick my hand out to shake his. He stares at it, smiling as though amused by the formality.

"Okay. Sure will." Rocky takes my hand, shaking it back.

"Do you want to go upstairs and check out her room with me before you go? I don't go in there much. We could see if she left the uniforms or key in there. And if she doesn't call or text me back by tomorrow, I'll ride over to Michelle's and check on her there, too, and go up to the school if I have to. My niece is usually pretty responsible, so I don't worry often. But this definitely doesn't seem like normal behavior for her . . ."

The thought of driving back to Michelle's trailer or facing off with her again sounds like a perfectly dreadful nightmare I don't want to live through. If Rocky can track her down for me, all the better. And a chance to snoop around for clues in Rebel's bedroom is too good to pass up.

"That would be great. Thanks."

Rocky leads the way upstairs, Sadie bounding at our heels.

The second floor is narrow, like a tunnel in the dark. Rocky, thankfully, flips on more lights at the top of the stairs, illuminating the long, dizzying hallway. "Her room is at the end there."

The last door on the left faces the back of the house, so it's not the one I saw earlier, lit up from the street. A wave of disappointment flows through me as I realize that I'm no closer to finding Rebel.

We pass by an open bedroom on the right that is well-lit and sparsely furnished, with a small air mattress on the floor and a dog bed full of toys, in what I assume is Rocky and Sadie's bedroom.

Rocky skips ahead of me and tries to pull his bedroom door shut, but Sadie pushes her way between our legs and darts inside. "Okay, go ahead, I guess," he says, grinning and shaking his head at the dog, then me.

Rocky keeps going all the way to the end of the hallway and opens the door to Rebel's room. Lights pop on, revealing a small, but crowded, space with yellow wallpapered walls and a neatly made twin bed. Stuffed animals are piled on top of the bed, and it makes my heart ache. For someone so old and mature, Rebel really is just a child.

For a moment, I try to remember what it was like—really like—to balance on that dreadful tightrope, the one between womanhood and girlhood.

Besides the stuffies on her bed, the rest of Rebel's room looks like the space of a grown-up. Makeup, perfume, and toiletries litter the top of one dresser. A desk stacked with schoolbooks and papers is pushed up against the edge of the wall.

For such a small room, Rebel tried to fit a lot in here, squeezing all parts of herself into this tiny space.

The smell of teenage angst—Eau de Rebel, her signature scent—permeates the air, thick and cloying, almost like we just missed her moments before.

Memories float back of our earlier conversations in my apartment, about her schoolwork. *It's not the school that's the problem,* she said. *It's this whole damn town.*

My own experiences at ND High were fraught with difficulties—struggling with the schoolwork, my classmates . . . and so much more.

"You okay?" Rocky asks, bringing me back to the present.

I blink, turning away from the door and nodding at him.

I spend so much time alone that I often forget to adjust my face in order to hide my emotions. Thinking back to ND High and my own teenage years brings out a whole lot of memories and a side to me that I don't want to retrace.

"Yeah. I'm just wondering where she might be. I'm worried about her," I say, trying on honesty for the first time since I arrived.

Rocky studies my face, unsure, and looks around the room. We're searching for something, but not sure what it is.

"Is there anything else going on? Did she mention that anything was wrong to you, while you were supervising her at the shoppe?" Rocky asks.

I shake my head. "No, nothing. I just . . . There was that incident at the canyon . . ."

"What incident?" he asks.

Yikes. Is it possible that he doesn't know about the dead girl they found there recently?

I open my mouth to explain, but then there's the loud trill of a cell phone ringing from downstairs.

"That could be her. See if you can find the uniforms and key, and I'll be back." Rocky and Sadie take off down the hallway, and I hear their footsteps on the wooden staircase.

I turn around and stare at the empty bedroom. *Where the hell are you, Rebel?*

There is a closed wooden door with a brass knob that undoubtedly leads to Rebel's closet. But I'm laser focused on the bed.

As soon as I hear Rocky downstairs talking on the phone, I drop to my knees beside the bed and plunge my hand between the mattress and box spring.

I flip through my mental pages of memory—some chapters of my teenage years were easier, but then there were those with sticky and hard-to-read pages, the ones I try to keep hidden away from others. Every teenager has secrets, but there are some hiding spots that transcend generations and time.

My fingers brush over the corner of something hard between the mattresses, pushed damn near the center of them. I'm looking for a diary, and this is the same spot where I used to hide mine, and half my teenage friends I remembered from my youth used a similar place for tucking away things they didn't want their parents to find. Cigarettes, joints, boys' phone numbers. For me, it was a diary with a lock and key.

I lean forward, stretching my whole arm between the mattresses until, finally, I'm able to get a grip on something small and rectangular. But it's not a diary. It's a cell phone.

It's small with a faux-diamond-studded pink case, and it looks like the very first version of the iPhone, or one of the firsts, with a smaller-than-normal touchscreen. I press the home button, but it remains dark. Why would Rebel hide her cell phone? Any normal teenager would have taken theirs with them, wouldn't they?

Rebel's parents don't strike me as the type to micromanage her phone usage, so what would be the reason for tucking it away from view, hidden between the mattresses?

For the first time, I consider that Rebel might have run away from home. She's nearly eighteen—barely a crime, and in many states, it is not a crime at all to run away from home at any age. But she wouldn't leave before completing her senior year, would she?

I think about those bruises on her cheek. The excuse about volleyball. If her mother or father gave her those bruises, she had every reason to want to ditch town. But still, would she leave her cell phone behind? I know I wouldn't.

In my mind, I play back that last day—her dropping off the notebook and telling me to read it. But I did read it—some of it. It was mostly the rantings of a young girl, complaining about the smell of meat in her homeroom classroom, going through the overly detailed mundane tasks she completed on her school checklist, complaining about the other girls in class . . .

Impulsively, I tuck the cell phone in the waistband of my leggings and go to explore the closet. Rocky is still downstairs talking to someone—hopefully, good news about Rebel—and I can hear the *wah wah wah* of his voice, but not the details of what he's saying.

I sink down on the scratchy green carpet in front of the closet and sift through a few shoeboxes and land mines of clothes that rest on the bottom of Rebel's closet floor. But the boxes contain actual shoes, and there's nothing suspect. We don't actually have a set uniform for the nut shoppe, but Candy does require aprons. There are six of them hanging in Rebel's closet, starchy white and clean, dangling from wire hangers on a metal bar. I grab a couple, just for good measure.

The closet is a bust.

The papers on the desk offer nothing further. I flip through math and science assignments. Page through a notebook full of loopy cursive—scientific definitions and dates. Organized notes that include bullet points. For someone so young, Rebel sure has neat handwriting. Something about it irks me, and I stare at the words on the page until they turn blurry.

The cell phone weighs heavily, pressed up against my skin, and I can't help feeling a hot rush of shame in my stomach and chest. What am I doing—stealing a young girl's cell phone? Peeping through her private things?

Nancy Drew never seemed like a creep when she was searching for clues, but then again, she was nothing like me. Good family, good instincts . . . and let's face it—the mysteries she solved were not as scary as some of the modern-day horrors we read about every day in the news.

Perhaps that's why I decided to write sci-fi instead of mystery or horror; the real world is so much scarier than fiction . . .

I catch a glimpse of myself in Rebel's mirror—standing in the middle of her bedroom, surrounded by her girlish belongings, and for a moment, I'm hit with an eerie feeling, one that I just can't shake. That I'm looking in the mirror, not at my own reflection, but at a much younger version of me. Not some middle-aged creep-o writer. But someone younger, needier. Someone with a secret to hide.

What were you hiding, Rebel? And from whom were you hiding it?

There's a five-by-seven photograph hooked to the top edge of her mirror. I move closer and pluck it off the glass. Earlier, I shoved my glasses onto the top of my head when I saw how hot Rocky was (although I'm ashamed to admit this even to myself). I slide the glasses back onto my face so I can get a good look at the picture.

It's Rebel in the photograph, standing arm in arm with three other girls. The photo is grainy, like it was printed from a cell phone on a printer running out of ink. I don't recognize the other girls—they look like any teenagers you'd see on the street, all around the same age as Rebel. Two are blonds, like Rebel, and the fourth is a redhead with a slight gap-toothed smile.

So she does have some friends after all, I think, breathing a sigh of relief.

Maybe Rebel isn't a troubled, lonely loser like me after all.

Here I am again—projecting my own weird neuroses onto a teenage girl. She's probably staying at one of her friend's houses this week, ditching work and school, and pissed off at her parents. If Michelle and Ronnie were my parents, I'd be pissed off too.

Hornsey isn't the kind of town people want to stay in—you either get stuck here, or you move away as soon as you can. I consider the possibility that Rebel couldn't wait, even just one more year. Hell, maybe she's halfway to California by now. Who knows.

I flip the group photo over, and there are names on the back: *Jane, Carrie, Christian, and Tami.*

Jane. So this was taken before she changed her name.

Turning the photo back over, I squint at the background behind the girls—it appears to have been taken inside a classroom. The background is hard to see, but there is a green chalkboard on the wall behind them. The letters written on the board are also hard to make out, but there are three letters I recognize.

S.S.S.

It takes a few seconds for it to come back to me, but when it does, it feels like a kick in the throat. A jolt of recognition.

The Story Seekers Society.

Is it truly possible . . . that Mr. Hobbes is still running his creepy little after-school writing club?

Memories come rushing back, moving so quickly that I have to stumble over to the bed to sit down.

There are stories that bubble beneath the surface, and then there are stories that blow the top off everything. Mr. Hobbes is one of those stories that I like to keep tucked away, close to the vest.

Mr. Hobbes, teacher of *Beowulf* and *Macbeth.* Lover of satire. Charmer of young female students. He was one of a few male teachers at an all-girl alternative school. Back then, he taught British literature and composition. Is it really possible that he's still teaching there after all these years?

He was a charismatic teacher. Well loved by all. When he taught me, he was young—only in his mid-twenties. But he seemed so old then to all of us, and mature. Girls were drawn to him. Not just because he was handsome, but also because he was skilled. There was a waiting list to join his classes. He offered private tutoring sessions after school, but the girls who really impressed him with their written stories were invited to a special club. A society, of sorts . . .

The Story Seekers Society. SSS. Is this who Rebel was writing her story for? Is Mr. Hobbes in charge of the contest?

The clicking sound of Sadie's nails on the wood wake me up from my trance. I jump up and run over to the mirror, replacing the photo on the glass. I'm just heading out with an armful of aprons when Rocky meets me at the top of the stairs.

"Did you find out anything?" I ask.

But I already know that something is wrong. Rocky's face is sheet white and sullen.

"That was Michelle I just talked to. She's been out of town for a nursing conference since last Sunday. She said that Rebel was supposedly staying with her friend Tamara from school, but as it turns out, that was a lie. She never had plans to stay with Tamara."

"And?" There's something more; I can see it written all over his face.

"Apparently, they found a dead girl a few days ago. Near Cooper's Canyon. It's been all over the news, but I had no idea," Rockys says, rubbing his cheeks with both hands, as though he can scrub the fear away.

"Yes, I saw the news story about the girl they found. But surely, it's not Rebel . . ."

"It's not," Rocky says firmly, jaw flexing.

I want to ask him how he can be so sure. How can we both act so certain?

I want to believe it's not Rebel, but there aren't any other missing girls in Hornsey . . .

"How can you be so sure?" I finally ask, voice barely above a whisper.

"Because they just identified the body, and it's not Rebel. The body belongs to Tamara Levy."

Before

The funny thing about being labeled a "bad girl" is that everyone expects you to get in trouble. Expectations are lowered. Deadlines are adjusted. Space is given, even when you don't ask for it.

I was sentenced to New Day after my seventh consecutive suspension for skipping class. Skipping is bad, sure. But it's not as bad as, say, calling in bomb threats, getting busted by the drug dogs during a locker search, or beating up kids on the bus—which was what I'd heard some girls at ND were in for.

There was this unspoken rule at ND: You don't talk about what had happened before. After all, that's the school motto—a new day; a new opportunity to turn it all around . . .

But the problem with keeping our past a secret was that it left a lot of room for interpretation. For example, there was a story going around about a certain new girl that involved a double dare, a pack of hot dogs, and a very pricey visit to the emergency room when one of the hot dogs broke.

Were any of the rumors really true? Probably not. We liked to embellish . . . Mostly, we liked to tell stories. Especially those of us who had a knack for writing.

My invitation to the writing club arrived on a Wednesday. I nearly missed it. Just a simple slip of paper, folded in half, stuck between the slits of my locker. I'd heard about the after-school club through the rumor mill.

It was invite only, and the teacher who ran it was everybody's favorite, of course.

I wanted to brag about the invitation to my friends, but I kept it secret, staying after school and creeping around the empty hallways. Perhaps, in my mind, I was hoping that when I showed up for it, it would be only me and him. But when I entered the room, I was disappointed to find it full of girls, most of whom I already recognized.

"Come in! Welcome. We're discussing Shakespeare," Mr. Hobbes said.

"Oh. Awesome." Truthfully, I'd read little to no Shakespeare, inside my classrooms or out of them.

"You can sit back here," someone said, as I wandered down the rows of desks.

"Oh." I recognized her. The mumbler in the back of the room in English, the one who'd made that joke about my bestie not knowing how to spell the word *pretentious*.

"Thanks." I sat down beside her. She was different from the other girls at ND—with her all-black clothes, mysterious graphic tees, and pierced septum.

"Did it hurt?" I said, pointing at her slightly too big but beautiful nose.

I expected her to act tough by saying no, but her eyes widened and she nodded. "Worst pain of my life," she admitted.

"And what's your favorite Shakespeare play?" Mr. Hobbes boomed. I turned my head toward the front of the class, horrified to realize he was looking straight at me.

"Umm . . ." My brain was racing. He'd invited me to this exclusive club, and I didn't even know one single Shakespearean play. What a loser!

I coughed, giving myself time to think.

What was that one story, the one about the son who kills his dad . . . ?

"*King Lear*," my new strange friend whispered, nudging my foot with her combat boot.

"*King Lear*," I said, proudly, hoping she was right and that was an actual play by Shakespeare.

"Ah. One of his best works. Lear had a thing for favorites," Hobbes said, smiling with all his teeth.

I promised myself I would read *King Lear* later, but days and weeks passed, and Shakespeare was the furthest thing from my mind. Our writing club slimmed down; Hobbes scared off the slackers and focused on those of us who he felt had real, raw writing talent.

But my new friend stuck around, and I quickly forgot about the other girls at ND, the ones who silently rooted for me to fail or who got me in trouble.

Act Four

She's in the Wind

Chapter Sixteen

I follow the familiar winding roads, driving on autopilot. My stomach is clenched in knots.

I'm glad that the girl they found isn't Rebel, but who's to say something didn't happen to Rebel too? If they were supposed to be together and one of them is now dead, where is the other one?

The car radio is no help. It's half past ten at night, and there are no local stations that are featuring any news stories.

I'm half tempted to call my mother, even though we're not scheduled to meet for dinner until tomorrow. She's not the kind of mom you lean on for emotional support, but she used to be a teacher before she retired, and she still has some local teaching friends who might have kept her in the loop.

Somebody has to know something. Such as, Where is Rebel James?

I press my foot to the gas, eager to get home and close myself off from the world. I need to think. Need to process this.

As I take a sharp curve on Edgewood, Rebel's cell phone slips from my waistband, slides across the console and passenger seat, and then falls between the seat and side door.

I nearly forgot about the phone.

What I really should do is go straight to the police and let them take a look at it. There's no good reason for a teenage girl to leave her phone behind like that, unless she was hiding from something or trying to get away from town. Did she really have plans to spend the weekend with Tamara, or was that just a ruse?

But again, I think back to all my daily encounters with Rebel. Never once did I see her pecking away at a cell phone, not during our writing sessions or while working at the store.

But, then again, she also never mentioned her friend Tamara.

The one who's currently lying dead in the morgue.

Trees and residential houses fade away. I pass the public park that I haven't been to in years. A merry-go-round gyrating eerily in the wind; no one in sight. Kids don't play outside like they used to, and who can blame them when there's young girls turning up dead only a few miles away, at Cooper's Canyon?

As I pull into my apartment complex, I'm hit with a temporary rush of relief. The body doesn't belong to Rebel.

Now that I'm home, maybe I can sit down and write for a little while, forget about Rebel and Tamara. Forget about everything while I disappear into a fictional world. A world that I can control, unlike the real one.

But then I remember that I don't write anymore. At least I haven't for a very long time.

I kick off my combat boots and make a beeline toward my bedroom. The computer is still on, the screen glowing white. But the words on the page haven't changed, and there's nothing new for me to read.

For a moment, I consider that, perhaps, I really did write those words—my brain was so foggy, half in and out of sleep and between dreams, it's possible. But then I remember the terrible grammar. No. No way.

I save the story as *Who the F Wrote This* and close it. Then I shut the computer off.

My stomach growls. Eating food at a time like this feels inappropriate. A girl is dead, yet my body is craving a cheeseburger. With pickles, onions, and extra mayo.

But the putrid smell in my kitchen has grown worse, and I still haven't tracked down the culprit. It smells like something rotting and dead. My stomach squeezes into knots, and my mind goes to a place I don't want it to go—imagining a young girl's body twisted and mangled like that pink bike I saw on TV.

At least it's not Rebel . . .

But a girl is dead and another is missing. And as far as I know, no new answers exist.

With my appetite gone, I remember the phone and go outside to the parking lot to retrieve it from the sideboard of my passenger seat. Back inside, it takes a few minutes for me to locate the correct type of charger from a drawer in my bedroom.

I attach the charger to the phone, and then I wait. But minutes pass by, and nothing happens. Perhaps, the phone was really, really low on battery and it will take a while to charge.

I force myself to undress, slip into one of my old college sweatshirts, and climb into my shaky bed.

My body rocks side to side on the water mattress, causing my stomach to twist more.

I don't want to look at the news updates on Tamara, but I have to.

My phone reveals a few missed texts from my mom, almost like she sensed I was thinking about reaching out to her earlier. For a moment, I expect her to have texted something about the local girl's death, but instead it's just another reminder that we have a scheduled dinner date. It's not like I ever forget—my social calendar is blank—but she feels compelled to tell me anyway.

Making Lasagna. See you tomorrow at 7.—Mom

I picture her elbow-deep in tomato sauce, stretching flesh-colored noodles across the pan.

I laugh, despite myself. I should really consider writing horror next. With the spaghetti monster as my central character. The heinous villain.

I sit up in bed, press my back to the pillows, and open up my news app.

> Tamara Levy, age 17. A senior at ND High School.
>
> The county corner, Raquelle Dracone, had identified her remains using her dental records and DNA provided from a toothbrush that her parents gave to police.
>
> Cause of death—still unknown.
>
> The local sheriff stated that her death was a tragedy, and a full investigation is underway.
>
> ND High School will have crisis counselors and grief specialists on staff tomorrow to provide support to students, teachers, and administrative staff who need it.
>
> Anyone with crucial information about Tamara Levy's untimely death is encouraged to reach out to Hornsey PD.

I search several other trustworthy local news sites, but they're all sharing the same generic information. Her cause of death is unknown.

No mention of the friend who was supposedly spending the weekend with her before she died. Has Michelle reported that bit of information to the police?

Is it possible that Tamara's death was simply a tragic accident? Parts of the canyon are steep, with dangerous curves and hundreds of ways to fall and get injured, especially on a dinky kid's bike.

But where, oh where, is Rebel? And why has nobody reported her missing?

I think back to Rocky's words—if Michelle is just recently returning from out of town to discover that Rebel isn't where she said she was going to be, then she might only now have become aware enough to report her daughter as missing.

But I knew and said nothing. I should have gone to the police myself.

From the first missed day of work, I knew something was wrong. The school should have reported it too . . . *Shoulda woulda coulda.* This is a game I can play all night, but there's no point to it now.

I glance over at Rebel's phone again, resting on my nightstand. When I turn it over, I'm shocked by another bird's-eye view into Rebel's life. The phone is barely breathing but it's on now—battery life at 2 percent. There's a screensaver on the lock screen and, unfortunately, a passcode prompt. I have no idea what Rebel would use as a passcode, so I can't unlock it. *Damn it.*

I stare at the picture Rebel picked for her screensaver, turning the phone side to side, to figure out what it is. I can't see the entire picture, not with the password prompt in the middle.

But it appears to be a picture she took of herself—not her face, but the tops of her knees and one of her hands. She's holding what looks like an ink pen in her hand, and resting on her knees is an open notebook. It looks like the same one she gave me before she disappeared.

"That damn story."

Sighing, I roll over in bed, struggling to pull myself out of it. Rebel's notebook is sitting on my dresser under a pile of other things—books and papers, receipts. I haven't looked at it since last week.

I open it back up to the front page and start from the top.

The main character is a girl—obviously, Rebel herself—getting ready for school and then riding the bus. She doesn't arrive at school until page three, the descriptive, boring sentences droning on and on. She's trying to set the scene here, but it's dull and lifeless. And she hasn't told me anything at all about the main character, besides a mirror-view, cheesy description in the first paragraph.

I take a long swig of water and cringe—even the plastic bottle that came out of the fridge smells rotten. Yuck.

I keep going . . . keep reading . . .

By the time I get to the tenth or eleventh page, the bell for first period has rung and the girl is taking her seat. She sits in the back of the room. The girl pulls out her neatly organized school notes and her science textbook . . . *wait.*

I flip the page forward and back and skip back to the beginning. The handwriting is small and neat, written in print. But something about it is making my brain itch.

Something about it is wrong.

My mind drifts back to those notepads I skimmed through in Rebel's room—the looping cursive, the stylistic handwriting that looked too mature for a girl her age . . .

I stare at the notebook pages in my hand, a sudden thought that just won't leave crawling into my skullcap.

The handwriting in this book looks completely different from the handwriting I saw earlier today . . . This writing looks childlike and careful; the other was written with a hurried but practiced hand.

I turn the notebook on its side, holding it by the ring-bound spine, and flipping through the pages, wildly. That's when a folded piece of paper falls out of it.

It appears to be a letter of some kind. I take a deep breath and read it.

> Here's the story you wanted! I hope that you're impressed. I wish I could promise you a happy ending, but this isn't some sort of fiction.
>
> Girls go missing every day and some of them die. You should know that better than anyone!
>
> I've never preferred fiction. Fiction is a fantasy, a lie, a twisted version of the truth. And we all know that truth can, sometimes, be ugly.
>
> What about your truth, huh? Is it squeaky clean, or murky?
>
> Or better yet—is it rotten from the inside out, like pumpkins in December?

Funny thing about pumpkins . . . they rot faster if you cut them. Did you know that?

If people simply left them alone, they would live longer. But what fun would that be?

No . . . We rip them from their taproots. We tear off the lateral roots, too. We poke the skin. We prod the flesh. We slice through its ribs, all the way to the soft and squishy middle. And we don't stop there!

No . . . We scoop out the seeds, and we scrape the guts, until the inside is hollow.

And don't forget about the face! That's the most important part!

The face is the part we show the world. It's the part that must be carved with precision.

Pumpkins are prettier when they smile. Don't you think?

Do you see where I'm going with this?!

While you were making up stories in your head, I was tearing REAL ones from my flesh.

You wanted truth, right? The skin and the guts; all the fleshy little bits of me.

Well, I'll give them to you, but it comes with a price. Don't say I didn't warn you!

And don't you dare ask me to smile.

But I'll try.

For you, I will try . . .

Perhaps, it's your turn to take a lesson from me. What is that saying? The master becomes the student, or is it the other way around?

Sincerely,

Your Favorite Student

The handwriting of the letter is the same as the handwriting I saw in Rebel's room—but the rest of the writing in the notebook doesn't match.

I read the letter again and again. What does it mean?

The writer of the letter seems a little unhinged. I used to like pumpkins, but the writer has ruined that for me now.

Or maybe the writing is not unhinged, but rather . . . angry. What was Rebel so angry about? And who was she angry with?

I can only think of one "teacher" she was writing for, and that was me. Is it possible she meant for me to read this?

I fold the letter in half and return it to the notebook.

If Rebel wanted me to read this story, then I'm going to read every single line of it. Maybe it will hold the clues I've been missing.

Chapter Seventeen

I lie on top of the covers, reading the story that Rebel asked me to read exactly one week ago, before she disappeared and Tamara was found dead in the canyon. I know I should have read it in full sooner, but it seemed unimportant at the time.

She said that I would understand after reading it, and I do. I understand that it sucks being a teenage girl. But I knew that already back when I *was* one.

The further along I get in the notebook, the more I realize that it is in fact a story—not just a journal-like monologue based on Rebel herself. Yes, the main character looks like her (based on that mirror-trope scene at the beginning), and yes, the school described in the pages seems familiar, but ND High is basically like any other small-town school in the United States, so I can't be completely sure. Are any of them really all that different?

The story is told from a first-person perspective, which is what I usually enjoy reading.

But the problem is, at no point in this story has Rebel revealed the first name of her main character. Not through dialogue with other kids at school, or in the home scenes either. With the differences in handwriting, I'm not even sure at this point if Rebel is the author at all . . .

The character, albeit similar to Rebel in personality and looks, has a different life. The girl in the story struggles with her schoolwork, she doesn't have an after-school job at a nut shoppe, and she lives with both of her parents, who are teachers.

Perhaps Rebel created a character who is a better version of herself. Better house. Better parents. I'm no stranger to making this kind of mistake myself—describing a character who is prettier, wittier, and more successful than me, but also so like me in every other way that it seems obvious to the reader.

The beginning pages were a snooze fest, and there doesn't appear to be much plot now either—more like a teenage girl's daily loggings and complaints . . . But considering the fact that I don't know who wrote it, my interest is piqued. Is this a student at New Day, either Rebel herself or one of her friends that I saw in the photo in her room?

I set the notebook aside, rub my eyes, and take another swig of stinky water. The clock on my bedside table reads 3:00 a.m. I'm due to be at the nut shoppe earlier than usual in the afternoon, and at some point, I need to get some rest.

The mystery phone still sits on the nightstand, too, the security code still taunting me. There's absolutely no way to know what it is, and my plan is to take the phone straight to the police station tomorrow.

If Rebel's mother hasn't reported her missing by tomorrow, I can at least try to report it myself. I can't figure out her passcode, but the police might be able to. And who knows? Maybe the police can even use the phone to track down her last known whereabouts.

If this were a crime novel, I would know what to do.

In the real world, nothing is that simple. I can't shake off the feeling that I'm overreacting to everything, and I'm already prone to an overly active imagination as it is.

My eyes are dry, like they're filled with sand, but I try to focus back on the pages.

It's what you would expect of a high school drama—PE sucks; school lunch is disgusting; the girls are jealous and snobby. I'm in and out of sleep, eyes opening and closing, struggling to follow the lines, when I turn the page and out falls another loose-leaf sheet of paper.

I sit up and rub my eyes, then read the words. I read them a second time and then a third. They're jarring, not only because of what they say but because of who they're directed at. The author has broken the fourth wall in their story, directing the character's voice directly at the reader. It's not unheard of, but it's quite bizarre, and the tone of the story has completely changed all of a sudden:

> Come close. Closer.
>
> Let me tell you something.
>
> You. Yes, YOU—the one who is reading this story.
>
> Things have changed here at ND High School. They're not like you remember.
>
> Yes, it's still the home of the Hornets. Still dead-last loser of the tri-county basketball finals. Our mascot is still that funny-looking hornet that actually looks like a fuzzy bumble bee with a chubby rump, and no stinger. We're still the Hornsey Hornets. But we are no longer the keepers of secrets. I know the truth about you. Yes, you—are you still here, reading?
>
> I have only one word for you: Saffron. I'm not talking about the spice, the one people use in those rock-hard Swedish cookies, or the color in a Crayola box. But I don't need to tell you that, do I? You know exactly which Saffron I mean. And Saffron was only the beginning.

Chapter Eighteen

Saffron Mulvaney. Not a spice or a color.

No . . . Saffron was a bunch of wild ideas bunched together and shaped into the form of a girl.

I know exactly what—or who—the writer, presumably Rebel, is referring to. But how did Rebel find out about Saffron? And does she know that we were friends in high school?

I can taste it, something awful in the back of my throat.

The urge to vomit is so strong that I roll out of bed and stumble down the hallway to the bathroom.

But the nausea passes, and all I can do is pace up and down, back and forth in my hallway, replaying every single page—every line—that I've read so far.

Nothing about this story has anything to do with what happened to Saffron Mulvaney. The two loose pages—the pumpkin carving one and the one about Saffron—seem personalized, and angry. Directed at me? Most likely.

What is the relevance of the notebook pages, and is it possible that Rebel authored both the pages in the notebook and the loose-leaf sheets of paper that fell out of it? Or could there be two different people telling this story?

One thing is clear—Rebel knows more about my past than she's led me to believe.

I want to stop reading. I want to drown all the pages in a tub full of water or take the notebook outside and burn it.

But instead, I'm going back to my room. I have to finish. Have to see this thing through.

First, I flip through the entire notebook, looking for more loose pages.

Part of me is disappointed when I find none.

Perhaps Rebel is meant to be a writer after all—with her proneness for embellishment and dramatic flair.

I flip back to the page I was on previously and keep reading.

I'm shocked to discover that, in my sleepy stupor, I nearly reached the end of the notebook. There are only a few pages left to go.

I expect more teenage ranting, or at the very least, a return to our no-name first-person POV story. But, once again, the author has switched gears, the story shifting to yet another viewpoint. This one is written in third-person, and the main character's name is Cordelia.

The name itself is confusing, considering the fact that the main character hasn't had a name thus far.

Is Cordelia the same schoolgirl who's been narrating the POV?

If Rebel were here, I could ask her to explain . . . but she's not. So I can't. Like all readers, I'm left to interpret the writer's intentions all by myself.

I read on, the story now told from a bird's-eye view, the narrator describing the young Cordelia as she follows a boy named Lear through the hallways of school. There are other students clogging the hallways with excitement as they head home for the day. Cordelia loses Lear in the crowd as she zigzags around the throng of students, ignoring those who try to speak with her.

She's on a mission—to follow Lear.

Cordelia's bike is secured to the rack outside. The bike has a crappy "banana boat seat," and it's two sizes too small for her. She's melancholy over losing Lear, but then she spots him in the distance. He's following the crooked sidewalk that snakes away from the school and leads to a pathway toward the canyon.

Pumping and huffing, Cordelia pedals to catch up with him.

Suddenly, the story shifts its point of view again. We're back to the nameless first-person POV. But it's clear from the start of this section that the story is told from a different view—not the girl named Cordelia who is following Lear, but the nameless narrator who is following both of them.

> She followed him to the canyon on her bike again, so she left me no other choice. I had to follow them both in my car, to see where they were going. Dodging side streets, watching her flash by on her bike between houses . . . for a moment, I hoped that she would change her mind, turn around, and go home. But no, she kept going just like she always does. She won't stop chasing after him and he won't stop letting himself get caught. It wasn't the first time I followed them for one of their Romeo and Juliet clandestine meetings and it won't be the last. But pretty soon I will make sure it's their final meeting, even if I have to kill them both to put an end to it.

My hands are shaking as I flip to the final page. But there are no lines left, no more pages. The last white sheet in the notebook is blank.

Did Rebel write these words? The last part sounds like the words of a potential killer—possibly, the person who followed Tamara Levy to the canyon . . . ?

The most concerning part of all is Rebel gave me this notebook days before Tamara Levy was discovered dead at Cooper's Canyon, her bike mangled beyond repair.

How could Rebel have known what would happen to Tamara unless she was involved?

Chapter Nineteen

I wake up in Fawn. The forest has grown thicker, wilder than I remember. There's something moving through the trees. Not the usual shifters and trolls. Not the flowering fairies. This is something dark. Something dangerous.

A big black shadow hovers above the trees. It's moving closer and closer . . . watching.

I throw my head back and howl, trying to scare it away.

◆ ◆ ◆

"You're late," Candy says, hands plugged on her hips as I enter the nut shoppe in a whoosh, tying my apron around my waist as I hurry around the counter.

"I know. I'm sorry."

I would have been much later had I followed through on my plan of going to the police station on my way to work. But after reading the details at the end of the notebook Rebel gave me, I can't help wondering if she's somehow involved in Tamara Levy's death. Should I turn over the notebook to the police too? I can't make up my mind . . .

If I show it to them, will they suspect her of murder? I know it's not my job to figure this out instead of the police, but as a writer, I know what it's like to have someone misinterpreting your words. Will the police assume the worst? And what if Rebel didn't even write it?

"Hello! Can you return to earth, please?" Candy snaps her fingers in front of my face to get my attention.

"Sorry," I say, again.

I freeze when I realize Candy's not alone. A young girl stands beside her.

After reading and rereading Rebel's bizarre and unsettling pages, I struggled to fall asleep, leaving me only a handful of hours to rest before the start of my shift, and what little sleep I got was riddled with bizarre dreams.

"Anyway, like I was saying . . . being late is unacceptable," Candy tells the girl, giving me a sideways look. The girl looks even younger than Rebel, with sandy-brown hair and a mouth full of braces. She's wearing a dirty white apron already.

"Emily, this is Adrian. She will be your trainer. She knows everything there is to know about my shoppe," Candy says.

"Adrianna," I correct her. I start to confess to my new trainee that I've barely worked here a month, but Candy puts up a hand to stop me, almost like she could sense what was coming.

"Adrian, this is Emily. She will be working here a few days a week, after school. Emily comes with her own fair bit of experience. She worked an entire summer at the car wash."

"Okay . . ."

Candy stares at me, waiting. Waiting for what? I don't know.

"W-welcome to the team," I stammer.

As Candy watches me like a hawk, I lead Emily around the store, pretending to be Rebel. *There's the cash register. There're the scoops. There's the scale for weighing candy and nuts . . .*

Eventually, Candy drifts back into her creepy little workshop in the back, securing the deadbolt behind her. For a moment, it crosses my mind that I've never seen what's back there. For all I know, she could be stashing young girls behind the Wonka door . . .

I sink down into a chair behind the register and rub the sleep grit from my eyes. Everyone has become a suspect, including Rebel herself, and I'm so tired that I'm not thinking clearly.

I should have called in sick today, but Candy isn't the most forgiving person, and I wouldn't put it past her to fire me on the spot. Despite all the stress over Rebel's whereabouts and the pages, I still need this job. My electric bill is due next week, and I have just enough to scrape up to pay it.

My stomach aches, missing Rebel's silly attitude and snarky put-downs. But those words she wrote . . . I'm haunted by them.

I think about her scribbling words on paper during our shifts—was she writing that bizarre story I read last night? What sense does that make?

"Did you work with that girl?" Emily asks. She's leaning against the fudge counter, elbows pressed to the glass. I'd nearly forgotten she was there.

"Who?"

"Plain Jane, the kids at school like to call her. But now she insists that everyone call her Rebel. I'm not sure why."

I sit up straighter in my chair. "You go to school with Rebel?"

Emilys shrugs. "I do, but I don't really know her. She's a senior and I'm a junior. I've definitely seen her around, though. She's hard to miss. Now everyone at school is talking . . ."

"What are they saying?" I press.

"That Tamara Levy was murdered, and now Rebel's gone missing too. Rebel's mom was up at the school today, and the cops were, too, asking people questions. She's considered a missing person now, I guess . . . because she was supposedly with the dead girl before she died."

Thank God. At least Michelle and the cops are finally trying to do something to find Rebel!

"What else are people saying?" I ask.

Emily looks around uncomfortably, like she isn't sure if she should be talking about this. She glances over her shoulder, at the closed door that Candy disappeared through.

Finally, she says, "Well, a buddy of mine's mom works for the sheriff's department. Supposedly, Tami was strangled. But nothing official has been shared yet, so don't say anything."

Tami.

It's such an obvious nickname for Tamara, but I'd never put two and two together.

Tami—the dead girl Tamara—was the pretty, young blond in that group photo taped to Rebel's mirror. So Rebel and Tamara—Tami—were friends after all.

Strangled.

I imagine a young girl's neck being twisted, around and around, mangled like the handlebars of that bike. Like the old bike Rebel described in the story, perhaps?

Something is rotten; I just don't know what it is.

Like that ripe, putrid stench emanating from my kitchen—I know it's there, if I could only find it . . . So close, but also far . . .

"Emily, do you know anyone at school who might want to hurt Tamara—Tami—or Rebel?"

Emily shook her head. "No, not really. I mean, ND has its fair share of bullies, sure. But, like I said, I didn't know Rebel well. Tami even less. They hung around with some other senior girls. Carrie and Christian, but Christian doesn't go to ND anymore. They were all in some after-school club, I think . . ."

Carrie and Christian. Were these the other two girls in the photo I saw in Rebel's bedroom?

"SSS. The Story Seekers Society?"

Emily shrugs again. "I don't know what it's called. There are a lot of after-school clubs offered at ND."

I remember the clubs from when I went there. But, unlike Rebel who played volleyball, I was interested in joining only one. And so was my friend Saffron.

A gaggle of customers come through the door, a mix of school-age kids around Rebel and Emily's age.

"Hey, Emily," a young brunette says, waving awkwardly.

"Hello," she says shyly, covering up her braces with her hand when she talks in a way that makes my heart ache.

The kids are looking around the shoppe, fingers smudging the glass cases and talking in hushed whispers.

"This is where she worked. I wonder what she knew . . ."

I try to hear their words, but it's a struggle, and I can't catch most of them.

Emily gives me a guilty look, like she's responsible for them.

Finally, the group of gawkers moves on, without making any purchases.

I show Emily how to tie a ribbon around our bags and how to use the scales, my mind still back in my apartment, going over and over those words. The mismatched handwriting . . .

What am I missing here?

"Candy gave me a disgusting apron on my first day too. I know where there are some better ones," I say, remembering Rebel's secret drawer beneath the nut case.

I get down on my knees, searching for it. It's tucked away out of view, and the floor is sticky and disgusting. Better sweep before Candy comes back here and realizes I gave up on the task after Rebel vanished.

"Ah. There it is." My fingers finally brush over the tiny knob of the drawer. I slide it open and look inside.

But there are no aprons in it.

There is something, though. Something shiny pushed all the way toward the back of the drawer.

"Hey, Emily. Can you go around the corner and check the register? Sometimes I forget to close the money drawer. Candy would kill me if someone stole money out of it," I say.

"Sure." Emily walks away, giving me a moment of privacy.

I have to pull the drawer all the way out to reach the object.

It's a cookie tin, similar to the one my Aunt Gina used for storing her needles and thread. I remove the canister and tug at the corner. It's difficult to open at first, and when the lid finally pops off, the metal lid slips from my fingers and hits the floor beside me with an ear-splitting bang.

Emily glances over but seems disinterested.

"Cash register is closed," she yells over to me, taking out her phone and scrolling.

"Thank you," I say quietly.

I look down at the tin, still kneeling on the floor by the hidden drawer.

Inside the tin is an array of items—a small silver key, half a pack of cigarettes, a folded-up newspaper article . . . and a note, folded up like origami. Just like Saffron used to do.

Did Rebel put these items here? Was she hiding them for some reason, or did she leave them for me to find?

As much as I want to inspect further, I don't have time or privacy. Sliding the lid back on, I close the hidden drawer and get on my feet.

While Emily's head is still bent, looking down at her phone, I walk over and stuff the tin down deep inside my backpack. For later.

Chapter Twenty

After work, I drive toward my mother's house for our dinner date. My head is somewhere else—lost in the pages of Rebel's story, trying to make sense of what she was trying to tell me or show me, along the way. Thinking about Saffron and what her connection might be to all this, if there is one.

Rebel's phone is still sitting on my nightstand at home. When I left for work, it was fully charged but exasperatedly inaccessible. Without the passcode, it's useless.

But maybe the contents of that tin will shine a light on whatever the hell Rebel's been hiding . . .

Instead of turning into my mother's cookie-cutter neighborhood, I drive right past it before I can change my mind. The grand entrance for her gated community whooshes by in my periphery as I follow the familiar curves that lead down the hill behind it, into the older neighborhoods of Hornsey.

I can't stomach my mother right now.

I haven't seen Aunt Gina in nearly six months, but going to her house makes so much more sense. I don't have to wear a mask with Gina . . . not in the same way I do with my mother. Gina's comfortable with who I am, and when I'm in her presence, I almost feel comfortable with myself too. But being around her also reminds me of my father, so there are times when I avoid her more than I should.

I park my car in front of Gina's two-story Federal-style home. But instead of going to the front door on the covered porch, I walk around to the back of the property, heading straight for the water.

Like a moth to a flame, my body seeks it out. Almost like it remembers.

The Whispering Sea.

It's been so long since I came to visit my father's sister, and years since I stood here in this spot—on the "beach" at the back of her property. Not a beach at all; rather, it's a man-made lake with a patch of sand and rock that was hauled in by the neighborhood's residents many years ago.

Over time, the sand has grown thin.

But it's the closest I've ever been to the ocean.

I slip my shoes off and step on the sand. Tiny black rocks cling to the soles of my feet, and sand squishes between my toes.

Nothing has ever felt so good.

The beach is deserted, too cold and windy for most of the nearby lakeside residents, especially in October.

The breeze that comes off the water is nostalgic, the slap of fishing boats thumping against the side of docks like a lullaby from my childhood.

I suck in the lake's oxygen and release my own stale batch of carbon dioxide.

I used to love coming here, when I was a kid. In fact, I wrote a few short stories while sitting right here on the "beach."

I have vague memories of kayaking and boating with my father when I was little. He and Aunt Gina grew up in this house. Even then, before I knew how hard it was to be an adult, I couldn't imagine what it must have felt like—living here, by the water, all the time. It seems like such a lucky break in life.

My mind drifts to Rebel—that run-down trailer on Cherry; the temporary fixer-upper she stays at on the weekends with her uncle, and sometimes her dad, when he comes around.

Some of us are born into luckier homes . . . luckier families. Some of us get lucky breaks. But many of us don't, and we don't get to choose our circumstances or our families.

I dig my toes into the sand, then edge up to the water. The frothy lake water hits the top of my feet with a shocking blow. It's icy cold, and tickling.

I almost feel like a normal, breathing human being again.

This is not the Whispering Sea.

This is some place infinitely better.

Or it used to be . . . before that summer with Saffron Mulvaney.

My eyes follow the edges of the lake, all the way around a muddy bend where a tall rock structure (also man-made) stands. I can still see her there, standing at the edge of it. Arms raised in a V. Not for *victory*, that's for sure.

Saffron never knew real victory. Her life was a series of painful moments, shuffled from one foster family to the next. She had no real friends at school, not until she joined SSS and we became acquainted at the alternative girls' school.

We were friends for less than a year before she died, but her death still resonates. People her age aren't supposed to die. Certainly not the way she did.

I take the origami letter out of my pocket. Even though I was never able to successfully make one myself, I'm a pro at knowing how to unfold it.

This isn't the first time I've unfolded one of Saffron's letters, but it will be the last, because I'll never get it folded back the way it was, shaped like a tiny little swan.

The paper is old and yellow, so I'm careful as I pull the tabs, even though my hands are shaking.

Finally, it's open, and I'm able to smooth it out just enough to read the words on the crinkly paper. It's too dark to see them clearly, but I already know what they say. I could recite them from memory . . .

It looks like the original letter Saffron left behind, but it can't be . . . can it? There's no way the police refolded it into its original birdlike shape, and only someone who knew Saffron well would have known to do this . . . Is it the real letter, or did someone construct this as a fake to mess with me? And if so, how did they know how to fold it exactly the way Saffron used to do?

"I saw you from the balcony." The voice comes from behind me.

I startle, wiping my face and folding up the letter, tucking it into my pocket before I turn around.

"Hi there," I say, trying not sniffle.

It's Aunt Gina, looking younger than when I saw her last. Her black hair is streaked with silvery bits of gray and cut into a neat bob with bangs. Her soft gray eyes sparkle in the light.

She slips her shoes off and steps on the sand, coming over to the water's edge to join me. If she saw the letter in my hand, she doesn't mention it.

Gina is the polar opposite of my mother. She's affectionate. Carefree. Nonjudgmental.

And still touchy, I realize, as she turns my face toward her and rubs her hands over my cheeks, before pulling me in for a tight hug.

"It's good to see you too," I say, whispering into her hair. She smells like coconut oil and jasmine. Some things never change.

Next, Gina pulls back and looks me over. Runs her hands over my hair, scans my body from head to toe.

It's not like when M-ee-Chelle or my mother does it; there's no judgment in Gina's eyes. She's looking at me with appreciation—and with something else my mother never does: *love.*

"If you had short hair and shorter eyelashes, you'd look just like him. Have I ever told you that before?"

She has.

Gina taps my nose and smiles sadly.

By *him*, I know she means her brother—my father.

I didn't come here to talk about my dad. I sigh. "How are you, Gina?"

"Fine. Great now that you're here, sweet girl."

"I'm sorry for just showing up like this. I wasn't sure if I was coming. It was a spur-of-the-moment decision . . ."

"Well, I'm glad you did." She wraps her arm around my shoulders and leads me up toward the house. For the first time in a long time, I feel safe. Cared for.

I fight the urge to turn back and look at the cliffside rock, jutting out over the water.

Mental note: This is what coming home feels like.

◆ ◆ ◆

Gina's making hand-tossed pizza, rolling out the dough, spinning it in the air like a pro, and stirring a rich red sauce on the stove that smells homey and fresh, and doesn't look like blood. I offer to help her, but she gives me a stern look. I know that look.

Everyone who has ever known Gina knows that she is the queen of the kitchen. She fancies herself to be a chef, and she doesn't want—or need—anyone's help when she's preparing a meal.

I'm waiting for her to ask me why I showed up here today, out of the blue. Or why I waited so long to come visit. But she doesn't. Deep down, she knows that when I'm struggling, I tend to isolate myself.

Unlike my mother, Gina respects my decisions and gives me space when I need it.

I send off a quick text to my mother. Sorry to miss dinner, but I got held over at work and I need the money. See you next week.

"How's writing?" Gina asks. It's a simple question. But not one I want to answer.

"Actually, I've been taking a break from it, giving my brain time to thaw."

"I'm surprised those characters of yours are letting you get away with that." Gina chuckles and winks at me.

Simply being around this woman makes me feel better.

Gina's kindness and the headiness of the lake water—the only version of the Whispering Sea I've ever truly known—is like getting a dose of medicine. The good stuff too.

I suppose that's the real reason I came—to feel better, even if only for a brief moment in time.

Gina knows me. She knows me in a way that my mother never could. Perhaps, in a way that my mother never wanted to.

She used to babysit me when I was little. And even when I was old enough to go to school, I'd still spend some weekends with her, from time to time.

If ever I was sick on a weekday, she's the one who showed up to relieve my mom and dad. Instead of making me lie in bed all day like Mom would when I was sick, she'd fix me a tray of crackers and set up the card table. I loved those crackers, and the sounds of her shuffling cards.

Each cracker would have a different topping—raspberry jelly, Swiss cheese, ham, turkey, peanut butter . . . but she'd always add a couple extra, strange things for laughs, like crackers with pickles or pineapple bits on them.

Aunt Gina loved cards—gin, rummy, spades . . . You name it, she played it. And she always played to win. Later, when I was a teenager, my mom told me she liked to gamble. "That's where she got all that money from, you know. It's a disgrace, if you ask me." My mom sniffed.

My mother never cared much for my father's sister, and she never worked hard to hide it.

I used to think that Gina and I had only one thing in common—my mother couldn't stand either of us. And vice versa.

"Have you talked to him?" I take a sip from a can of Diet Coke, trying not to look at her.

She knows I never ask about my father. But it's been a long time, and I want to know how he is. I have a right to ask questions, don't I?

"You know . . . I think he's doing well. I really do. I don't talk to him as often as I'd like to, but he seems okay."

"Is he married yet? New kids?" My words sound angrier than I intended when I spit them out.

Mental note: This is what *bitter* looks like.

Gina pretends not to notice, focused on chopping a pile of black olives. "No, not married. No new kids. He's working on an oil rig and staying sober. That's why I haven't heard much from him: He's away on a job. He seems to like the long weeks away for work. It probably keeps his demons at bay."

"Well, if you ask me, that man deserves a little time with his demons . . ."

"You're more like him than you realize, Adrianna. Certainly, more like him than that mother of yours. He used to write too. Did I ever tell you that?" she asks.

No, she didn't. And for some reason, that bit of information comes as a shock.

"My father? Really? I never saw him write down a damn thing in his life. Not even a grocery list."

Gina smiles. "Well, he always did it in private, you see. When we were kids, he'd hole up in the bathroom closet. He'd let the water run for an hour, making our mother think he was taking a bath, all the while scribbling in those notebooks of his. He would come out of the bath even dirtier than when he went in." She giggles, eyes watery as she remembers this version of my father—a version I've never known.

I wish I had memories like that.

I'm sure that if I try really hard, I can remember good times with my father.

The fishing and kayaking . . . But most of those memories are tied up in my memories of this place and of Gina. He would mostly spend his time on the water drinking beer, while I had fun by myself or with Gina.

But my heart simply won't let me think about the good times that are specific to him—it's easier to stick with the bad. My anger is my shield, and I have every right to be pissed off at a father who picked up and left when things got bad with my mother. Just because he left her didn't mean that he had a right to leave me too.

I shake my head at Gina. Still disbelieving this tidbit of personal information about my father, the writer. To me, my father always seemed sensible—the opposite of a writer. He worked in a factory when I was younger and spent his days off drinking beer on the couch. He was like any other dad in the United States, I suppose. Blue collar. Stern when he had to be. Not around as much as he should have been.

The idea of him hiding in a closet somewhere, lost in a story or poem, shattered that image of him. Or, maybe, it did the opposite of shatter—maybe it repaired it a little.

"What did he write about?" I asked.

Gina decorated the pizza with olives and small bits of sausage, smiling. "Well, one day he left his notebook in the closet. I always knew he was faking his baths, but I didn't know what he was up to. Figured he was reading porn mags, or something of that nature. So, when I found his notebook, I locked the bathroom door, sat down on the toilet, and started reading it. I read through every single page. They were silly stories with superheroes, but I enjoyed them. But, oh . . . when he found out later, he was furious. He was so embarrassed that he shredded some of his notebooks. There were poems too, romantic ones . . . I think that's what he was mostly ashamed of. He had the writing bug, just like you. He's not the perfect father . . . but there are some similarities there, beyond your looks."

"No. I'm nothing like him," I interject.

"But you do have pieces of him in you. Believe it or not, you do."

We're quiet for several minutes. I can almost hear the choppy waves of the lake breaking against the docks outside, foaming over the sand and broken rocks. I'm reminded again of broken bodies, and I close my eyes until the images pass.

Like the lake, my father was pretending—pretending to be something he was not. It's not the beach or the ocean; it's a small, man-made lake with a fake beach. And my father—he was just a man, pretending to be someone who could take care of me. Until the facade got to be too much . . .

If he wanted to be a good father, then he would have been. Simple as that.

I don't want to cry, but I can feel a dam giving way inside me, threatening to explode from within. I can't write and Rebel is missing, and I don't want to think about the past. I feel lonely. So damn lonely . . .

Sensing my distress, Gina clears her throat. "You always were a storyteller, Adrianna. I don't care what your mom says. You were *born* to be a writer. Do you remember how much you loved fairy tales?"

I smile, still choking back a sob. "It was one fairy tale in particular," I whisper. In truth, I was less of a fairy-tale kid and more a fan of Aesop's fables.

"Ah, yes. *Alice's Adventures in Wonderland.* You were always walking around, banging on the bark of trees, wondering when it was your turn to go to Wonderland. Why do you think that story was your favorite?" she asks.

That's an easy one. "Alice had it rough from the start. She's too small; she's too big. She just can't get it right. And everyone, even the flawed characters in Wonderland, doubt who she is and what she's capable of. In Wonderland, as in life, she follows the twisted path she's given. She makes choices along the way; for better or worse, those choices are her own. In the end, she becomes her own hero. That's why I liked it." I shrug, spinning my soda can in circles.

My phone chimes once, twice. My mother—probably angry that I didn't come to dinner. Oh well.

"And don't forget the best part about being Alice. Anytime life gets tough, she can always find her way back to her imaginary friends. She can lose herself in a story—just like you." Gina points her spatula at me, giving me a knowing look.

Yes, like me. Well, the old me. Now I'm stuck in the real world, unable to check out when I want to.

Gina finishes decorating her pizza and then pops it into the oven. "You'll stay for dinner?" she asks.

I agree to stay, but I'm feeling distracted. I can't stop thinking about stories. My mind used to be so full of them, but now it's focused on only one in particular—a true one that I fear will not have a happy ending.

What happened to Rebel? Is she lying dead somewhere near Cooper's Canyon, just like Tami?

◆ ◆ ◆

By the time I make it out of my aunt's house, heart softened and belly full, there are dark clouds in the sky—real ones, not like the imaginary monstrous ones in Fawn.

These clouds look angry, murderous . . . and bulging at the seams.

There's a storm brewing somewhere—in the town of Hornsey, and also inside me.

As good as it was to spend time with Aunt Gina, I have a bad feeling. It feels like the kind of day when bad things happen.

So, when I park in front of my apartment and see the police cruiser waiting there for me, I'm not in the least bit surprised.

Chapter Twenty-One

"I'm Detective Dawson. This is my partner, Detective McCabe," the female detective says.

Dawson looks too young and hot to be a cop. She has pale blue eyes and long black hair streaked with red-hot highlights. Even in business attire—attire that screams, *I'm a cop!*—she reminds me of *those* girls. Like the kind who could kick Officer Shannon's fictional ass and look way cooler doing it.

Dawson's partner, on the other hand, is an ugly old troll of a man. With his arms crossed over his chest, I can't help noticing the pit stains on his shirt. McCabe scrunches up his face at me, with beady little eyes, during our introduction.

The officers were standing on my narrow front porch, waiting for me when I arrived. They're still blocking the door of my apartment, preventing me from going inside and escaping this bad version of a crime novel that has become my life.

I haven't done anything wrong, but I feel like I have. I feel like a criminal standing in the spotlight.

My mind is whirring—trying to come up with the right character to emulate. Someone to conjure up in this moment. But no one seems right for this.

My favorite characters tend to be good guys, not the ones being hassled at the front door of their apartments by police.

"How can I help you?" I say, keeping my voice level even though I want to scream.

"May we come in?" McCabe asks. The way he's leaning against my door, like he's about to shove his way through even if I say no, gives me the impression that I don't have a choice in the matter.

"Yes, of course."

They step aside, watching me unlock my front door. My hands are shaking uncontrollably, and I can hear the thump of my own heart beating in my ear drums.

Mental note: This is what *scared shitless* looks like.

You've done nothing wrong, I remind myself. This is a good thing. Hopefully, they're looking for Rebel and wanting to ask me some questions since I worked at the nut-and-fudge shoppe with her.

I lead the officers through my messy living room and into the compact kitchen in the back. I forgot about the smell. I'm reminded now, as the rotten stench overwhelms my sinuses and makes McCabe scrunch his nose up at me harder.

Thunder rumbles outside, making the windows of my apartment rattle. Fat drops of rain begin pounding on the rooftop of the building.

Something bad is coming . . . something terrible.

Or maybe it's already here.

Please don't let Rebel be dead. Please.

In a trancelike state, I lead the officers over to a place where we can sit and talk.

Unfortunately, my dining room table is tiny. It can seat only two, but I pull one chair out and plop down in it anyway, manners be damned. I'm unable to stand up any longer, and my heart feels as though it might beat its way right out of my chest.

"You can sit. I'll stand," Dawson says, motioning for McCabe to take the other seat.

"No. *You* sit. I'll stand," Detective McCabe grumbles, nose twitchy as he looks around. Probably trying to locate the smell.

Me too, officer. Me too.

Something stinks in Hornsey, and it's permeating my apartment—and my entire life.

Detective Dawson gives her partner a weary look and sits down across from me. I catch myself studying her features. She's a great upgrade from Officer Shannon and perfect for a sequel, if I ever get back to writing about Loon . . .

"What's your relationship with Rebel James, and do you know where she is?" she says, not beating around the bush.

There it is. The question I knew was coming. It's the million-dollar question, isn't it?

We all want to know where she is, Detective. Including me.

They wouldn't be here, asking questions about Rebel, if she were already dead. They're looking for her, trying to find her . . . right? This has to be a good thing.

"We were coworkers," I say. "I haven't seen her, but I would like to know where she is too. She hasn't been at work . . ."

It's the truth. But we were so much more than that. I want to say *friends*, but does being friends with a seventeen-year-old when you're my age make you creepy? I consider the possibility that my own viewpoint might be skewed. It's not unusual for adults and young people to be friends when they work together, unless boundaries are crossed. Even though Michelle was upset about her coming over, I don't feel like I've crossed any until recently, snooping around her room and keeping secrets . . .

"Coworkers, you say. So she never came to your apartment? You only saw her at work, then?" These questions come from Detective McCabe. He's looking everywhere in my kitchen and dining room, anywhere but directly at me, still seeking out the source of the stink, probably.

"Yes. Rebel has been here. She needed help with a school writing contest, and I'm a writer, so . . ."

"According to the school, there was no such project. Her mother mentioned the contest in her interview and the time she was spending with you, so we followed up with Principal Nally about it. We spoke with her teachers too."

McCabe's eyes finally zero in on mine, and the coldness I see behind them is jarring.

I take a deep breath. "Are you sure about that?"

"Yes, we're certain," Dawson answers for him.

I feel like one of the rogue trolls who live in Fawn, less than a foot tall. In that universe, Detective McCabe would look like a giant, towering over the village square.

Is it really possible . . . that the whole story Rebel told me about the writing contest was a lie? But, if so, to what end? Why would Rebel lie about that? There was nothing for her to gain from it, surely.

"So, tell us about your recent phone call to the high school asking about Rebel. What was your motivation there?" McCabe asks. His partner is watching me, her face soft and thoughtful, but his eyes are like lasers, zapping my soul. As I remember making that phone call, I realize that there are a few more boundaries I crossed than I initially realized.

This is a question I wasn't expecting, but I should have been. Calling the school pretending to be someone else was an unwise decision, but I only did it out of my concern for Rebel.

"Rebel didn't show up at work. Recently, she turned up for one of our writing sessions with a bruise on her cheek. I was worried about her, so I wanted to make sure she was okay. That's all. That's why I called the school asking for information . . ."

"Do you have it?" Dawson clears her throat.

"Have what?" My brain feels foggy all of a sudden. Did I miss something crucial in the interview, or am I just so damned tired that I can't keep up with their line of questioning?

"The project you all were working on. Do you have a copy of it?" Dawson asks.

Without a second thought, I'm shaking my head. "No. Rebel kept her writing mostly private. I don't have anything."

But less than a few feet away is the door to my bedroom, and her notebook is probably still lying where I left it this morning, right next to my bed.

Liar, liar, pants on fire.

I'm not ready to show them the notebook. I don't understand its contents myself, but I don't think Rebel would follow someone to the canyon to do them harm. Until I know more, I don't feel comfortable sharing it with these aggressive cops.

"We couldn't find any recent writing projects on which she was working. Not at school, or her locker, and not at her mom's or dad's either. But we're just getting started . . ."

I sit there quietly, unsure what to say in this moment.

But then a tiny voice inside me is saying, *It's not the story they're worried about—it's you. They don't believe anything you're telling them now . . .*

"Here's what I don't understand," McCabe says. "You say that you were worried about your coworker, and that makes sense, Ms. McMahon, it really does. Calling the school is a little weird, I'll admit, but I can sort of understand that too. But why did you impersonate a police officer? That is a federal offense. Did you know that?"

My breath catches in my throat. It feels like there's a lump in my gullet, too big and rotten to swallow.

Maybe the stench that's permeating my life is coming from deep inside me . . .

"I didn't hurt Rebel. Or that other girl either. I don't even know Tamara Levy. And I pretended to be a cop because I knew they wouldn't give me any information on the phone unless I was family."

"Exactly," McCabe says, slamming his hands on the tiny table in front of me and causing it to rock side to side on its flimsy wooden legs. "Normal adults who aren't family don't call schools trying to get information about little kids. Information like, for instance, the child's secondary address. Only weirdos do that!" he says.

I clench my jaw. "Or concerned friends. I was worried about her. Pretty sure I'm the only one who was at that time. No one else seemed to notice she was gone. Why did it take her mother and father so long to report her missing?"

Dawson clears her throat to get our attention and flashes a sweet-looking smile. "You know, it's not uncommon for people who commit murder to insert themselves into an investigation. They try to get close to the family, call police . . . They like to know what's going on."

I stare at her, slack jawed. Is this real life, or have I entered some sort of sick and twisted murder mystery?

"Are you saying Rebel's dead? That someone killed her? I thought you found only one body. And there's no information about what happened yet in the news . . ."

"We're not saying she's dead. But we are investigating the murder of Tamara Levy. And I don't think you killed anyone, Adrianna," McCabe says, lowering the volume of his voice.

Suddenly, their roles have switched, and McCabe is trying to play the good cop.

"But if something happened, something you're not telling us . . . that could help us figure out what happened to these girls, you would tell us, right?" he pries.

I nodded. "Of course I would. I only want to make sure she's safe. And I feel terrible about what happened to that other girl at the canyon. I saw the picture of her bike on TV . . ."

"You seem to know a lot about Tamara's murder for someone who claims not to know her," Dawson says, voice steely.

"I've been watching the news reports. Just like everybody else." I scoot my chair in closer, staring back at her.

I won't let them intimidate me. After all, I have nothing to hide.

"Have you ever been married, Adrianna? Ever had a boyfriend? Because, from what I hear, you're quite the loner these days. Not close to too many people," Dawson says.

"I'm a writer. So what?" My hands are balled into tiny fists on my lap. My fingernails are digging into my own flesh. It's scary to think that these two small-town cops are in charge of finding Rebel! They'll never find her if they're wasting time harassing people like me instead!

"You said you would do anything to help find her, right?" Dawson asks, voice soft like butter again.

I nod.

"But you have a history of not being very cooperative with law enforcement, and this isn't the first time you've been connected to a local tragedy. I know about Saffron Mulvaney," she says.

The name feels like a blow to the chest. What is the likelihood that, after all these years, her name would come up twice in a twenty-four-hour period?

"I was a kid. Saffron died. End of story," I snap.

"There were suspicions though . . . and her parents blamed you for her death for a while," Dawson adds.

"Parents blame a lot of things on other people. Lots of finger pointing, but none in the right direction. That's how it was back then, and that's how it's looking again now! I think I'm done here, Detectives. Should I hire a lawyer?"

I push my chair back and stand up. I don't need a character for this one—I'm done being pushed around. The anger I feel is very real, and I want them to get the hell out of my apartment.

The police tried to bully me back then when I was young, after Saffron died at the lake, and I cried like a baby during their questions. But I have no tears left for them.

"I'm done here," I say again, slower this time.

"Are you sure about that?" McCabe has changed his stance since I got on my feet. He's spreading his legs, one hand resting on his gun, fingers twitching.

I can't help thinking about all those stories in the news, about cops overreacting and shooting people for no good reason.

Mental note: This is what you call *trigger happy.*

I try to imagine the way it would feel—like taking a hot punch to the gut, blood gurgling out of my midsection, foamy like the Whispering Sea . . .

Don't cry. Please don't cry, Adrianna. Hold yourself together now.

But my eyes are watering, not out of sadness or fear, but anger.

"I'm sure. I have nothing else to tell you," I say, looking from Dawson to McCabe, then back to Dawson.

"Here's the thing, Adrianna, I don't think you really want to help us find Rebel at all. If you did, you'd tell us why you're in possession of her cell phone. You see, we aren't pretend detectives. We're real ones. And we tracked down the location of Rebel's phone. The phone was off and impossible to track, but then it came back on. And guess what? The ping led us straight to you."

Dawson flashes a wolfish smile, showing all her teeth.

Chapter Twenty-Two

The stolen cell phone still sits on my nightstand, where I put it this afternoon before leaving before work.

I can feel the officers' eyes boring holes in my back as they hover in the doorway of my bedroom, watching me retrieve it. My body shakes, not just from fear but something else—shame. I feel violated by them seeing my private bed space, and I'm humiliated that they think I'm a thief, or worse, a potential kidnapper. Scratch that—killer.

"It's useless. It's passcode protected," I say, handing over the sleek pink phone to McCabe.

"We'll be the judge of that," Dawson says. She doesn't move from the doorway, and for a moment, I panic, like maybe they'll hold me hostage in this room forever, trying to force a confession out of me.

"Technically, we could arrest you for withholding evidence. Do you understand how serious this is?" Dawson moves closer—so close I can smell her fruity-scented deodorant.

I would help them if I could. I want to know that Rebel is out there somewhere, safe and sound.

"More questions are coming soon, so make sure you don't skip town," McCabe warns. It feels like I'm in one of those small-town horror films where rural cops have it out for the wrong suspect.

I'm afraid of being arrested, but I'm also tired and ashamed. At this point, I'll do anything to get them out of this apartment and away from me, just so I can be alone with my thoughts.

Writers are professional liars—we take bits of the truth and mix those bits with fiction to produce a believable lie. Perhaps that's why this one slips so easily off my tongue. "I found it at the nut shoppe in a drawer under the cabinet. I assumed that it belonged to Rebel, but I wasn't sure. According to Candy, who owns the shoppe, she fired Rebel for being a no-call, no-show, so I brought the phone back here to my apartment, where my chargers were, and plugged it in. I was going to return it to her, or bring it down to the police station, but I couldn't even verify if it was hers or not. After all, like I said, it's passcode protected. I never saw her with a phone at work, and the picture on the save screen is ambiguous, at best."

McCabe and Dawson exchange a look, then stare at me, waiting for me to say more.

"That's all I know," I say, with a shrug.

Dawson moves aside to let me go, and I walk straight to my front door.

"I have to work tomorrow, so I'm going to have to ask you two to leave now."

"Anything else you're hiding? Now is the time to share," Dawson warns.

I shake my head resolutely. They already caught me with one thing of Rebel's, and that made me look guilty. I'm definitely not about to fess up to the notebook too.

It's not until the door of my apartment is locked and the police car has pulled away from the apartment complex that I feel like I can breathe again. I collapse on the sofa and close my eyes, wishing I was anywhere but here.

◆ ◆ ◆

My eyes are swollen and dry from crying, sticky lids taped together and a whir of buzzing voices in my head as I strain to pry them open. I must have fallen asleep on the pleather sofa; my right cheek is pressed against it, and I peel my face off the material quickly, like it's a BAND-AID I've been dreading.

My focus sharpens, and I zero in on a familiar face.

Rebel's mother, Michelle, is staring back at me.

She's on my TV screen, talking in a sweet voice that sounds nothing like the M-ee-Chelle I met on our first encounter.

"Not the kind of jump scare I envisioned starting my day off with," I mutter, fumbling for the remote control and turning the volume up.

Michelle's voice fills my living room. As much as I want to say she's faking her distress, the desperation in her voice sounds genuine, like she's truly in pain.

On the screen, Michelle is surrounded by cameras, and the background is familiar—she's standing in front of the trailer on Cherry Street.

Why is she on TV talking to reporters? Shouldn't she be out there looking for her daughter instead?

But then I hear what she's saying, and my chest grows heavy with shame. I turn the volume up even higher so I can catch every single one of her words.

"My daughter's name is Jane James. But that name never really suited her. She wanted everyone to call her Rebel, including me. Although I didn't like it at first, I'll be the first to admit that the name fits her perfectly," Michelle says, choking on the words as she appears to fight back sobs.

"It fits . . . because my daughter has always known how to stand apart from the crowd. Even when I asked her not to, she did anyway. I wanted her to blend in. To have a happy life . . . but Rebel is who she is. She stands up for people, and she is her own person." There's a pause, and some rude reporter shoves the mic so close to Michelle's face that it threatens to smudge her red lipstick.

"My daughter is a lovely person. She's not perfect, not by any means, and sometimes we fought. But she is loved . . . Rebel, honey. If you're watching this, we love you. Both your father and I do. And we just want you to come home. Come home, Rebel."

A tall man with salt-and-pepper hair that vaguely resembles his brother, Rocky, comes into view. He sidles up next to Michelle and looks directly into the camera. For the first time, I'm looking at Rebel's father, Ronnie James.

"Name's Ronnie. I'm Jane—Rebel's dad. Baby, if you're out there somewhere, please come home. We aren't angry. We just want to know that you're safe. Even if you don't want to come home, just let us know where you are. Let us rest more easily."

Something about her father irks me. Perhaps, it's the way his speech focuses on how her being missing affects him. *Let us rest more easily.*

But what about Rebel—how is she resting these days? If she is on the run, what exactly is she running from? Or whom?

I don't know her parents well, but I do know that it took them longer than it should have to report her missing.

In true crime cases, it's always someone close to the victim—could the parents know more than they're saying?

In the background, there are a few more people standing off to the side of the trailer. I recognize a man who is pacing back and forth—Rocky. Sadie's with him, tugging at the leash in his hand.

The reporter asks Ronnie a question about Tamara Levy and her relationship with Rebel.

"Yes, we know about Tami. The girls were school friends, but I know Rebel had nothing to do with that girl's death. And I know my daughter is still alive. Don't ask me how I know; I just do. Fathers know these things," Ronnie says.

Fathers know these things. But do they?

Why would Rebel lie to her parents and say she was staying at Tami's house in the first place?

If she wasn't with Tami, then she's a liar. And if she *was* with Tami . . . well, it could be her body they're finding next. Both those options aren't good ones. What I really need is a third one. Another alternative to this horror show . . .

I squeeze my eyes shut, trying not to think about Rebel being dead somewhere or on the run from the person who hurt Tami.

I try not to think about those detectives and the accusatory looks in their eyes when they brought up the cell phone.

Having it in my possession made me look like a suspect, but maybe, in the long run, it's a good thing the police have it now.

Maybe now that the phone is in their hands, they can find a way to bypass the passcode and see when and why Rebel vanished from our lives.

Michelle's nasally voice fills my ears once again. "Please. Rebel," she begs, "if you're watching this, come home. Or just call, sweetheart. That's all we want. I want to know that you're alive and well."

And that's all I want too. Am I a suspect? Maybe.

But am I guilty? No.

I glance over at my backpack in the corner. The cookie tin is still inside it. I probably should have handed that over to the police, too, along with the notebook, but I didn't. That and the letter from Saffron . . .

But the police already know about the letter from the past. Nothing can be done to bring back Saffron. And frankly, there's nothing inside that tin that would be helpful in finding Rebel either.

The key inside the tin? No idea what it can open.

The cigarettes—stale, but still smokable. After my run-in with the cops last night, I could probably use a heady dose of nicotine to calm my nerves.

The only thing left inside the tin is the folded-up newspaper article. It's old, dated for the year 2005.

Young Girl's Tragic Death Rocks the Town of Hornsey.

Another reference to Saffron.

I remember the article from when it ran in the paper, vaguely.

The headline back in 2005 was a true one. Saffron's death rocked us all. Me, especially.

On that summer day when she died in the lake behind my father's childhood home, I was there. I saw it. I saw the whole thing happening, and I did nothing to stop it.

I didn't kill Saffron. But I didn't save her either . . .

Chapter Twenty-Three

I wake up in Star Creek. It's been a while since I came here. Nothing looks the same.

There's a pentagram burned into the center of the football field. Townspeople are holding hands, chanting. They've formed a chain of hate. The words are muffled, but they sound like, "Let her die, let her die . . ."

I try to push through the rows of people. Must. Break. The. Chain. Must get to the center of the circle. Because there's something dead or dying in the middle; something stinks. I can smell it—*feel* it—even though I can't see it.

"Let me through, please," I beg. Nobody moves. Nobody cares. They're too busy chanting, repeating those hateful words.

Red rover, red rover, let Adrianna come over.

I shove through with my head down low, like a bull with horns. I'm breaking arms. Ripping hands from their sockets. Push and pull, until I fall face first in the middle of the wicked circle.

But there's nothing there in the middle, just a gaping black hole. Should I dive inside it and see where she went? Or should I turn around and try to fight my way back home?

◆ ◆ ◆

I wake up chanting—*panting*. Struggling to catch my breath. Details of the dream are murky. I try to hold on to it, but the details are fading fast.

Trying to remember dreams is like chasing shadows: pointless.

It's practically evening by the time I climb out of bed, but I make a pot of coffee anyway.

The sun glitters through the windows; nothing is prettier than a setting sun, and there are no traces of last night's storm. The weather's so nice it should be a crime. Rebel deserves a storm. A storm that takes out houses and rips trees from their roots. Tamara Levy deserves that too.

There's a small balcony that I rarely use attached to my kitchen. It's so narrow, you can barely turn around or bend your legs out there. But I carry my coffee and the pack of stale cigarettes out there, anyway.

I force down the piping-hot coffee, punishing my taste buds.

Birds are chirping. Don't they know that somebody died? And that somebody else is missing?

I know I'm being ridiculous, but this is a feeling I know all too well.

When I realized that my dad was never coming home, I had a funeral of sorts. I put together a bouquet of dandelions and stood in the field behind our house, saying a silent prayer. Letting him go.

I thought it would make me feel better, but things only grew worse. Normal everyday things made me angry—just like I'm feeling today. After my dad left . . . when I saw people out shopping or watched my mother making dinner or watching TV, I'd get so pissed off. *Don't they know my father's dead and gone from my life? Why is everyone acting so damned normal?*

But he's not dead, is he? That's what Saffron said, when she overheard me telling one of our classmates that I didn't have a father.

No. He's not dead, Saffron. He's worse than dead—he stopped loving me. What could be worse than that?

Saffron was fatherless too; both of us attended an alternative high school because we couldn't cut it in a normal school setting. She was the only girl at ND who was genuinely kind to me, but also who challenged me at times.

And then she went and died too. How dare she?

Standing here now, clenching my teeth at the singsong chirping of birds, I can't help feeling sorry for myself.

I'm projecting. Rebel isn't my father or Saffron. She's a young girl. A girl with her whole life ahead of her. And she's probably going to be back any day now . . .

I'm gripping the coffee mug so hard I'm surprised the cup doesn't shatter to pieces.

"Did you hear the news?" says a voice.

I startle, coffee sloshing onto my hands and burning my skin.

It's my neighbor, Patty. She's standing two balconies over, leaning over the side of it. She's puffing on a long vape pen, curls of vapor around her head.

"There's been a lot of news lately. Which part do you mean?" I ask wearily.

"They found another body today, while they were out there searching for the missing girl." She's smiling as she says it, as though she thinks she's in an episode of *True Detective.*

"Whose body?" I ask.

She shrugs. "Well, that's obvious, isn't? It has to be the other missing girl. They found her in the forest, less than a mile from where the first one was."

I dump my coffee over the side, wordlessly. The birds are silent now, almost like they know that another storm is coming and that this time, I expect them to react accordingly.

Chapter Twenty-Four

"The body of a young girl discovered last week at Cooper's Canyon has been identified as high school senior, Tamara Levy. Or Tami, as her friends liked to call her. Hornsey PD has yet to hold a press conference or give a formal statement about how Tami died and if residents of Hornsey should be living in fear, locking their doors at night. Inside sources, close to the investigation, revealed that the death has been ruled a homicide, with the young victim suffering blunt force trauma—most likely the impact of a vehicle, which also destroyed a bicycle identified as belonging to Tami. Sources reveal that it wasn't the impact that killed her. That poor young girl, who must have been in so much pain and suffering from her injuries, was then strangled by an unknown assailant."

I'm sitting on the sofa, knees tucked to my chest, flipping from station to station, trying to confirm—or please deny—my neighbor's recent claims.

They're talking about Tami on the news, not Rebel.

But then a big red bulletin flashes across the bottom of my screen.

Breaking News!

The reporter on my TV screen taps an invisible earpiece, then says, "Viewers, please stand by for more breaking news. We will return momentarily after this quick commercial break."

I'm so angry that I want to jump through my TV screen and strangle the reporter myself.

I pace back and forth. Back and forth. Waiting for an update I don't want to see. *Please don't tell me it's true. Please! Another body?! It can't be possible, can it?*

Finally, the reporter's back on my screen, repeating the same sentence as before about breaking news. Only this time, the school picture of a young girl pops up in the upper right-hand corner of the screen. It's Tami. The same girl from Rebel's photo in her bedroom, just like I suspected.

And then I watch, in horror, as a second school photo pops up on the screen beside it.

The reporter clears her throat, looking off camera as though someone is giving her an update from behind the scenes.

"Take it off there. Why is her picture there . . . ?" I say, the words whispered and wheezing.

"We have breaking news," the reporter says, again, "and it's not the kind of news I was hoping to share with all of you today."

"Come on!" I scream, tossing the couch pillow at the screen. I stare at the smiling photo of Rebel on my screen.

Rebel and Tami look a little bit alike, with long blond hair and piercing blue eyes. I don't want to imagine Rebel mangled and dead, but my mind won't stop flashing with the worst images it can conjure up in this moment.

"One girl is dead in the town of Hornsey, a victim of murder. And another young girl has been missing too. Jane James, whose friends called her Rebel, has been missing for days now."

More like a week, if her mother had reported it when it happened, I think angrily.

"We are now hearing reports of a second body. Police are swarming Cooper's Canyon and the surrounding areas, but we have no further details at this time. We have reporters on the ground at the scene, and we will update shortly. Our hopes and prayers are with the families of both Tamara Levy and Jane James. Sources say that the girls were friends, but neither the families nor the school will offer further comment at this time on the relationship between the girls. This is an ongoing investigation, so please stay tuned."

There are thoughts rushing in, a gut-twisting pain in my head. I feel helpless, unsure what to do in this moment.

Impulsively, I grab my keys and backpack by the front door and head outside. I'm going to drive to the canyon and see it for myself.

Chapter Twenty-Five

Cooper's Canyon is only a few short miles from me, but I can't get close to it. There are TV news vans on every corner and a glitter show of police lights, blocking traffic from getting through the front entrance of the forestry.

I park two blocks away, between a pickup truck that looks similar to Rocky's and a news van for Channel 8. There are other vans, too, and they're not all local. I recognize several vehicles sporting national-network logos.

So, one dead girl from a Podunk town wasn't enough to interest people, but two dead girls is what it takes, apparently. Two pretty young girls, faces splayed on the nightly news, just enough to get people excited.

It's been years since I've gone to Cooper's Canyon. I'm not sure that anyone should label it a canyon, as it's three miles' worth of knobby tracks and hills, a great place for bike riders, ATV lovers, hikers, and those who want a private spot to make out.

People are standing on the sides of the street, and some of them are walking toward the chaotic crime scene.

I try to keep my head down, tucked low to my chest and inconspicuous, but I only make it half a block on foot before police sirens whir behind me.

It's Detective Dawson's face I see behind the wheel, black-and-red ponytail stretched so tight on her head that it's forcing her face into a jack-o'-lantern type of grin. I know that smile isn't for me.

"Adrianna McMahon, fancy seeing you again so soon," Dawson says, leaning her head out the window. She parks her cruiser right there in the middle of the road, steps out of it, and walks toward me.

I turn around and keep walking, but she catches up in no time.

"You know," she says, falling in step beside me, "killers are also more likely to return to the scene of their crime. Did you know that?"

"Oh, fuck off!" I whip around so quickly that she's startled, and I can't help smiling for a brief second.

Until I remember why I'm here. Until I remember that it might be Rebel lying out there in the forestry somewhere, dead like her friend Tami.

"Watch your mouth, ma'am," Dawson says. She takes a step back from me, looking weary.

I wonder if she learned that Wild West stance from watching that troll-like partner of hers, McCabe.

"I'm sorry," I say, putting my hands up in a "don't shoot" posture. "Look, detective, Rebel was my friend. We worked together, and I helped her with her writing project; whether that project was real or not doesn't matter to me. I'm here for the same reason you are, and all these other gawkers. I want to know if the body they found belongs to her."

Dawson looks past me at the other bystanders and the glittering lights up ahead. "They don't know whose body it is yet. We've been combing the area for clues to help track down Tamara's killer, so finding another body might just be a coincidence."

"Coincidence? That's bullshit and you know it," I say, holding back a laugh. Is this lady for real?

"It wouldn't be the first body found at Cooper's Canyon. Every few years, there's a hiker who gets injured out there on a trail or, sometimes, even homeless encampments where we find a body months later, succumbed to the elements."

I pause, considering that. I've never heard those news stories around here, not that I pay much attention. It's unsettling what catches the attention of the news media these days, and what doesn't.

"Is that what they think? It's an unhoused person or a hiker who had an injury?" I can't hide the hopefulness in my tone. As devastating as either of those possibilities might be, both sound better than the alternative—Rebel dead, battered and choked like her friend.

"They," she said, emphasizing the word, "aren't sharing any information with the public. And that includes you."

"Her uncle is here. I saw his truck parked back there. Is someone here to look at the body . . . to see if they can identify it at least . . . ?"

Dawson frowns. "I don't know anything yet. We're cooperating with the state guys now. This is turning out to be a big case. If we need your assistance, Adrianna, or if we have any further questions, we know where you live. And where you work. The best thing for you to do right now is go back home and stay out of the way. Everybody needs to give the medical examiner and officers on scene space to do their jobs. You care about your so-called friend, right?"

I nod.

"Then stay out of my fucking way so I can try to figure out where she is—dead or alive—and then I'll figure out who the hell is responsible for making her disappear. Got it?"

She doesn't wait for a response, pushing past me with a hard shove.

When I look around, people are watching. But that's the last thing I care about.

Slowly, I walk back toward my car, staring at the ground.

As I'm climbing behind the wheel, contemplating another stale cigarette from Rebel's secret stash, I see a familiar face pulling up in a blue sedan, parking across the street from me.

I would recognize that face anywhere . . .

Twenty-two years ago, I thought he was the most handsome man I'd ever met. One of the smartest too. He could enchant anyone . . . like a snake charmer. But that light vanished pretty quickly when he showed his true colors. And seeing him here, now, is like seeing a ghost of the man. He's not the kind of ghost from my past I want to revisit.

Mr. Hobbes sits in his car, still gripping the wheel and staring straight ahead at the same gaggle of reporters and police lights I was earlier.

My breath catches in my throat as he turns his head, seemingly looking in my direction.

But he's not the only ghost living in this town . . . His eyes brush right over me, not recognizing the young girl who used to adore him all those years ago.

I'm not that version of me anymore. Sweet. Naive. Young and beautiful.

I used to hang on to his words like they were gospel. But those days are gone.

He doesn't even know who I am.

I lock the door of my car and start the engine, keeping my eyes on him. I wasn't the only girl who adored him back during my school days—Saffron had a crush on him, too, before she died. Is he still at the school, teaching English and still in charge of the SSS club?

"Are you still adored by pretty young girls, Mr. Hobbes? And most importantly, do you adore them back like you once did me?" My question hangs in the air, unheard and unanswered.

A few minutes later, Mr. Hobbes puts his car in drive, does a U-turn, and drives right past me. I hold my breath as he goes.

He's heading in the other direction, away from the chaotic crime scene.

I wait a few seconds; then I put my car in gear and do the same.

It's time to follow this creep and see what he's been up to after all these years . . .

Before

"This is one of the best things I've ever read," Mr. Hobbes said, his eyes studying me carefully. I stared at the words on the page in front of me, then looked back up at him. Did he really mean it?

For a moment, I thought he might accuse me of cheating. After all, it wouldn't be the first time a kid at ND got caught plagiarizing a paper or copying off their seatmate's test.

"Really?"

He nodded. "I know that reading aloud makes you nervous in class, but I love hearing your voice when you're reading your own work. You say things with such conviction."

"Really?" I repeated, too flabbergasted to come up with any other words.

"Really. That's why I held you after class. I was hoping you could read it for me while I record you doing it. I'm putting together a documentary of sorts, filled with the best stories and poetry. Only the best of the best . . ."

I bit my lip to keep myself from saying something I'd regret.

There was something so special about a handsome man like Hobbes, with his writing talent and experience, taking an interest in me. Decidedly, I picked up the paper and stood up from my desk, carefully adjusting my short skirt. "Now?"

Hobbes held up one finger and walked behind his desk. Carefully, he used a key to unlock a drawer in his desk, and then he pulled out a handheld video camera. He held it up to his face, covering one eye, then pressed a button and pointed a finger at me to begin.

"*We are the girls your mother warned you about*," I said slowly. I glanced up from the paper and looked into the lens, wondering what I looked like on the other side of it.

He motioned with his hand for me to continue.

"*The girls with sly grins and secrets. We stay up late and we miss school. We tell lies about where we're going. We drain our parents' vodka, then we fill it with water. We kiss boys. Too many boys. Some of us, the really rebellious ones, kiss girls too.*" My cheeks burned as I followed the words on the paper. I was too ashamed to look up but determined to finish.

"*We are restless in the legs and tantrum prone. We all come from different backgrounds, but we have one thing in common. We were cast in these roles by our parents, shipped off to New Day to be reshaped. Reborn. They want us to learn math and science. Rules and grace. But we all know the real reason we were sent here. They didn't send us here to make us better. They sent us here to save our souls.*"

I folded the paper in half and looked up, ready to smile for the video. But he was no longer filming. The camera was resting on his desk.

"Come here," he said. His words were forceful, like he wouldn't take no for an answer. But did I really even want to say no, at this point?

He wasn't the first to make a move—no, it was me, leaning over his desk, brushing my lips over his . . .

Chapter Twenty-Six

A group of girls huddles around a collage of pictures that are balanced on what looks like an artist's easel.

The photos feature Tamara Levy, in all her various stages of life. Singing at her first-grade talent show, buck toothed and beaming. Chubby-faced middle-schooler. Cheerleading pictures from her freshman year. And then the rest of high school, in what appears to be her most recent photos—wearing heavier makeup, dark liner smudged on the bottom of her lids, tongue stuck out at the photographer playfully.

In some of the photos, she's standing shoulder to shoulder with other girls. A few of them I recognize from the photo I saw at Rebel's dad and uncle's house. Pretty girls with their prom-queen smiles. They look both broken and unbreakable at the same time. I envy them—these girls and friend groups. I never really had anything like that, at least nothing real. Saffron was it—all I really had back then.

Arms slung over shoulders, bone-white teeth, shiny pink lips spread with laughter. Camaraderie.

They were happy and innocent, at least for a little while.

Tamara Levy was loved. And for the first time, she feels like—*becomes*—a real-life person in my mind, not just a dead girl adjacent to Rebel.

Her death is a tragedy.

No one should ever die that young . . . and certainly, not at the hands of another person.

An entire life of a young girl wiped out in an instant and then summed up by a few cardboard displays covered in recently printed photos that probably came from social media or her friends' cell phone albums. The whole scene seems sadly inadequate when compared to the gravity of what occurred.

I've parked in the familiar lot of ND High School, where I followed my former high school English teacher. Before I can change my mind, I shoot off a text to Candy: Sick. Won't be in tonight. It's totally unprofessional, but my life feels like it's unraveling and I can't face the shoppe. Not today.

I stare at the memorial scene unfolding before me as I linger in the lot near my car, where I can see the crowd gathering but still avoid joining them.

Mr. Hobbes is attending the vigil, or "celebration of life," being held on the front entryway of ND High.

I nearly forgot that the celebration was being held today.

I watched him exit his car, plaster on that cheap, fake smile of his—then readjust it to something somber—and then, finally, he joined the cluster of students and teachers who surrounded the photos.

Another girl is talking at the front of the crowd, near the memorial boards, but she's talking so low that I can only catch pieces from where I'm parked.

Mr. Hobbes is lost in the crowd somewhere now, too, and I've forgotten why I even followed him in the first place.

I'm like a ghost as I cross the familiar paved lot where I spent so many memorable—and also, terrible—years of my youth. Nobody turns around and looks at me as I edge closer, scurrying up to the back of the huddle to see what's being said about Tami.

Up close, her photos reveal that she was a lovely girl. Dirty-blond hair. Bold blue eyes. A playful smile. Unlike Rebel, she looks more well kept—eyes less haunted by life, and wearing more expensive clothes.

But there's only so much you can gather from a picture.

Just a simple flash. A moment in time, our best side on display—the sides we choose to show the world.

"We all loved her," the girl is saying. "Tami had so many best friends. I'm just grateful that I can count myself among them." She pauses, sniffling and covering her mouth with her hands.

As the crowd shifts, I spot Mr. Hobbes. He is standing directly behind the girl who is speaking. It looks like his hand is resting on the small of her back. He's consoling her. Ugh.

Other girls move in closer, too, huddling around the crier. She looks vaguely familiar.

I study her features as she brushes her hair off her face and looks around at the crowd with a tepid smile. "I just miss her so much, you know? I know that all of you miss her too," she says, voice cracking.

It took me a minute, but now I recognize her. *Carrie.* The third girl in the group whose photo was featured on Rebel's mirror.

My eyes shift to the photos on the collage. Tamara was also in the group photo Rebel kept in her room—but now she's dead.

One dead. One missing. One in tears and surrounded by friends. But where is the fourth girl from the photo—the cute redhead who stuck out like a sore thumb, with her wild hair and gap-toothed smile?

I look around the gaggle of kids—a couple of boys who might be friends or family to the victim, but mostly girls since it's an all-girl school. A few stray teachers are standing around in clusters or pairs. But I don't see the redhead . . . *Christian,* I think her name was, written in ink on the back of the photo. That new girl working at the shoppe said that Christian stopped attending ND, but I was so distracted that I forgot to ask why . . .

If I could only talk to Christian or Carrie one-on-one, maybe they would have some information about Rebel's potential whereabouts. Teenagers are secretive—maybe the other girls know something but don't want to share it with their parents or the police. Maybe they're afraid to get Rebel in trouble.

But speaking of trouble . . . asking more questions and snooping around is bound to cause me more grief and hassle from the lovely Detective Dawson, and that's the last thing I need. She told me to stay out of her way, but I'm not sure if I can listen.

It can't be Rebel's body they found today. It just can't . . .

My brain won't allow me to accept it, not after the relief I felt after discovering the first body wasn't hers.

The kids are talking in whispered huddles now, wandering farther and farther away from the memorial boards. I scoot in closer to view them and slide my glasses on.

There aren't many pictures of Rebel featured on the board—but my eyes zero in on two.

Both pictures are small candid shots of Rebel and Tami. I notice that Rebel isn't in any of the pictures with the other girls, just the two with Tami.

Did she not fit in with the other girls in the group? If so, why not?

They must have gotten along at some point because they took that group photo in the classroom.

I think about Rebel's attitude: her lack of interest in talking to other teens at the shoppe, her lack of a cell phone most of the time.

Coming from someone who's been a loner their whole life, it takes one to know one.

Rebel is sort of like me—an outcast.

There's a wave of whispers behind me, and someone says, "I heard she was missing some fingers and toes. That the scene was gruesome." I'm not sure if they're referring to Tami's crime scene or the new one. Rumors spread in small towns; I know that better than anyone.

"Do you think Tami was pregnant? She did gain some weight after she quit the cheer team . . ." says another voice in the crowd.

Yikes.

When I'm certain no one is watching me, I drift over to the front entrance of the school building and tug on the doors. Part of me is shocked to find the doors of the school unlocked, but another part is not. ND High was always open in the evenings, a place for kids to come and go, for after-school sporting events and meetings for clubs.

I'm hit with a weird sensation that I'm not entering a building at all, but rather being sucked into a time loop . . . a dark loop from my past.

The first thing I notice when I enter the school is the smell. That earthy aroma of poorly ventilated, stagnant air that permeates public school buildings. It stirs up a familiar ache in my chest. A desire for friendship and structure, but also terrible memories, too, recalling how difficult it was to fit in and make it through those last couple of years at ND . . .

The waxy smell of floor wax mixed with disinfectants. Chalk, paint, dust.

Whatever that smell is, it brings me right back to my last year of high school . . .

It was an exciting year—the thrill of knowing everything was a "last." That pretty soon I would no longer haunt these hallways, slam shut the doors of my locker, or see the same few hundred small-town faces in the hallway every single morning.

Being a senior is liberating. And like me, Rebel and Tami were so close to their last and final days—but those *lasts* should have been for high school, not their last days alive on earth.

Toward the end of my senior year, there was heavy sadness too. Part of my life was fading away, albeit a part of it I wanted to let go of. After Saffron died, I could barely remember those final few months leading up to graduation.

Fluorescent lights buzz overhead.

The hallway is deserted, but if I close my eyes and concentrate, I can almost imagine the squeak of sneakers, the drone of voices carrying through the entire building . . .

I can picture Rebel moving ahead of me, head ducked as she zigs and zags through crowds of students, walking alone toward an open classroom.

But no, that's not right—she wasn't alone here. She had some friends, at least. Tamara, Carrie, Christian . . . the girls from the writers' club that were in that group photo.

A large plaque on the wall greets me at the front of the center hallway, and it's not new to me—I've seen it hundreds of times, but it never fails to annoy me. I'm just shocked that, in this day and age, it still hangs there: **Being a woman is a matter of birth. Being a lady is a choice you make.**

"How inspiring," I mutter, brushing my fingers over the plaque, tracing the brass letters.

The main entryway breaks off into corridors. Everything looks the same as I remember, mostly. Updated paint and carpet, but they're just replicas of what used to be.

There is a staircase straight ahead, with one set of stairs leading up and another down. The upper rooms used to be classrooms; the bottom floor's hallway led to an open rec area for special occasions, with TVs on rolling carts, Ping-Pong tables, and a half-ass version of a school library with only boring classics to choose from.

Rows of lockers line each side of the central hallway, the floors spackled by eerie moonlight that pours in from the high-resting windows above the rows. The lockers look smaller than I remember.

The vast emptiness of the hallway, with the closed and darkened classroom doors, fills me with an eerie feeling. If you've seen one school, you've seen them all—cold cinder block walls. The crush of bodies in a narrow hallway. But this place feels different when it's empty, or maybe it's just different because I know I don't belong here. This part of my old life is gone, dead.

"Hello?" My voice echoes through the long hallway.

I am met with heavy silence in return.

Eyeballing the lockers, I wonder how difficult it would be to track down the one belonging to Rebel. Those detectives, so busy drilling me with questions . . . Shouldn't they be here instead, searching her locker more thoroughly and questioning her friends?

I hope they've been investigating her teachers and classmates. Not just me. Just because those detectives are assholes, doesn't make them incapables. At least I hope, for Tami's and Rebel's sakes, they have some inkling of what they're doing when it comes to this investigation.

I wait a few minutes, standing there in the abandoned hallway, ears perked for any sound of life. Nothing.

The first classroom is dark, the door locked tight. I peek through the sliver pane of glass. It looks completely unchanged from my school days here. The early 2000s interior and vibe are still there, filling my stomach with butterflies. It's an eerie feeling—the sensation of being in two places at once . . . the past and the present.

I can't shake the feeling that I shouldn't be here . . . don't belong here . . . but also that I've already been here, in this exact moment, many times before . . .

I follow the long, narrow hallway to its end, passing the same wooden door marked **Counselor's Office** that was there decades ago.

Marina Dobbs, my high school counselor. The one person I could always run to for help, back then. *Anger is sadness turned inside out. Tell me, Adrianna—when you had that outburst in class today, what were you feeling sad about?*

Around the corner, three doors down. I stop in front of another familiar door. Mr. Hobbes's English classroom.

There are no guarantees that he still uses the same room, not after all these years. Changes happen all the time in public schools. Renovations, swapping out classrooms, teachers moving from one subject area to the next . . .

But I can't see Mr. Hobbes moving. He would never give up his infamous corner room, the one without windows. His own dark little cave.

I turn the knob, expecting it to be locked like the other one I tried. But the knob twists easily in my hand, and the door creaks open noisily.

After glancing up and down the hall first, I quickly slip inside the room and secure the door back behind me.

Just in case Mr. Hobbes or a custodian shows up, I decide to leave the lights in the classroom off. No one will suspect I'm in here if they walk by it . . . just another empty classroom, Hobbes's little learning cave, closed after hours . . .

Taking out my cell phone, I use the flashlight app, keeping it close to the floor, and shine it around the room to get a better look.

There are no windows in this particular room, just like I remember, giving the entire space a claustrophobic vibe. *I like to keep my classes small. Intimate,* I can remember Mr. Hobbes telling us.

I remember the way that word sounded in his mouth—*intimate.* There was something erotic—almost forbidden—in the way he described it. *We're alone here. With him. No one else can see or hear us,* I could remember thinking to myself back then. What a strange thought to have. And I wasn't the only one who felt that way: other girls snickering when he said it, looks exchanged between friends. *Oh, Mr. Hobbes. He's the hot one, right?* I can remember one of my classmates asking me in the hallway.

The first thing I notice about his room are more smells. Stale and acrid, a familiar scent of eraser dust, and industrial cleaners.

How many days did I spend in this very room my senior year—enraptured by his teachings, both in the classroom and out of it—during after-school meetings for the writers' club?

I move toward the forbidden zone in the room—his desk—scooting around tightly arranged desks and plastic chairs to get there.

My eyes wander over the walls, taking in those cinder blocks with the same, or similar, posters on them—Shakespeare, Hemingway, Poe. Mr. Hobbes challenged us, and we, of course, loved him for it.

A book is simply a kaleidoscope of lies, he told us. *A collection of the author's real world—simply shattered into pieces and rearranged into this Frankenstein version of itself. Every writer, no matter what they tell you. And believe me when I say this, writers lie! Every writer, every single one, is a liar! They're telling you a story about themselves—a fucked-up version of the truth—even when they don't intend to. Writing isn't about stories. It's about life! My life. Your life.*

I remember him poking a finger at Saffron's chest when he said that part, and I can also remember feeling jealous that it wasn't directed at me.

It took us a while to get over hearing a teacher say the word *fuck*. Or a teacher acting like lying was a normal and healthy thing for us to do—if we wanted to be writers.

"What a crock of shit," I mutter under my breath, walking around the backside of his desk. I tug on his desk drawers, disappointed to find each and every single one locked.

My mind wanders back to that quote by the front door. **BEING A LADY IS A CHOICE . . .**

Is it though? And what does that even mean?!

Mr. Hobbes, the great feminist. But, if that were true, then why did we spend all our time reading books by stuffy old men?

I shine my flashlight at the chalkboard behind me, but it's bare, wiped clean by Mr. Hobbes himself, or one of the custodians.

I move to the rows of tiny desks. The tops are clear, but inside some of them there are notebooks and colored pens, some scribbled writing too.

Geena is a big fat whore, someone wrote inside their desk.

Rhonda you suck! is scribbled on another.

Johnique sucked Dustin Henderson's tiny dick, is written in teeny-tiny print on the inner lip of one desk.

I peek inside the desk nearest the teacher's desk.

NONE OF US BELONG HERE, someone wrote inside it.

The words look angry, as though written hastily by someone who was pissed off. Rebel, perhaps?

But none of the desks are clearly assigned. No indications of which desk, if any, Rebel sat in.

I'm just about to head out when I hear the squeak of footsteps in the hallway. I yelp, struggling to turn off the flashlight app and dropping my phone in the process. The phone strikes the edge of my boot and goes skidding under Mr. Hobbes's desk.

Instinctually, I drop to my knees and crawl behind it.

The linoleum is sticky with filth, and I scramble around on my hands and knees in the dark, trying to find a place to hide if Mr. Hobbes, or someone else, comes inside and discovers me here.

I sense movement before I feel it. Holding my breath, I press my right cheek flat on the floor, staring under the desk toward the tiny strip of light coming from under the classroom door.

I don't move, don't breathe.

Years of public school have ingrained lifelong fears of mass shooters into the deepest core of my soul. We did countless drills a few years after Columbine. "Intruder Alerts"—that's what they call them now.

Stay away from windows and doors.

Move to the safest part of the room.

Drop to the floor.

Stay out of the line of vision if an intruder opens the door.

Remain as quiet as possible.

Stay calm (what a joke!).

I can't hear any sounds coming from the hallway, and the strip of natural light reveals nothing as I stare at the one-inch gap underneath the classroom door from where my face is pressed on the floor.

I'm about to chalk it up to paranoia and climb to my feet when a dark shadow passes by the door.

I gulp. What will I say if Mr. Hobbes enters the room? It's been so many years . . . What would I say after all this time, and would he know who I was, if I was standing right in front of him? How would I explain my presence here?

But, finally, the dark shadow of feet disappears. I wait several minutes before I snatch up my phone and get on my feet, releasing a breath, long and slow.

I don't walk out of ND High School—I run. Slipping out the classroom door, I take off down the hallway, muscle memory leading the way through the familiar curve of hallways. Instead of going out the front way, where I run the risk of seeing Hobbes or the grieving students, I switch left, heading for the side exit.

As a teen, the side exit was the way to go if you were skipping class or sneaking a cigarette. Bordering the side of the school, away from the main parking lot, and surrounded by thick oak trees, it is sure to provide an easy escape. And when the coast is clear, I'll circle around the building from outside and go back to my car.

But as I burst through the double glass doors of the side exit, I'm met by a familiar face. Detective McCabe.

McCabe takes one confused look at me and says, "Well, hello again, Adrianna . . ."

But I'm already gone, running past him.

Chapter Twenty-Seven

I haven't run since high school.

I can remember grunting and groaning, complaining how hard it was even then. Once a week, Ms. Machiatti would make us run a mile in PE. I was usually one of the last to finish.

But now, charging through the side lot of ND High School, my body feels wired. Electric.

Cold wind strikes my face, hair flying around and sticking to the corners of my lips. I can feel the fear slipping away the harder I run, replaced with something stronger. Tami's smiling face on that memory board. Rebel. All of them—so happy and carefree, trying to enjoy their final year of high school. My heart is filled with so much rage. They didn't deserve this!

I keep going, burning off the anger—no, sadness, according to Miss Marina Dobbs.

Maybe if I run hard and fast enough, I can escape what I already know—what my mind must accept but can't.

She's dead. Rebel is dead, and some monster killed her, just like they did Tamara Levy.

So much of the anger that burns inside me stems from my time spent right *here*—at this godforsaken school. This town. Rebel was right all along: It's not just the teachers or the school. It's all of it . . . the whole damn town. Hell, maybe the entire country.

There are monsters walking among us, waiting to snuff the life out of girls and women. Waiting to wipe the pretty smiles off their faces, to take away what could have been . . . a life unfulfilled. For Rebel, a life barely started.

But as I run, gasping for breath, it's not just the recent horror of these local crimes that plagues me. It's all of it . . . everything.

The writer's block. The lost jobs. The student loans in default. The empty frame in a drawer somewhere that's supposed to contain my degree.

My shitty relationship with my mom. My no-relationship with my dad.

Tamara. Rebel.

Saffron.

I never saw the letter that she left behind, but I heard about it. I know every single word of her suicide letter because we all did. Her parents, the police, the teachers.

I was questioned and harassed—made to hear those words, again and again . . .

I pump my arms, pushing through the stabbing pain in my left side, lungs burning.

It feels so good . . .

Forget it all, Adrianna. Just let go. There's nothing you can do . . . Isn't that what Miss Dobbs told me? *She's gone and she's not coming back. But you're here, and you have a life to live.*

By the time I circle the entire building and make it back to my car, my breathing sounds asthmatic. I expected McCabe, or even Dawson, to be there waiting.

Waiting to question me some more.

But the parking lot is dark and mostly empty, only a few stragglers from the memorial hanging around. A few kids smoking cigarettes. They look up when they see me, faces clouded with fear.

I'm no longer one of them—I'm one of the monsters, an adult who doesn't understand. What could be scarier than that?

I climb in my car, slam the door shut, and lock myself in.

The cardboard memorial displays from the front entryway are all gone. There are orange pools of light under the halogen lamps.

I look over to the spot where Hobbes was parked earlier. But he's gone too.

So it wasn't him coming into the classroom earlier . . . probably just a custodian. I'm so paranoid these days. But who could blame me, at this point?

◆ ◆ ◆

The drive home is a blur. By the time I let myself inside my apartment, I'm too exhausted to think about—or worry about—anything. I drop my backpack on the floor and slide off my boots.

But that's when I hear a crunching sound, like broken glass. The sound is coming from my bedroom!

I freeze.

"Who's there?" My breath sticks in my chest. Still clutching the keys in my right hand, I slip the sharp side of the house key between my fingers. I'm ready to take jabs at someone if I have to.

I take a couple of steps forward, ears pricked. And that's when I hear someone moving around in there—someone's in there! Oh my God, I didn't imagine the sound . . . It's real.

"Hey!" I shout, just as there's an unmistakable screech, like someone opening a window.

What I should do is run away. But instead, I run toward the sound.

"Rebel!" I shout, bursting into the room, key pointed out in front of me like the world's tiniest sword.

My bedroom is empty, but the window is wide open. Curtains blow in the breeze.

Broken glass shards lie scattered on the floor beneath the window.

It takes a moment to unfreeze my body, but then I'm running toward the window, stepping on broken glass with only my socks to protect me. I peer out the window and shout her name in the wind. "Rebel!"

But there's no one out there.

Where the hell could they have gone?

I lean as far out as I dare, looking left, then right. Still seeing no one at all, not even a neighbor or car passing by. Is someone out there right now . . . watching me as I look for them?

I turn around and look at the damage.

There's broken glass all over the windowsill and tracked to the doorway. Tiny glass shards stuck in the soles of my feet. I wince at the streams of blood coming off my feet.

The window is wide open, but from here, I can see a fist-sized hole in the glass.

Someone punched their way through it to get to the lock, then opened the window up the rest of the way to get in—and out in a hurry once they were already inside.

But who? Why?!

Clothes that were in my drawers earlier are now strewn across the carpet in random lumpy piles.

Some of the drawers have been yanked all the way out, a couple hanging at awkward angles where they were ripped off the track by the intruder.

My bed was unmade before I left, but now it looks even more rumpled.

I open up the drawer in my nightstand, looking for the small bit of jewelry I own—my mom's wedding ring and a few fake strands of pearls.

The jewelry's all there.

There's nothing here worthing robbing me for, and there's really only one thing in my entire apartment of any value at all . . . my computer.

But it's still there too, the screen turned off.

I have Rebel's notebook and the contents of the tin in my backpack with me, so those are safe.

But when I look down at the floor beside the computer, I notice the modem lights flashing.

Tiptoeing over to it, I take a nervous seat at my desk.

The phantom writer might be back. What message or story did they leave for me this time?

I flip the computer screen on and lean in . . .

But then I jump back immediately, slamming against the chair as I try to get away from the screen.

Have you ever seen something you couldn't unsee? A flash of a picture, or maybe a scary scene from a movie? Something that chills you to the bone and sticks with you, digging its claws into your marrow and refusing to let go?

Well, that's what this is, only it's much worse than any picture or movie.

A milky-white face fills my screen. It's dead and bloated, eyes lifeless. One electric-blue eye bulges from its socket.

And the arms—they're tiny and curled, like a dinosaur stance, clutched close to the chest. The body is twisted and broken, barely recognizable.

But I know exactly what I'm looking at.

The backdrop is dirt and moss. A blurry shade of tree limbs in the distance.

This is a photograph of Tamara Levy at the kill site in Cooper's Canyon.

For some ungodly reason, there's a picture of her dead body on my computer screen.

Chapter Twenty-Eight

From across the room, with my glasses off, the image on my computer is just a big blurry blob.

That's how I'd like it to stay. I never want to see that again.

I don't want to see it. Limbs. Hair. Blood. Those pretty bone-white teeth. That electric-blue eye.

I'm panting now. Pacing back and forth in front of the broken glass. I know I have cuts all over my feet, but I can't feel any pain.

I need to look at the picture again.

No! I need to call the police.

But my body is wired, jolted by fear and adrenaline. Was Tamara's killer just in my apartment? Who else would have that kind of picture of her?

Slowly, I force myself to count to a hundred. Closing my eyes, I focus on the numbers, trying to even out my breaths.

When I reach one hundred, I shake my hands out and jog in place. Put my glasses back on. I'm like Rocky—the boxer, not the hot uncle—preparing to get my ass kicked or my mind blown. I have to look at the picture again, even though I don't want to.

I creep over to the computer. I'm walking on my tiptoes now, like a ballerina, dancing toward a death show . . .

Tamara's face is still there on my screen, looking dead as ever.

I'm afraid to touch the mouse. Afraid to lose the evidence. But I have to see where this image came from.

Was it an email? I usually stay logged onto Gmail, since I live alone. Maybe I left my email open on the desktop . . .

But it's not an email. I check my inbox to confirm that it wasn't sent to me. But there's a file name at the top of my screen—DeadGirl1.

Someone broke inside my apartment and uploaded this themselves. Just like when they left me that weird little story . . .

Even though Tamara looks different because she's dead, like something out of a wax museum, I know the girl in the picture is her.

Flashes of her smiling face, pompoms raised in a V over her head, snap before my eyes. Tamara with a microphone, lips parting as she sang onstage. She was just a kid.

A collage of moments . . . moments that, when added together, became the story of her life. A story that ended violently. Someone gave her a dreadful ending, and for some sick reason, they wanted me to see it for myself.

My hands are shaking as I scroll up to the File tab and save the image again. *Just in case it disappears.*

I need to show the police when they get here. They need to collect fingerprints, analyze the file itself . . .

I take a deep breath, and then I close out the picture. Pulling up the search bar, I look for the file named DeadGirl1.

It's still there—saved in my downloaded files, which is where I usually keep documents my editor sends me. Most of my own personal files are saved to my Desktop, neatly labeled according to book titles.

The cursor hovers over the file name, my hand still quivering. I right click it and pull up as much information as I can about the original image. It's a JPEG.

I gasp, jerking back in my seat.

The image has a time stamp on it. It's from a week ago.

According to this, it's been on my computer all this time. But how . . . how is that even possible?!

Before Tamara Levy was even identified as the dead girl at Cooper's Canyon.

I remember those words on my screen—the ones I originally thought Rebel wrote to me. Yes, that's the night. The same night.

Whoever typed those words also added this image to my computer.

It's been here all along; I just didn't know it.

The killer broke into my apartment and opened this file. They wanted me to see the dead girl for myself because I clearly wasn't paying attention to anything that had been downloaded on my computer, just that half-written story.

Tamara's killer has been inside my apartment—not once, but twice.

Chapter Twenty-Nine

I maximize the picture, looking for clues.

The backdrop is fuzzy. It's clearly the canyon, but there's nothing and no one else in the picture. Just Tamara, deceased.

There are dark streaks in her dirty-blond hair. Streaks of blood, perhaps?

My head is swimming, overpowered by the terrifying image but furious all the same. What sort of monster did this to a young girl like Tami? And why would someone put this on my computer, almost like they're taunting me with it . . . ?

There's a hint of curl on the ends of Tamara's hair, almost like it's wet. Hands drawn up, mouth stretched in horror.

A defensive posture. This wasn't a simple hit-and-run someone did with their car.

Someone chased her down with their vehicle. And then they finished the job.

Her eyes and mouth were open. She knew she was going to die. She saw the monster who did this, and she was scared.

Her clothes look dirty and torn, like she's been in some sort of fight.

Fighting for her life.

Unfortunately, it was a fight she couldn't win. Someone overpowered her, someone . . . I notice a thin blue piece of material around her neck. I force myself to move closer, face pressed to the screen, trying to absorb all the details.

Not material. Wire. Someone wrapped a wire around her neck.

It's so tight that you can barely see it after death; it's embedded in the bloated gray skin around it.

The sound of the refrigerator running causes me to jump out of my seat.

I move through the house, panting and flipping on lights.

I know the killer/intruder is gone now, but if they came in twice, they'll certainly come back again.

My body is shaking—anger, fear, sadness . . . ?

I need to call McCabe and Dawson, but I just ran away from McCabe like an unhinged zealot when I spotted him at the school . . .

That time stamp. They'll think I did it. I know they will!

Those small-town cops will try to blame her murder on me!

But if I don't tell them, then there's no chance of them gathering fingerprints or tracking down who left this file.

I make a quick decision—I'll go to my mother's and call the police from there. My mother will be pissed, but the last thing she wants is to be embarrassed or to have her reputation tarnished. I'll ask her to hire a lawyer. Someone who can help me deal with these shit-bag cops and keep me from getting blamed for murder.

Anxiously, I move around my bedroom, stuffing extra clothes into my backpack, along with my toothbrush. I snatch up my keys and cell phone, then whip open the front door of my apartment.

McCabe is standing on my front porch, Dawson in the shadows behind him.

"You ran from me once today. You won't run a second time," he warns, pointed teeth gleaming in the dark.

Chapter Thirty

"Someone broke into my apartment . . ."

"Someone broke into your apartment," Dawson mimics back at me.

McCabe turns me around, slamming me against my front door, and starts patting me down.

"Where were you headed to with this backpack full of stuff?" Dawson asks.

I can see her from the corner of my eye, pilfering through the half-ass pile of things I just tossed into the bag.

"I was going to my mother's house because I was scared. Someone broke in. Go see for yourself! There's broken glass everywhere in my room. My feet are bleeding! And there's a photo on my computer that someone else put there." I close my eyes, but images of the dead girl's face are burned in my cerebral cortex. "I'm pretty sure the photo was taken by the killer, and I think it's Tamara Levy."

My words are panicked and wheezy.

McCabe is done patting me down. He and Dawson are exchanging worried looks.

"Stay right there," Dawson warns, unhooking a radio from her standard-issue police belt and walking a few feet away. From here, McCabe and I listen as she requests backup from the command center. "And send over the forensics from Northern County who were at the canyon earlier. We need everyone you got on this. We might have potential fingerprints. DNA . . ."

She lowers her voice and keeps talking.

Thank God. At least they're going to try to figure out who did this.

Who was inside my apartment, and were the killer and the intruder one and the same?

Detective Dawson walks back over to us. McCabe is gripping my shoulder with his big bear paw, squeezing harder than necessary.

"Put her in the cruiser for now. After the other crews come, we'll have someone take her to the station," Dawson says.

McCabe leads me over to the cop car and opens the door. Blood squishes between my toes from walking on the broken glass, but my body is fueled by too much adrenaline to feel the pain of it. "I'm not going to handcuff you, but if you try anything, I will," he barks.

"I won't." My voice trembles with fear.

I duck my head and climb into the back of the cruiser. When the door slams shut behind me, I'm all alone, and I'm hit with a sudden, strange flutter of relief.

At least I'm safe from the killer in here, and thank God they're going to process my apartment and look for clues . . .

Chapter Thirty-One

My stomach is in knots, growling every couple minutes. It seems impossible to be hungry at a moment like this, but I honestly can't remember the last time I ate anything.

I've been at the police station all night, holed up in an empty interview room.

No one has offered me food or drink. No one has been here at all.

It's almost like the entire station is empty . . . or the entire town is deserted. Like on Narcel, I'm all alone on my own planet with nowhere to go, nothing to do . . .

I don't know which is worse—the annoying hum of the overhead lights, the mind-numbing silence, or the not-knowing feeling in my gut.

Every few minutes, I stand up and pace the room, shaking the numb feeling from my legs and the burning sensation from my bloody feet, all the while praying that the slight amount of pressure I feel in my bladder doesn't get worse anytime soon.

In the far-right corner of the room is a camera. Occasionally, it makes a whirring noise as it moves side to side.

"Can someone please come talk to me? I have a right to know! And I really need to pee."

I stand on the tips of my toes, getting my face as close as possible to the camera.

"I have rights." I say the words slowly, baring my teeth. "I'm trying to be helpful. But if you're going to hold me here, I demand to see a lawyer," I say.

I have no money for a lawyer. Who am I kidding? Earlier, before being confronted by the detectives, I actually felt scared enough to consider going home to my mother's house and asking her for help and safety. But all I want to do now is go back home, crawl into bed, and pretend those images I saw were just a bad movie, or a bad dream . . . none of this is real. It can't be . . .

This eight-by-eight room is essentially a cell, because I can't get in or out, and I'm all alone.

The only company I have is my intrusive thoughts and flashes of a mangled dead girl.

Just as I'm considering smashing the camera with my fist, the door to the room springs open.

Detective McCabe enters the room. He looks less gleeful than earlier, his face a somber and unreadable mask.

Wordlessly, he takes a seat at the small table in the middle of the room. "Come sit down, please," he says. He removes the cap from his ink pen and pulls out a pad of paper.

Begrudgingly, I take a seat at the metal table across from him, wishing it were his partner instead. Detective Dawson is a stone-cold bitch, but at least she hasn't manhandled me, like McCabe did earlier with his meaty man hands.

But he surprises me with his next words.

"Adrianna, you're lucky you weren't killed tonight. That's the honest truth. I'm sure that whoever killed Tamara was also inside your apartment tonight. But what I'm not sure about is the why. And why the hell didn't you call 911 right away?"

I'm shocked by his demeanor. Does this mean I'm no longer a suspect . . . ? But how could that be?

"I just got home and found the image. I was in shock . . . I was scared. I was running out of my apartment and trying to get somewhere safe when you met me at the door. And, let's be honest, Detective, you aren't my biggest fan. I was going to call you guys, but the first thing on my mind was getting out of there in case the killer came back."

I'm expecting disbelief or some sort of snarky pushback, but McCabe offers none of that. He sighs deeply, massaging the stubble on his chin. He looks totally and completely exhausted.

"Do you know who put that picture on there yet?" I ask.

McCabe shakes his head. "Someone has been accessing your computer. They were on there tonight, just like you said. From what we can tell, the only fingerprints in your apartment belong to you and one other person."

One other person.

"The killer, you mean?"

McCabe stares at me, his eyes black and expressionless. "Rebel James," he says flatly.

"I already told you, she was there before . . . before the murder and before she went missing."

"Someone wanted to share that image with you. Why do you think that is?" McCabe asks, switching gears.

Oh, I see where this is going. I've been downgraded from killer to accomplice now. Great.

"I honestly have no idea, and that's the complete truth," I say.

McCabe purses his lips and cocks his head, studying me. It's a look I can't quite define. It's almost like he's toying with me . . . but why? What does he know that I do not?

"The other body in the canyon. Whose body is it?" I ask, scared to hear his answer.

"We still don't know. There are some . . . complications . . . with the identification process."

"What complications?" I press.

"I'm not at liberty to discuss this case with you at this time. We have limited information, as the case is still active. Very active," he says.

I wait for him to say more, and finally . . . he does.

"Adrianna, when is the last time you were in contact with Rebel James?"

"I answered this already," I say, sighing deeply.

"Are you sure she hasn't reached out since then? Or come by to visit you? Her fingerprints are all over your apartment."

Ah. So that's what this is about.

"I told you and your partner that we were working on a project for the writing contest," I explain, again.

"Yes, that's right. The fake writing contest."

I cleared my throat. "Mr. Christopher Hobbes. He's a teacher at the school. Teaches high school English. He was a creep back when I went to school there, and I'm sure he's still a creep now too. Rebel had him for English, and she was also in an after-school writers' club that Mr. Hobbes is in charge of. Tamara, I believe, was also in the group. So were two other girls: Christian and Carrie, but I don't know their last names. Have you questioned Mr. Hobbes or either of those girls yet? You need to talk to people other than me because I only know exactly what I've told you already. I have nothing new to add!"

"We've spoken to the teacher, as well as many other teachers and students at the school. I know that Rebel didn't have many friends. She had a falling out with some of her friends months ago, and the other girls you mentioned . . ." Detective McCabe stops and writes down their names on a pad of paper. "I'll look into it. But right now, I need you to be as honest as you can. If you're still in contact with Rebel, then I suggest you share that with me right now."

Wait. If he thinks I'm still in contact with Rebel, then that means he thinks there's a chance that she's still alive. Then maybe that body they found after Tamara didn't belong to Rebel after all. Oh, please let that be true . . .

"I will reach out to you right away if I hear from her. And frankly, I hope I do because I'm worried about her safety," I say.

McCabe nods, but he looks weary, and I suspect he doesn't believe me. What does he know that I don't?

"You came to my apartment when I didn't call for help. Why? Were you coming to question me again?" I ask.

"For one thing, you ran from me at the school. Why?"

I shake my head, trying to forget. "Memories, bad ones. I was trying to outrun my own ghosts."

"Is that so?" McCabe raises his eyebrows.

"Is that the only reason you came to my apartment?"

McCabe grunts. "Dawson got a tip right after you left the school. That you were hiding something in your apartment and needed to be looked at further as a suspect."

"Excuse me? Who?"

McCabe holds up a hand. He's not going to tell me anything above the bare minimum; he's made all of that very clear.

"I thought you might be hiding the girl there. She and Tami were friends. I thought maybe something happened . . . she did something she might regret and that you were helping her hide."

"I would never do that," I say, dully. But I'm not sure if that's the truth. If Rebel had come to me because she was in trouble, would I have helped her? Maybe.

"The person who called said I was hiding something, but I'm not. Maybe they broke into my apartment and tried to frame me so that you would find the gruesome photo in my apartment and think I'm the killer. I wasn't supposed to be home; I was supposed to be working at the shoppe, but I called in. I showed up and caught them in the act . . ."

McCabe frowns. "That sounds a little far fetched."

But does it? At this point, nothing seems impossible. "I'm telling you . . . it's true."

"But who would do that, Adrianna? Who has it out for you?"

Good question. I'm not very well liked, but I don't have really have any enemies. At least not anymore . . .

"We also talked to the uncle. Rocky James. When we showed him a picture of you, he thought you were his niece's boss. It seems you were at his house, impersonating Rebel's supervisor. Can you understand why this all makes you look very suspicious?"

I open my mouth to defend myself, but then I close it. He's right—I have made myself look sketchy and untrustworthy.

"I was just trying to get some information about Rebel's whereabouts, and just like when I called the school, I thought I would be able to get more info out of him if I lied . . ."

"Well, he wasn't too happy about it. Neither is the family. The mom and dad have pointed the finger at you as some loner type who spends their time grooming teenagers and luring them to your apartment . . ."

I pinch my eyes shut. This is all so ridiculous . . . but I can also understand what it's like not to trust people, and the family has a right to be scared. And I don't blame Rocky for being pissed at me about the lies.

The door to the interview room swings open again. Dawson steps into the room, eyes gleaming. "Found it!" she says, holding up a plastic bag of what looks like a matted clump of hair but smells like rotten meat.

"Found what?" McCabe asks, with a tired groan.

Dawson walks over and drops the bag onto the table, right in front of me. Bile rises in my throat as I stare at it. The beady eyes popping out of its head, the twisted limbs, and the mess of hair . . . my mind drifts back to those horrific images of Tamara.

"It was just a big, fat rat living under your refrigerator. The smell in your apartment! It was right there all along, under our noses," she says, looking positively pleased with herself.

McCabe rolls his eyes at her and turns back to face me. "If Rebel contacts you, please let us know right away. And, Adrianna? Be careful. Because we think Rebel might be involved in these murders. Not as a victim, but possibly the perpetrator."

Act Five

She's Hiding in Plain Sight

Chapter Thirty-Two

The sun is rising, a whole night lost, as I exit the concrete box that calls itself a police station.

I'm free to go, as McCabe said. But not to my apartment. It's still being processed as a potential crime scene.

According to Dawson, it will be days before I'm allowed to go back inside.

There are ten missed calls on my cell phone. My mother and Gina—no voicemails left behind. A few numbers I don't recognize, and two calls from my agent. I can see the text readout from the voicemail she left. Adrianna, OMG. Your town is making national headlines. A real-life true crime story is happening in your own backyard. This is exciting! Well, not exciting, exactly . . . that's not what I mean. But you should call me. Please? This might be something I can work with. There are potential book deals in the air. Can you smell them?

I hold down on the power button until the screen turns black. I'm scheduled to work in less than two hours. Maybe if I walk there now, Candy will let me clock in early. Plus, there are bathrooms at the shoppe and the mall that the shoppe's inside of. I can wash my hands and face . . . catch my breath for a while. Maybe pick up a sandwich and soda somewhere . . .

The shoppe is only one mile away. I'm walking on cracks in the sidewalk, every step a burning, painful reminder of the cuts I endured from the glass. I should probably bandage them up soon before they get infected . . .

I'm moving with my head down, like a hound dog following a scent.

Step on a crack and break your mother's back.

"It's you!" someone shouts from across the street.

I freeze, unsure if I should run or keep walking, maybe sit on the ground and hide my face. I just want to hide away from the world. Forget that image I saw on my computer. Forget what those detectives said about Rebel . . .

But someone is crossing the road, waving me down, shouting my name.

"Adrianna, right?" The girl stops in front of me, out of breath from her jog.

Her hair is twisted into two adorable side buns, and her lips are glossy pink. Girls these days look like girls from my generation, but like an updated version. Teenage beauty 2.0.

Scratch that—it must be like version 7.0 by now.

"I'm sorry, do I know you?" She looks familiar, but my brain is fuzzy from lack of sleep and (probably) stress, and I need to get to work since I'm headed there on foot.

"I'm Carrie. I went to school with Tamara."

"Oh, right. Carrie." The girl who stood at the memorial board. The crier. She's also one of the friends in the group photo I saw in Rebel's bedroom.

Carrie sticks her hand out, and I shake it wearily, thinking about how dirty mine probably is, after gripping the sides of that filthy table in the interview room.

"I heard about what happened. I'm sorry."

"Oh?" I rub my eyes, patience growing thin. "Heard what exactly?"

"That Tami's killer broke into your apartment. I'm glad that you're safe," Carrie says.

"Oh, right. Yeah, thanks. Hey, I have to get to work."

"The nut shoppe, right? Rebel was in my writers' group. She was excited when Candy agreed to hire you," Carrie says.

"Were you and Rebel friends? I saw some photos of the two of you at the memorial. I thought maybe you'd heard from her. Or someone else might have heard something, through the teenage grapevine . . . one of your friends from school, perhaps?" I ask.

Carrie shakes her head. "No, I wish. I'd love to know where she is so I can find out what she knows about Tami. Tami was my best friend."

Apparently, when someone dies, everybody becomes their new best friend.

"So, you weren't friends with Rebel?" I ask, trying to get the conversation back on track.

Carrie shrugs. "We hung out some after school with the writers' club, but we weren't close."

Close enough for Rebel to hang a photo of the group on her bedroom mirror . . .

I bet she'll change her tune if Rebel winds up dead. Suddenly, she'll have *two* former best friends to cry about. From what I can tell, it seems like they were friends—based on the pic in Rebel's room and my new coworker's account of the girls' relationship at school. Is Carrie hiding something too? Does she know more about Tami's death and Rebel's disappearance than she's letting on?

I rub my temples. I know I'm being unfairly judgmental, but I don't have time for this. My head hurts and so do my feet, and I need to get to work, especially after calling in yesterday.

But I also can't afford to pass up this opportunity to ask Carrie more questions.

"How many girls were in the club, besides you and Rebel?" I ask.

Carrie narrows her eyes at me, suspiciously, as though my question is unfounded.

"I just want to figure this out too," I say, shifting from one sore foot to the other.

"There were only four of us, actually. Me, Rebel, Tami, and Christian Lorde. But Christian Lorde moved back to Louisiana last year, and the writers' group shriveled down to three. Now it's only me, so what's the point anymore, ya know? The group is currently taking a break. Not that we had a choice . . . It breaks my heart just to think about it now."

Carries picks at a hangnail, then examines her manicure. She doesn't look too heartbroken, if you ask me. But what do I know about teenage girls anymore? I used to be one, but these girls have changed—they're smarter than I was. More secretive . . .

"Is anyone else from your school missing? Anyone besides Rebel?" I ask.

Carries looks up at the sky, as though she's thinking. "I don't keep up with everyone at school. I'm pretty busy. School, sports, clubs, band . . . you know how it is."

Not really.

"No one?"

Carries frowns. "No one that I can think of. Rebel was kind of snarky and mean sometimes, but I hope the body they found wasn't hers. Nobody deserves something like that. I know that Tami didn't deserve it." Her lips twitch; her eyes crinkle. Okay, maybe she is upset after all. It's hard to tell these days, and I'm suspicious of everyone I encounter.

Please don't cry. I don't have time for it, and my emotional bandwidth is spent.

But instead, I say, "There, there. It'll be okay," and offer Carrie an awkward pat on the back because it's the right thing to do.

"I'm sorry for focusing so much on Tami. But like I said, she was my best friend. I'm sure you're upset about Rebel. She was your biggest fan! She literally begged that boss of hers to hire you before . . ." Carries says, voice brightening.

I don't like the way she's referring to Rebel in past tense. And I'm not sure what she means by *my fan*?

"What are you talking about?" I say.

Carrie gives me a strange look. "Oh. Well, Candy hates anything and everything to do with computers. She asked Rebel to post the job on Indeed and try to find the best fit for it."

"But . . ." I think back to how the job came about. Yes, I put my résumé on Indeed and made it public for local employers to view. But hardly anyone reached out to me, so I contacted nearly a dozen places that were hiring and did their online application process through Indeed.

Now that I think about it, I can't even remember directly applying to the nut shoppe before I received a call from Candy, out of the blue, scheduling an interview.

"I didn't know that Rebel was involved in the process of getting me hired. I just assumed that was Candy's doing," I say, slowly, still trying to process this update.

I knew she'd read my books, but I certainly didn't know she considered herself a "fan."

"Well, I had no idea who you were when she mentioned you to the club members and told us that she was working with you at the shoppe. I'd never heard of your books, and Rebel usually reads nonfiction in her spare time. Like I said, I wasn't familiar with your work, no offense," she says, blushing. "But we were impressed that she knew a real-life writer."

"No offense taken. Look, Carrie, I need to go to work. But can I ask you something else? Why would someone want to hurt your best friend? Did Tami have any enemies?"

It's a lot more than one question, but what I really want to know is *why*.

Why would someone in a small town like Hornsey hurt a young girl like this?

"No. Absolutely none. Everybody loved her, especially me. I was her best friend," Carrie says, making sure I don't forget. "Heaven gained an angel with that one," she continues, and I wonder which one of her seventy-two-year-old Southern grannies she picked up that expression from.

"Indeed, it did. Sorry for your loss, Carrie," I say.

I walk the rest of the way to work in a daze.

Nothing about my life feels real anymore. It shouldn't have come as such a shock that Rebel knew who I was and encouraged Candy to hire me. After all, she pointed out, *You're that writer, aren't ya*, on our very first day of work.

But with the fake writing contest, her recent disappearance, the murder, and someone targeting me at my apartment . . . I feel like I'm missing something, a very critical piece to this puzzle.

Candy's ready and waiting when I get to the shoppe.

But today I'm early instead of late, so how much can she really complain?

Although, I am missing my apron and probably stink a bit, since I didn't have time to freshen up or use deodorant—or sleep—after leaving the police station.

Candy blocks me from coming behind the counter. "Don't come any further," she warns, holding up one finger with a pointed red acrylic nail.

"Why not?" I ask dully. But I can sense it, what's coming down the pike . . .

"Guilty or not, I can't have you here in this store. The whole town knows you were at the police station all night last night, being questioned by the cops. And your other friend who ditched out on work—she's still gone and missing! I'm starting to think both of you are in cahoots, a bunch of devil-worshipping weirdos," Candy says.

Devil worship? This lady really is stuck in the eighties.

"Are you serious?" I say, but it's already clear from Candy's demeanor that there's no turning back now. Having me here is bad for business, and ultimately, all she cares about is herself and her shoppe.

"Fine. I'll just take my last payday then," I say, crossing my arms over my chest.

I expect her to refuse—after all, who am I going to complain to if she doesn't fork over my illegal money?

Candy nods. "Stay right there."

She disappears in the back room, and I look around the shoppe, feeling nostalgic. It was a lousy job for sure, but I'll miss it. More than anything, I'll miss joking around with Rebel and having a good time while we worked.

But those days were gone already, so there's nothing to lose at this point—besides a crappy paycheck that's barely covering the rent of my currently-a-crime-scene apartment that I can't even go to.

God. My life sucks so bad right now, and it only seems to be getting worse.

"Here," Candy says, coming out of the back room with an envelope of cash and an army green backpack in her hand. "Take your money and take this too."

"That's not mine," I say, plucking the envelope from her fingers and pointing at the bag.

"No, but it's hers. Your friend, Rebel. She left it in the store the last time she worked here, so I put it in the back for her. If you see her, will you make sure she gets it? There's a bank envelope with some money in there. I counted it, but I didn't take any of it!" she says defensively, thrusting the bag into my hands.

"Maybe you should have given this to the police a week ago when you found it here," I say, looking over the backpack before slipping it over my shoulder. Now I have two packs to carry on my long walk home, since I don't even have a car to drive. Or a job.

Or a home to walk to, I remember, cursing under my breath.

"I don't deal with police, honey. Or the Feds. Fuck the government. Every single last branch of it. They're lizard people. You know that, right?"

I wince. And she calls us the weirdos.

"Thanks for the money." I turn and limp out of the shoppe, my feet aching but not as much as my heart as I exit Candy's for the very last time.

Chapter Thirty-Three

As I cross the parking lot of the mall and walk toward Main Street, I spot several TV news vans passing by, and a few parked in front of local restaurants and shops.

So my agent wasn't lying after all—the deaths have sparked the nation's interest, and that interest only seems to be growing.

With two backpacks to carry and a head that feels like a bowling ball on my shoulders, I begin the long trek. The last thing I want to do is run into reporters asking questions, or those detectives again.

I make a quick turn, weaving between a Dollar General and a used bookstore, and enter the woods instead. It'll take me longer to get to my mom's house this way, but it's not like I'm in a hurry, and taking a detour will provide me with some much-needed alone time to think.

The woods adjacent to my mother's house stretch on for miles and miles, connecting this whole damn town. They're deep and wide, thicker in some areas than others.

It suddenly occurs to me that if I were running away, or hiding, the woods are exactly where I would go. Is it possible that Rebel's hiding for some reason? Does she know something about the murders?

Like that disgusting rat in my kitchen—so close, but also far.

For the first time, I allow myself to entertain the idea that she might be involved in that young girl's death. Is Rebel really capable of murder?

I think about that body in the picture—the horror on Tami's face and the damage sustained to her body.

No way could a teenage girl inflict that kind of horror on another. It just doesn't seem possible . . .

The kind of rage, and hatred, it would take to do that sort of thing . . . I never saw that kind of anger or violence emanating from Rebel. The letter she wrote me—*Your Favorite Student*—the one that fell out of the notebook . . . Yes, it was a little unhinged, I'll admit. But it was the writing of a young girl filled with anger and pain, not the budding words of a killer. At least, I don't think it was . . .

Leaves and twigs crunch under my feet. It's been a long time since I entered these woods, but I know them well. I snuck out, both from school and home, skulking away to these woods all the time as a teenager.

There are four-wheeler trails that get narrow and twisty, and if you follow them for a bit, the paths eventually merge and take you all the way up to the canyon where those bodies were found.

I shiver at the thought. Following in the footsteps of a killer . . . could the monster who hurt Tami, and possibly Rebel, be someone local?

I let my mind drift back to Rebel's letter. *Home of the Hornets . . . but no longer keepers of the secrets . . .*

The secrets had to involve ND High, but what were the girls hiding?

What is your secret, Rebel?

The trees above create a protective canopy, only small slivers of sunlight pouring down on me. I follow the sounds of birdsong and walk a familiar trail, the one I know leads to a small creek in the woods.

The creek was where I used to go when I wanted to smoke a joint or just be alone with my thoughts for a while. I'd perch on an overturned tree trunk, writing in my notebook, all while feeling cut off from the world around me.

I wish I could say that I feel differently, now that I'm an adult. But I don't. Not really.

That *difference* has morphed and changed, but it's still there—always has been.

I used to love writing out here. But now, I haven't written in months, and I don't even have any paper.

All I have is this damned backpack stuffed with clothes, and this mysterious backpack that belongs to Rebel.

The last thing I need is to run into Detective Dawson and Detective McCabe again, and this time with a backpack belonging to a missing, possibly dead girl.

Even though Rebel's gone, she's left clues everywhere. If only I knew how to unravel them and piece them back together . . . how to make sense of it all . . .

I follow the trail through the forest, gripping her backpack in my hands.

It feels unusually heavy, and I'm eager to look inside it.

The trail is softer than usual, the forest floor becoming like soup under my feet.

By the time I make it to the creek bed, the bits of sky I can see through the trees are pink and cloudless. Morning has morphed into late afternoon.

My old tree trunk is gone, so I plop down on the ground beside the creek bed, not caring how muddy my butt gets.

The front compartments of the backpack are filled with random things you would expect to find in a kid's schoolbag: pencils, pens, erasers, a lighter—okay, that's not normal, but not so strange either.

I unzip the main part of the backpack and am surprised not to find any papers at all. There are no folders or books inside. Just a small metal lockbox and a large white envelope.

I look inside the envelope first. Candy wasn't lying about the money—the envelope is stuffed with cash. Like Candy, I count it too.

There are a lot of bills wadded together, but they're not big ones. Mostly ones and fives. A few tens and twenties.

Sadly, the thick wad of cash amounts to less than three hundred dollars. Not a shabby amount of money by any means, but not a treasure either.

I think back to what Rocky said—about her saving up for a new motorbike. Perhaps, this is where she kept it, tucked away in the backpack she carried to and from work, never wanting to leave it behind, at school or home. Protecting her savings for the bike with her life.

My heart aches in my chest. Rebel wouldn't leave the money behind, just like she wouldn't leave her cell phone either.

Maybe she really is dead after all . . .

I place the envelope back in the bag carefully, and then I remove the heavy box. This is what was weighing down the pack.

Strangely enough, the lid of the box looks dirty, as though someone dug it up from their backyard.

I stare at it, wondering. Nothing about this makes sense.

The box is small, like one of those cash boxes you see people using at little booths in the mall or concession stands at basketball games.

I pick at the lock on the box with my fingernail. I could probably bust it open if I hit it hard enough, against a tree or with a hammer.

Struck with an idea, I sit the box aside and reach for my own backpack. I throw out the clothes and toiletries from the top and dig around in the bottom of the bag.

Despite my fears after the break-in, I wasn't daft—I stowed some of the items belonging to Rebel and the notebook in my bag.

I dig deeper, relieved when my fingers brush against the cold metal key I carelessly dropped in the bottom of my pack.

If this key doesn't open the box, then I don't know what will.

I slip the small silver key into the lock and turn it. The metal lid springs open with a creak.

There's not a lot in the box. No cash. What could be more important to stow away in her lockbox than the money she was saving for her the bike she so desperately wanted?

There is a tiny handheld spiral notebook. A few loose photographs and a plastic baggie with a folded piece of paper inside.

I take the tiny notebook out first, turning it over and back. There's a big sparkly neon unicorn on the front cover. It looks like something *those* girls always carried in elementary school—the bright colorful ones with Lisa Frank's name scrawled across the front.

But this is a cheaper version. And honestly, it's not Rebel's style. At least I don't think it is.

But it's full of Rebel's scribbled writing.

I flip through the pages. This isn't what she wrote during our "lessons," but it looks like she was jotting down stuff, dates and times. An address I recognize from my childhood. An address for a school friend, but not one of Rebel's . . . One of mine. Saffron was bumped from foster family to care home during her mother's addiction "spells," but every once in a while, her mother would straighten up her act and Saffron would get to go back home . . . Why does Rebel have this address? Was she talking to Saffron's biological mother?

I set the notebook aside for a minute, reaching for the pictures in the bottom of the box. The photos are facedown.

They're creased and worn, like maybe they were crumpled up by accident or left outside for a while.

The first photograph is of Rebel herself. Sitting on a porch swing, hands neatly folded in her lap. Her smile is tight and strained, but pleasant, and she's clearly putting on a show for the picture.

The next photo is closer up, and she's staring right into the lens at whoever took it, almost like she's looking at my very soul.

I will her lips to move, to form the words, to tell me where she is . . . *Where are you Rebel?*

My hands are shaking as I lift out the other photos and hold them up into the sunlight.

The first one is Rebel again, but this one is very different. She's shirtless, wearing only a bra and pajama shorts, and looks asleep, almost doll-like, lying on someone's bed. Her bed, maybe?

But then I remember that I've been to her father's house and this bed looks nothing like hers.

My stomach curls as I look at the photo. The bedding is dark in color, masculine almost.

It's possible that it could have been taken from her bedroom at her mom's. But by whom? A boy she liked? Or maybe a girl?

It looks strangely intimate and heinously inappropriate for someone to have of a young girl.

It's not unheard of for teens to take risqué, intimate photos even when they know they're not supposed to. But these photos look like they were taken without Rebel's knowledge or, possibly, even her consent. She looks . . . practically dead in the photographs. Dead or asleep, in her underwear. Splayed in a weird position.

My hands shake uncontrollably as I reach for another photo in the box. It's another inappropriate one, but this one isn't Rebel. And it's two girls in the photo this time, not just one.

This time it's Tami and Carrie. Their eyes are open, very much alive, but they're also half dressed and they look tired. Almost like they'd been drugged.

I turn the photos over where I can't see them, feeling like I might puke.

Who the hell took these photos, and why did Rebel have them in her backpack?

But as I lift out the last photo in the box, I find my answer. Part of me knew who it was all along . . .

The final photo is a girl I recognize—it's me, but it's not me. It's a version of the girl I once was . . .

Vomit springs from my mouth and nose.

He still had my photo after all this time . . . or someone else had it. Why was Rebel holding on to this?

Shaking and mouth sour with bile, I remove the baggie from the box. A tiny square of paper is inside, thin as a feather.

I unfold it and spread it open on my lap.

It's handwritten, but it looks to be a photocopy of the original.

It's an ad. *For a writing contest.* My skin prickles.

I skim the details as my heart pounds in my chest.
There really was a writing contest. She didn't lie, after all.
There's a date on the bottom of the flier. *December 1st is the deadline.*
The story calls for three thousand words or less, written in English.
The theme—*young love.*

Chapter Thirty-Four

I stare at the flier, turning it over and back. It's strange. I've never entered a writing contest before, but it seems like there should be a physical address or an email address or some actual details for how the writer should send in their submission.

Also, shouldn't there be a sponsor of some sort, a person in charge of the contest?

If it was a writing contest hosted by a teacher at school—like that weirdo, Mr. Hobbes—then why isn't his name on it?

It doesn't say who is hosting the contest or what the purpose of it is. There's no mention of any prize money, like Rebel said there was.

It's like someone threw it together and printed off a few copies . . . but who?

Rebel's face swims before my eyes. That excited glow in her cheeks, the nervous lilt to her voice as she told me about the prize money. *Nearly two hundred dollars,* she told me.

They act like she was a troubled teen. But they used to say that about me too.

Rebel was excited about something she was working on; it meant a lot to her. And someone clearly created this writing contest, even if other teachers or students didn't know about it.

I should have asked Carrie about it when I saw her on the street, but I was tired and leery. I'll track her down soon and ask more questions.

Most importantly, who took those creepy, inappropriate photos of her and her friends? Is it a coincidence that two of those people are now dead or missing?

The photos are damning . . . I should look at them again, but I don't want to.

I wonder if it's possible that the photos of the girls were taken by other friends, or even another teen they liked. But there's something so unsettling about them. Photos like these shouldn't exist of girls their age, and Rebel should never have been in them. But my picture is here too . . . Is it possible they were all taken by the same person?

Rebel obviously knew about the photos, since she was carrying them around in a lockbox, with the key kept separately in a tin in the secret drawer under the nut case.

She clearly knew they needed to be kept hidden . . . so why did she keep them? Why were they taken in the first place?

Rebel filled her lockbox with photos and this flier instead of the money that she so desperately needed for her new motorbike. These photos were important to her—more important than money, obviously.

Rebel isn't a killer—at least I hope not. But I'm more convinced than ever that she's in grave danger, and so are, possibly, the remaining girls from the writing group.

One is dead, one is missing, and there's another dead body yet to be identified.

And I don't believe in coincidences. Never have.

I know Carrie. But what about the fourth girl in the group pic—the one who moved away? I think back to my conversation on the sidewalk with Carrie . . .

Carrie said that Christian Lorde moved away to Louisiana.

Could Christian have taken these photographs of her writers' group members? Does she know who hurt Tami and where Rebel went?

When I was a teenager, it was impossible to track people down if they moved away from Hornsey. But nowadays, with social media, it's pretty easy to find someone. I need to find Christian Lorde and ask her some questions, as soon as possible.

I tuck the photos and flier back into the lockbox, lock it, and put it back inside Rebel's backpack. Nobody needs to see those photos, ever. Except, possibly, the police.

I turn my cell phone back on, ignoring the cacophony of texts and voicemails coming through—more from Mom, Gina, and my agent, presumably, and I pull up Instagram. I barely use it, but I have the app, and I know how to search for people.

It takes less than a minute to find Christian Lorde's profile.

Carrie wasn't lying—her location is listed as Baton Rouge, Louisiana, and I recognize her profile pic as one of the same ones from the memorial board.

Why did you skip town, Christian? And what do you know?

Before I can change my mind, I click on her page and send her a message: Hi Christian. My name is Adrianna, and I was helping Rebel with her project for the writing contest. I'm not sure if you've heard the news, but she's missing. And one of your other friends is dead. I know you moved away, but I was hoping you could tell me more about your time spent in the writing group. Did you know about the contest, or did that occur after you moved away? Also, have you heard anything at all from Rebel lately? Or anyone else who might know where she is? We are desperately searching for answers in Hornsey and could use your help here. Please respond when you can. I'm not a reporter. I worked with Rebel and we were friends.

I click Send, then turn my phone back off.

◆ ◆ ◆

There are all these different versions of me walking around this town.

There is the angry teen. The college student. The dropout. The writer.

The daughter. The mentor. The friend. The whore.

And don't forget, my personal favorite, the murder suspect . . .

Somewhere in this town, there's a seventeen-year-old version of me walking around. Full of love and yearning. But also full of anger and pain.

As I trek past the trees lining Brickston Park, I can almost see her, that younger version of me—hiding behind a tree in the park, face pressed against the bark and panties down around her ankles. Meeting up with boys, trying to feel something, *anything*.

And a few miles from here, back at the high school . . . that same version drifts from classroom to classroom. She actually believes that her high school English teacher is going to leave his wife and be with her. He made promises; he kissed her behind the closed door of his classroom.

The boys in the park don't kiss like Mr. Hobbes; they're rough and mean, and they tease her for going to an all-girl school—*the bad-girl school,* they call it. She thinks that Mr. Hobbes's softness when they kiss means he's not the same as those boys.

And he's not—he's *worse*. Because she actually trusts him.

Back then, Mr. Hobbes was not that much older than me. I was a teenage girl on the cusp of adulthood, and he was in his mid-twenties.

It didn't feel like a crime. It didn't even seem that weird to me.

But when we were alone in his car, outside those classroom halls, something changed. He was gripping my hips so hard that I could feel the cold metal of his wedding ring digging into my skin. That ring left its mark, a thin purple bruise that was more painful than it looked and left the kind of scars that you can't really see. The kind you feel deep inside you.

What happened with him caused more than a bruise—my parents' relationship unraveled shortly after that, ripping my family apart and making me feel guilty even though I know it's not my fault. Hell, it ripped my mom apart. When I finally told her the truth about Mr. Hobbes, she was so angry. But not at Mr. Hobbes. She was angry with me. After all, I was the one with a history of promiscuity. This wasn't my first rodeo. Two years prior, I'd been expelled from Boulder Creek and sent to ND as an alternative. It was a last resort.

How could you do this, after all the chances I've given you? And now you have to go to that school for delinquents. It's so embarrassing! my mother had said. *How could you be so stupid?*

She blamed me, treating me as though I were on level footing with the teacher who was supposed to be the authority figure.

In my mind, although I never talked about it, I agreed with her at the time—for a long time. I felt like I *was* a willing participant. Sure, he shouldn't have done it. He was an adult. He was married. He was a teacher. But he was young, too, and I was . . . I was . . .

"A fucking kid," I say, through clenched teeth. A kid who deserved a teacher with boundaries, not the kind who invites you into his car and pulls over on the side of the road and takes advantage of the trust you put into him.

I turn away from the park and stalk toward my mother's house. I wanted to avoid going to see her, but there's really no other choice.

My apartment is a crime scene. My car's still there, too, but the keys are inside the apartment, left behind after my interrogation with police. I should go home and break in to get the keys, but I can't afford more trouble, and, truthfully, I'm not ready to see that hellhole again.

I look frightening with my hair sweaty and wild, unslept, and unshowered. I look positively feral, just like I did as a teen. But maybe that is exactly what my mother deserves—to see me for who I really am. The version of me that she helped create.

You were asking for it, she told me. *How could you be so stupid?*

I remember everything she said to me that day, as I cried into my hands and held my head down in shame.

What did I expect, when I told her the truth? I thought she would be shocked—even angry. But I never thought she would blame me.

That's not how things like that are supposed to go.

There's this TV version of what grooming looks like, and then there's the real version. The part when you're a kid . . . a girl who feels like a woman . . . and it happens so subtly that you don't know it's happening until it's over.

I thought that as time passed, as I grew older and wiser, I would finally see the light—I would finally stop blaming myself for what happened. But it's still there—that gnawing guilt.

That guilt festers inside me. And ever since it happened, ever since I told my mom, things between us have never been the same. I still blame myself, sometimes—even now. Because I find it hard to believe that this man, this teacher . . . could be doing it to someone else.

I thought I was the only one. I thought I was special. But none of us are. We're just generations of women passing around trauma like a blowtorch. And it's possible . . . very possible, that Mr. Hobbes was involved with what happened to those girls. Could he have been grooming one of the girls? Maybe they threatened to expose him . . . ?

By the time I make it to my mother's house, it's nighttime, and I'm shocked to realize that I'd been roaming the woods for hours. I haven't slept much this week, and every single bone in my body aches.

I know I could have called Mom or Aunt Gina to come pick me up. But I needed this time to think . . . to figure out my next steps.

I walk along the creek that runs behind my mother's house and squat down beside it. I poke at the water with a stick, feeling childish.

I don't want to go inside and talk to her. My real hope is that she's already in bed and I can just use my spare key to go inside and lock myself away in her guest bedroom for the night.

I step over my mother's flower bed and skirt around the hydrangea bushes, and then I enter her home, straight through the unlocked front door, without even knocking.

Chapter Thirty-Five

"Mom?" I lean against her closed bedroom door, pressing my lips against the cold white wood.

She used to drink a lot after she and Dad got divorced. After he moved away and left both of us for good. Sometimes the only conversations we had all day were done with a closed door between us.

"Mom?" I repeat, waiting to see if she'll answer. *Please just be asleep. That would be the easiest thing.*

"Adrianna?" my mother says.

I can tell she's standing right there on the other side of the door, only inches away from me, listening. There are traces of anger and sadness in the way she says "Adrianna."

"Of course it's Adrianna. Who else would it be, Mom?"

There is a sniffling sound on the other side of the door.

"Mom?"

It's been years since I saw—or heard—my mother cry. But she used to do a lot of it.

Sometimes, I think that's why she arranges these weekly preplanned dinners. For one hour every week, she can hold it together—the drinking and the depression—in order to act like a normal mother. Well, normal if you consider carefully controlled emotions, never talking about the past, and sweeping all bad things under the rug to be *normal.*

"Open up, Mom. It's okay."

There's a clicking sound on the other side of the door. Nervously, I turn the knob, letting myself into her bedroom. It's been years since I've stepped inside it—her inner sanctum. Unlike the rest of the house, my mother's room is a total mess—clothes and makeup strewn everywhere, stuff pouring out of closets and drawers.

If you want to know how well someone has it together, check out what's behind their closed bedroom door. Behind the polished wood and the scrubbed counters, beyond the well-swept floors in the main rooms of my mother's house, she's falling apart inside, and perhaps, she always has been.

My mother's sitting on her bed, her face a puffy pink color. I stare at her, feeling a mixture of sadness and relief. Relief for finding out that she's still human after all.

"Mom. Talk to me." I sit down next to her on the bed. I try to reach out a hand, try to console her. But she turns away, still sniffling.

"I never was a good mother to you. Not back then, and not now. All I ever wanted was for you to be happy. Happy and successful. Better than me. But I've failed you, in every way possible. And I thought . . . I thought . . ."

I'm stunned. My mother never admits her faults, and she rarely apologizes. I had no idea she blamed herself for my failures and mistakes, but hearing her say it feels strangely . . . satisfying.

"You thought what?" I'm genuinely confused but trying to be gentle. My mother is more fragile than she's let on.

"I heard that the killer broke into your apartment. That you left the police station, but nobody saw where you went. I thought you were dead, Adrianna! That maybe you . . . you . . ."

"What, Mom?"

"I don't know. I thought maybe the killer got you. Or maybe you killed yourself, just like that friend of yours back in high school," she says.

"Saffron." Her name tastes funny in my mouth. I haven't talked about her out loud in years, and my mother and I never spoke about her after it happened. "I'm sorry if I scared you today. I'm okay . . . I just had to take care of some things. The police wanted to ask questions about the girl who's missing since she came to me for help with her writing. And, Mom? I would never kill myself like Saffron. I promise."

There were times when I worried that not me, but she, my mother, would do something drastic, when she was going through the worst of her depression, after Dad cut and ran.

I watched Saffron jump from the ledge. I watched her flail in the air for what felt like minutes, and then she sunk like a rock. According to the divers who fished her out of the lake, half her skull was crushed. She hit her head as she soon as she broke the surface of the water, on the sharp rocks that jut out from the man-made lake. I hope she didn't endure more suffering in those final moments than the suffering she was already going through with her mental health. But I guess I'll never know the truth, or what she was thinking before it happened.

She never came back up from the water, and by the time I'd gotten my Aunt Gina to come help, there was no saving her. Gina couldn't find her in the water, and it was nearly a whole day later when she was finally pulled from the lake.

I never was the same after Saffron died. I don't think anyone could be, after losing someone like that and seeing it happen.

Saffron was troubled, like me. We ran around in some of the same circles—with wild, mean boys from other schools and reckless girls. Saffron had a history of trying to hurt herself. She had shared that with me one night when she came for a sleepover.

But I thought she was doing better, and I had no idea that she planned on jumping that day. I wish I could have done more to save her.

My mother takes my hands in hers, looking me straight in the eye. "What can I do to help you get through this, Adrianna? I'm sorry that your father isn't here."

Suddenly, I'm twenty years younger and feeling something akin to déjà vu. How many times did my mother blame his leaving on what went wrong in my life?

If only your father had been here, this wouldn't have happened.

It's not my fault he left me all alone to deal with you on my own . . .

"Hell no, he's not here, Mom," I say. "But, do you know what? That's okay. He left when things got hard, but you didn't. We didn't need him then, and we don't need him now. You weren't perfect. Far from it. But you've always been there for me, in your weird little way. I don't need Dad. I just need you. And there's nothing I need you to do right now, but just to be here for me. That's it, Mom. That's all I've ever needed . . ."

This is a conversation we should have had years ago—but here it is. Better late than never, I guess.

I don't always like my mother, but I do love her. I want her to be better than she is, and in this moment, on this awful day—when I've lost my job, my sense of safety, my apartment, and maybe even my friend—I need her the most.

"My mother was horrible to me," she says abruptly. My mother's eyes are lost, staring over at the stack of photo albums in the corner of her room. I've never seen her open one of those photo albums in her life, but I've opened them. When she wasn't around. I know they contain a treasure trove of pictures from when she was a little girl. Photos of her own mom and dad. Her brothers and sisters.

I never met my maternal grandparents, and now I understand why.

"I wanted to be better than she was. Better for you. But look at me! I'm just the same, just as bad . . . unable to prevent awful things from happening to my own daughter."

"Not anymore. You can choose to change. We both can. And it's not your fault," I say, squeezing her hand.

Generations of women passing down trauma. At some point, it has to end. Maybe we can put a stop to it.

Her expression softens. "I hope so. I really do."

She grips me in the best hug she's ever given me, and it lasts so long that I can feel myself falling into her arms . . . and falling off to sleep right there in her bed, while she holds me close, the way I always wanted her to.

Chapter Thirty-Six

My apartment looks different, like an empty shell. A ghost of its former self. It's been stripped of all its warmth. What little warmth it had in the first place.

I take inventory.

Dishes—check.

Clothes—check.

Towels—check.

Canned goods—check.

Cleaning supplies—check.

Books—check.

My sanity—still up for grabs.

Everything in my apartment is labeled in neat yellow tubs. I'm not normally this organized, but Mom has been overseeing the move. She's helped with the packing some, but mostly she's just been ordering me around. I've let her do it, relieved to not have to be in charge of my own life for a little while.

Something has changed between me and my mother over the last few days, since our little cry in the bedroom. Something has softened, grown easier between us . . . and it feels like something I've needed for a very long time.

"I think we're all ready to go," Mom says, from where she's standing in the living room.

I watch the movers she paid carry the tubs and boxes, one by one, out to the moving van. We easily could have done this ourselves—I don't own that much stuff and Mom's house isn't far at all—but she insisted, so I let her schedule and pay for it anyway.

My mother seems determined to organize this move, down to the last little detail. I think that having something to do, a list to complete, things to check off feels more manageable to her. Unlike the rest of what's been going on in my life, and the entire town. She doesn't know what to say or do about those things, but she knows how to make a list and check it twice. Or thrice.

Reporters have knocked on her front door countless times, and some of them have managed to get my phone number. They want to talk to everybody who knew Rebel or Tami, anybody who might know more about the other dead body near the canyon. The one the police still have not identified.

But nothing has changed, as far as the investigation goes, and I haven't heard from Detectives McCabe or Dawson in nearly a week, since I walked out of that police station.

An assistant from the police department called me, to let me know my apartment had been released, so I could go back inside.

The rotting odor is gone, and it's no longer a crime scene—but I can't live here anymore, not after my illusion of safety was destroyed, and it's not like I was doing a great job of paying the monthly rent anyway.

I notified my landlord that I was moving out of there, for good.

My waterbed was drained. It's wadded up in a ball by the curb next to the garbage cans. Good riddance.

Mom follows the movers in and out, watching them like a hawk.

Motionless in the living room, I watch my shitty apartment turn into an empty, hollowed-out space. I won't miss it. Staying with my mother is not ideal, and Aunt Gina offered for me to stay there too. But being at Mom's place is only temporary, and it makes the most sense right now. Mom offered to help me get a lawyer if I need one, and she seems much better lately, springing into action to get me moved out of this place and swatting away pesky reporters.

At least the killer, or whoever broke into my apartment and left me that heinous photo like a macabre gift in the first place, won't come back to this place.

I'm going to stay at Mom's until I can get some money saved up. I filled out some new applications on a different website and removed my old profile from Indeed. If the killer is stalking me, he's going to have to do it at my mother's house.

It's been only a short while, but I fear that the case is going cold. There have been no new updates. No harassing visits from McCabe or Dawson.

There have been nearly a hundred "Rebel sightings" all throughout the US. Right now, it's front-page national news, but soon people will forget. Updates from page one will move to page seven and eventually disappear altogether. And none of the coverage matters if there aren't any real progress or updates. Still no word on if the other body in the canyon belongs to her.

I won't forget. I can't. I need to know what happened to her, for better or worse. Eventually, I will find out the truth.

I turn my attention to my mother. She looks heated, pointing a crooked finger at one of the movers. I can't help feeling sorry for them, but I'm relieved her finger's pointed at them instead of me.

"No, those aren't coming," she tells them. "You can just throw them away." My mother's standing by the open front door of my apartment, where she can act like she's the overseer of a construction crew.

I drift outside, where the moving truck is parked at the curb, to see what the fuss is about.

It's a stack of reading material, but not my books. Stuff from my closet that the movers shoved inside a single box. College brochures, my high school cap and gown, my acceptance letter from Indiana University Bloomington.

When I was younger, I used to believe in the lie. *The lie* that if you go to college, you can be anything you want to be, which results in what we all *really* want—*to live happily ever after.*

I blame it on my first-grade teacher. I blame it on my mom. I blame it on those damned sappy commercials of troubled kids tossing graduation caps into the air.

No one tells you the truth behind the lie—that once you get the degree, you'll get a tiny pay raise and a nicer job, but no one can promise you a nicer life.

You can't be anything you want to be, not always. For example, when I was five, I wanted to be a ballerina. Mom stuck me in classes and bought me the pink pointy shoes.

But no matter how much I wanted it, no matter how much I practiced, I was always behind. Not to mention the fact that I'm five feet tall now. Ballerinas are tall. And thin. I am neither of those things.

So, instead of accepting the lie for what it was, I simply changed the dream. I wanted to be a veterinarian, but the colleges around here don't offer the right classes for it. So I finally decided on psychology. *I want to help people,* I told the admissions counselor.

Don't we all? she replied.

I remember thinking she had a bad attitude, but now I smile as I remember it. I was only starting my college journey then, but she already had it figured it out. She knew about the lie, and I didn't. I was so naive.

The whole writing thing came about much later, when I was in a dark and lonely spot after high school. I'd always loved books and writing, but for the first time, I decided to take it seriously. And I found real joy in it. Until recently.

I think about Narcel, Loon, Star Creek . . . *Maybe I can start writing again.* Once I'm settled in at Mom's and this Rebel mystery is resolved.

I'm not myself unless I'm writing—and maybe that's the cure. Maybe writing will fix me again, like it did last time I felt broken.

"She's right, guys. Throw all that out. I don't need it anymore," I tell the movers, pointing at the old college stuff. That's a version of my life I'm ready to let go of.

But Rebel isn't one. I still want to know the truth. I also want to know who killed Tami—and why.

I take one last look at my shitty apartment. Although nothing spectacular happened in it, I wrote my last few novels here. That has to count for something.

I have everything I own, and it's all coming with me to Mom's. Well, except for one thing: my computer. The police still have it, but I don't really want it back anyway. I'll buy a new one when I have the money for it.

I don't want to see that image of the dead girl ever again, anyway.

The old desk my computer sat on looks haunting without the monitor and CPU. I pull out the keyboard drawer, one last time for good measure. Shockingly, the investigators missed the keyboard itself. It's still sitting on the tray where it was the last time I was here, when I clicked it and then saw those disgusting photos . . .

My stomach twists in knots as I remember those frightful images.

I know what I should do—call McCabe or Dawson so they can come get the keyboard. But good keyboards aren't cheap, and they didn't find any other fingerprints anyway . . . Maybe if I start writing again at Mom's, I can do it on my own familiar keys.

When I lift the keyboard, I'm surprised to find something taped to the tray underneath. I recognize it—a USB stick. But it doesn't belong to me. I peel it off from where it is taped. Did the killer leave this behind for me on the night they broke in? I don't have a computer to plug it into anymore to check, but I know I need to take a look.

"Someone is at the door for you," my mother says. I startle, nearly dropping the USB.

"Okay, I'm coming. Just taking one last look . . ." When she's gone, I tuck the USB into my back pocket, take one last look at my bedroom, and leave the keyboard behind.

"Who is it?" I say, stepping out into the hallway. But I can already see Rocky's six-foot frame standing in the front doorway.

My mother gives me a confused look, then excuses herself to the kitchen.

"Hi there," I say, clutching my hands in front of me. What the hell is Rocky James doing here?

He looks the way he did when I first met him, covered in dirt and grime from doing construction. But this time, he isn't smiling.

"You lied to me. Why?" he says, looking around the nearly empty living room, as though it will contain some crucial clue to the mystery of his niece's disappearance.

"I'm sorry. It seemed like a good idea at the time. I was so worried about Rebel and I thought telling you I was her boss would give me more authority and help me find some answers . . ."

Rocky's anger deflates, and it looks like he might cry.

"They're giving up on her. I just know it!" he says, rubbing at his cheeks.

"They're not. They won't," I say, assuming he means the police. But part of me worries that he might be right.

"Have you heard anything? Any clues?" Rocky asks, desperately.

I shake my head. "No, I'm sorry. I'm moving to my mom's, but it's not too far from here. I won't stop looking for her, either, I promise. And if I do find out something, I promise I'll call you and this time I won't tell lies. Okay?"

Rocky nods. "Okay," he says solemnly. It looks like he wants to say more, but my mom—who has probably been listening on the other side of the kitchen door this whole time—enters the room.

"Adrianna, I'm paying the movers by the hour. We have no more time to waste," she says. She gives Rocky a disapproving glare and then taps at the nonexistent watch on her wrist.

"I have to get going anyway. Sadie's in the truck. Talk to you later," Rocky says, and then he's gone.

Chapter Thirty-Seven

I wake up on Narcel. It's cold—colder than usual. The ground is dry and gray. My voice echoes for miles, breath forming tiny little puff clouds around my head.

It's empty. Dead. No one lives here anymore.

No one except . . .

"Adrianna?" The voice is small, fragile. Familiar.

Rebel. She's lying on the edge of a rocky cliff, peering down at me from above. Looking up, all I can see are her eyes and nose. She sticks her head out farther, revealing her bow-shaped lips. "It's cold here," she whispers.

Her head wobbles back and forth at the edge. Then it rolls right off the side of the cliff, landing in the water below.

◆ ◆ ◆

I wake up in Mom's guest room, shaking uncontrollably. The clock on the nightstand reads 12:07 p.m.

Mom has been waking me up early the last few days. *Making sure you're productive,* she says.

But she must have decided to let me sleep in today, probably because of yesterday's front-page news: The body they found in the canyon has not yet been identified. Identification has been complicated by several factors, especially one in particular—the most recent corpse they found had been dismembered, and not all parts have been recovered. Police are unsure if the killer kept some body parts or if animals scavenged the scene. The killer is escalating . . .

I tiptoe over to the living room window and peek outside.

There are no news vans or police vehicles out there today, thankfully.

Throwing my clothes and shoes on, I make my way downstairs. Mom is in the kitchen, scrubbing a cast iron skillet with soap and water. I cringe.

"Did you sleep okay?" she asks me, without looking up.

I want to ask her to turn the news on, but I know she's been trying to avoid it herself and wants me to do the same. In her mind, if we don't see or hear the awful things that are happening in Hornsey, then maybe we can pretend they're not true.

I say, "I'm going to head out early today. I plan to start writing again soon, and I need to buy a new computer. But don't worry, I won't be gone long."

Mom's face relaxes as she turns around to look at me. "Okay. But don't talk to any reporters in town if you see them, okay? I heard they've been swarming people, trying to get answers . . . They're like damned vultures."

I can't say I blame them. I want answers too. At least somebody around here isn't sweeping it under the rug . . .

"I won't talk to anyone while I'm out," I promise.

◆ ◆ ◆

As soon as I sit down in the driver's seat, I remember the USB in my back jeans pocket. I lift my butt up and take it out, not wanting to damage it.

Checking out what is on this USB stick is my main goal for the day. I slip it inside my glove box, pushing images of severed limbs and heads out of my mind. I might not like what I find on that stick, but I won't turn and look the other way. I have to know what's on it.

I didn't tell my mom this, but there's not a place in town that will take my credit. I can't get a loan for a new computer, not at Best Buy or Target. Not even at that chintzy rent-by-the-week type place down in the valley. So I told a lie. Wouldn't be the first time I was dishonest.

I park in front of Hornsey Public Library, surprised by how full the parking lot is for a weekday afternoon.

I haven't been to the library since I was a teenager. At that age, I came here as an excuse to get away from home. I loved to read. Always have. But I didn't do much reading at the library then. It was more of a place to escape to, a place that felt safer than school.

It's funny how memories come rushing back, even ones I thought I'd forgotten. As I step inside, I walk right past me—that troubled-teen version of me—slumped in a bean bag in the YA section, headphones blasting music. Something angry, I'm sure.

I wave at my ghost and keep going.

There are three round tables in the middle of the library. They are full of teens. I can see myself sitting at one of those tables, Saffron beside me, huddled whispers in the hallowed halls of the library. This always felt like a place where secrets could stay safe.

But it's not me or my friends sitting at the table. I'm not a little kid anymore.

That's another day—another life entirely. And the table is full of a group around Rebel's age, but none of its faces are familiar.

The library is full of other people, too, browsing the shelves and looking at the world's worst VHS, DVD, and audiobook collection.

I can't remember the library ever looking this crowded before, nowhere near it.

When I was a teen, there was one computer. But now there are rows and rows of terminals. Unfortunately, though, every single one of them is full.

Over to the right, in the children's book section, there is one lone computer. But it's also being used by a child who looks five or six.

I walk up to the counter to talk to the librarian.

"Are there any computers open?" I ask, even though I already know the answer.

The lady behind the desk is your stereotypical librarian. Glasses perched on the edge of her nose, mouth drawn down in a perpetual frown. "You can put your name on the list and wait your turn," she says, pushing a sign-up sheet across the counter toward me.

"Is it normally this crowded in here?" I ask, scribbling my name on the sheet.

She taps a pencil next to my name, pursing her lips. "No, but today is not a typical day. The kids got out of school early. It's the yearly parent-teacher conferences for the entire district. Not to mention the fact that everyone in a twenty-mile radius who doesn't own a computer or TV comes here when there's big news in town."

I think about the dismembered body in the woods.

That definitely qualifies as a big news day, in any town in the United States.

So I wait my turn, making my way down the first aisle of books, perusing the titles. They are in alphabetical order according to the author's last name.

I peek my head around the bookshelves. The computer terminals are still all in use. From this angle, I can see what some of the internet surfers are looking at—all of it is news.

The dead body in the woods.

Dismemberment...

My stomach is twisted in knots.

Do they think Rebel is guilty, or do they think the cut-up body belongs to her?

"Adrianna. Terminal one is now open." The librarian's dull voice rings out from across the room.

"Oh! Okay. Thanks," I mumble.

The librarian points at the solo computer terminal in the children's book section.

I couldn't have had better luck—that is exactly the one I wanted. The one where I can have the most privacy, away from the other nosy townspeople.

I take a seat at the computer desk, squeezing my butt into the tiny chair. There's a small sticky note attached to the screen with the username and password for the terminal written in big red ink.

I punch in the name and password and bend down low to locate the port. I slide the USB stick inside it.

This isn't the ideal place to do this, but the police still have my computer, and there's no way my mom is going to let me use hers at home either.

My mother is worried about my mental health. This morning, I heard her talking to Dr. Raoul about me. He's been our family physician for as long as I can remember, but I stopped seeing him when I was seventeen. In fact, I'm surprised he's still alive. He prescribed me mood stabilizers and Ritalin as a kid, neither of which I enjoyed taking.

My guess is that my mother was asking him to prescribe something to me again, even though I'm a grown-ass adult who can make my own appointments and find my own doctor. And make my own decision about which medicines I want to take and which ones I don't.

She should consider having him prescribe something to her . . .

A dialogue box pops open on the desktop. Taking a deep breath, trying to push away memories of what I'd found last time I got on a computer, I click on Removable Disk E: Drive.

I open an unnamed folder. It contains two files.

The first one I recognize, because I've already seen it—at home on my own computer. DeadGirl1.

But this time there's a second file too. This one is named DeadGirl2.

I lean back in my chair, biting my fist with my hand. What am I going to see this time?

I look around to make sure no one is behind me, and then I click on the second file.

Instantly, an image pops up.

A bloody scene.

As I edge closer to the screen, my brain feels like scrambled eggs. I'm struggling to comprehend what I'm seeing, to piece it all back together.

An arm. It's not attached to a body.

A partial leg. It ends at the knee cap.

A torso. Jagged hunks of skin and gristle clinging to where a neck should have been.

Without realizing it, I'm standing up from my seat.

Someone screams—a bloodcurdling, bone-chilling sort of cry.

It takes a moment to realize the scream is coming from my own mouth.

Act Six

She's Gone to Pieces

Chapter Thirty-Eight

Loon is never lonely. There are headless clowns without arms, running around on rotten stumps for legs. Outrunning them used to be easy, but now, my feet are sutured to the ground. Every movement involves the rip of stitches, the blood making the floor even stickier.

I don't know where I am in Loon, but I know where I am going: the circus tent.

The flaps of the entrance widen, fluttering in the wind. I'm sucked inside before I can change my mind—through the entrance and floating through crowds, all the way to the center of the ring I go.

There's an audience of frozen faces in the stands; they are watching the magician. He's holding a flimsy, rusted saw above his head. He brings it down, lower. Lower.

There's a woman lying on a table in front of him.

I try to run toward her, try to help. But the sutures have regenerated, and once again, I'm stuck.

The magician lays the saw across her neck. Oh, so gentle.

And then he begins—chiseling below her chin, sawing through gristle and bone. He's trying to remove her head.

She doesn't fight. She doesn't even make a sound.

I can't pull my eyes away from the gruesome scene, no sutures needed for my lids. I'm too horrified to look, too mesmerized to look away.

He's grunting, struggling with his saw. He's sweating as he tries to saw through bone. Eventually, the audience becomes frustrated and bored, and so does he. So he changes tactics—using the saw like an axe instead.

He's hacking at the now semiheadless woman.

Her head—what's left of it—slowly begins to turn. One of her eyes meets mine. It's bright and blue.

Rebel blinks, the sound of her eyelids opening and closing like shutters on a camera.

◆ ◆ ◆

I wake up in a jail cell. Not the cell Officer Shannon uses to put away the twisted clowns in the make-believe town of Loon. I'm in a *real* jail this time—Grayson County in the town of Hornsey, to be exact.

I've lived in this town most of my life, but I've never been inside the actual jail part of the police precinct.

It stinks in here, like sweat and desperation.

Mental note: This is what rock bottom looks like.

And this is what "suspicion of murder" looks like.

I've apparently been charged, but no one is sharing details . . .

All I can think about are those jagged hunks of skin, that dangling detached arm . . .

That was more than *murder*. Whoever killed that person and created those photos did more than kill—they maimed and tortured . . . they did the *unthinkable.*

There isn't a name for crimes that heinous . . .

I'm lying on a stiff metal cot when I hear the clinking sound of keys and the door to my cell slides open.

"Lawyer's here. Time to get up," the guard says.

My neck is as stiff as a stalk of corn, like someone's been hacking at it with a blade. My legs and arms are achy from where the police wrestled me to the ground in the library like some sort of savage beast. Although, I will admit, I was howling uncontrollably like an animal by the time they arrived.

Groaning, I pull myself up from the cot and get on my feet. There's a petite woman in tall heels and a pantsuit waiting on the other side of my cell door, next to the guard. She looks out of place in the jail. She looks out of place in this Podunk town in general.

The guard leads me out of my tiny dungeon, and the three of us walk down a long, narrow hallway, past a small office and another row of cells. We wait for someone to buzz us through nearly five sets of doors.

Finally, I'm led into a cramped, windowless room with two plastic chairs, both of which are bolted to the floor.

"Fifteen minutes," the guard says. Then he locks us both inside. The woman and I eye each other warily, then sit down across from each other.

She pulls out a yellow legal tablet and an ink pen. I've got nothing on me, except the stink of desperation.

"My name is Rita Ackerman. I'm your mother's attorney. Now I'm your attorney, too, if you'll have me," the woman says.

My mother's attorney. I wonder if this woman was involved in my mother and father's divorce, or if my mother has needed a lawyer for other things she doesn't talk about. Both seem possible.

"Like I have a choice, at this point. Is my mother paying you? I hope so, because I can't."

"She is. She paid half my retainer, and your Aunt Gina paid the other. Lucky you, with two people who care so much about you," she says.

"Or maybe . . . they care more about protecting their own reputations," I say bitterly.

But it's not completely true. My mother and I have turned some sort of new leaf recently, and Aunt Gina doesn't give a damn about what the townsfolk in Hornsey think about me or her.

"Yes. Please, be my lawyer," I say, trying on politeness for a change.

Rita slides a stack of consent forms my way. I barely look at them as I sign.

"The cops can't really think I did this. Why would I go to a public library, open up an image of someone *I* killed, and then scream at the top of my lungs if I were the killer? What sense does that make, Rita?"

Rita sighs deeply. She's tired of me already.

Join the club, Rita.

"I'm inclined to agree with you, Adrianna. For the record, I don't think you are responsible for these murders. But I do think it's pretty strange that there's one dead girl's picture on your computer and two dead girls' pictures on your thumb drive," she says.

"It wasn't *my* thumb drive." There's a crack in one of my lenses from my scuffle with police. I take my glasses off, rubbing the tender skin on my nose. The optometrist might refuse to make me a new pair now that I'm an accused killer.

I was shocked by the image. And more shocked when the police came rushing in and started grabbing me, while I was still in the middle of freaking out.

I can remember struggling with the police. Screaming incoherently. Fighting back as they tried to put handcuffs on me. It's not that I was angry with them; I was angry with the killer. I was angry with the world.

Library patrons just stood there, watching. Mouths gaped open. They were probably enjoying my demise. I can see the headlines now: The Rise and Fall of a Middle-Age Semisuccessful Writer Turned Killer.

"You're a smart girl. Surely you know that library computers are monitored," Rita says.

"Truthfully, I was too focused on solving the mystery to care."

"Whose USB stick was it, then?" Rita asked.

So I tell her about the backpack and how it arrived in my possession, and what I found in the box that came inside it. I also explain how the detectives missed the keyboard and the USB hidden away underneath it.

Rita listens to the story intently.

"I'll talk to the owner. Candy, was it? But you must know—there are serious implications here. Inappropriate photographs were found in the backpack you were carrying, as I'm sure you know. The fact that you were in possession of a USB with both murder victims' photographs. The fact that you never once went to the police with any of this—they had to come to you. And you tried to fight them in the library, like you had something to hide. It's quite a mess, Adrianna."

My body shakes, with fear, but also rage. "The police also told me they thought Rebel was a killer or possibly involved in Tamara's death when they interviewed me. They don't know what they're doing. They're just reaching for something . . . anything to grab on to."

"Then stop giving them something to grab on to, Adrianna," Rita says firmly.

I slap my hands on the table, making Rita jump. "The only way I can do that is to stick my head in the sand, and I won't do that. Rebel had those photos for a reason. There was a teacher at the school. He and I had an inappropriate relationship while I was in high school. One of those photos is of me, even though it's hard to tell because it was taken decades ago! He's still there, now, teaching. He also happens to be Rebel and Tami's teacher, and the leader of the writers' club, something called SSS, which stands for *the Story Seekers Society*. That's what he called it back then, and that's what he's probably still calling it now. He was a young teacher back then, and I was a wild teen getting through my senior year by the skin of my teeth. I blamed myself for what happened. My mother blamed me too. But all this needs to be looked into in case he's involved," I say.

"Did you all report this to the school, or to the police when you were a teenager?"

I shake my head, and she lets out a long, overly dramatic sigh.

"My point is, Rita, I think it's possible that Mr. Hobbes is involved in what happened to these girls. Rebel was collecting things—pictures, stories . . . proof! She had a notebook that belonged to someone—herself or one of his students! I'm sure the cops found that in my bag too. She was planning to take him down, I know it. She was researching me and my background. She knew about a friend of mine who killed herself back then, Saffron Mulvaney."

"Whoa. Slow down a bit. Let's focus on you," Rita says.

"But that's the problem. I've been too focused on me! Rebel was trying to tell me something when she came to my apartment with her notebook. She was trying to tell me something . . . to show me . . . warn me. I've been trying to pick up the pieces of what Rebel was collecting, but I'm missing something. I'm missing . . ."

"Wait a second. Slow down, okay? I want you to write down some dates for me." Rita pushes a blank sheet of paper and a pen my way. "Police have now determined that Tami was dead several days before she was actually found. Which means that it's possible Rebel found those photos—or took those photos—before the discovery of the body and put them on your computer and left you the USB," Rita says.

I stare at her, still processing. That bit of information hasn't been shared on the news, and it changes things.

Did Rebel follow Tami into the canyon? Did she see her get murdered and take photos of it?

It takes me a full minute to remember the date of the first "break-in," when the intruder only left a childish story behind (but also an image that I didn't discover until later), but then it comes to me, and I scribble it down for her.

"It would really help if we could figure out where Rebel is. I'm of the belief that the most obvious option is probably the right one. That chopped-up body in the canyon that they're struggling to identify probably belongs to her, and you should prepare yourself for that. No more freak-outs." But none of this makes sense—if the USB belonged to Rebel, then she certainly didn't have a picture of her own torn-up body.

"No more freak-outs," I say, keeping a straight face.

She acts as though I *chose* to act like a wild animal.

The guard returns, bringing our meeting to a close.

"I'll get your bond set in a couple days, and then you'll be out of here while we wait for your court date. It's not about what they say you did or what they think you did, Adrianna. It's all about what they can prove. Suspicion of murder is not enough. They can't show intent or prove that actions were taken to commit murder. Hell, they haven't even made a positive ID on the victim. Just hang on for a couple more days," Rita says, gathering her papers.

She's right, but all I hear is *a couple days.*

◆ ◆ ◆

I don't want to spend a *couple minutes* in this place, much less a *couple days.* The jail smells like urine and bleach, and something dead and dying.

Maybe we're all dying in here . . . the life we once knew being siphoned out of us, little by little . . .

There is a stainless-steel toilet in the corner of my cell. No mirror, no clock. No real sense of time. No glimmers of humanity.

There's a camera in the corner that whirs and follows me whenever I go to the bathroom. In the tiny mail-slot-sized hole in the door, I can see the guards sitting around in a central office space. They play cards, tell nasty jokes, and watch girls piss on camera.

I feel like a caged animal. I wasn't murderous before I arrived, but I'm feeling it now.

My mind starts to wander, even when I'm awake. It's like lucid dreaming, only with my eyes open.

The stains on the ceiling form tiny patterns. Mold sprouts from the corners. Water stains look like clouds, weird shapes forming in them. Rebel's mouth and nose, two splotches form her eyes. The shapes grow wavy and blurred.

I imagine her lips moving, trying to tell me something.

Trying to tell me why she's dead.

That arm. That leg . . . That torso. The ones I saw in the photograph . . .

Bile burns in the back of my throat.

Suddenly, the door to my cell bangs open again. It's a different guard this time, a stocky woman.

"Detective's here to see you," she barks.

Detective Dawson peers out from behind the guard, her expression unreadable. This time, we don't go into a private room. Dawson steps right inside the cell with me, nose wrinkling at the smell.

"I'd offer you something to drink, but my choices are limited," I say, waving my arms at the toilet.

She takes an awkward seat on the cot, leaving me standing. I could almost imagine that she's the prisoner now, stuck in my hellish cell.

There's a manila file folder in Dawson's hand, the edge of a glossy photo poking out.

"If that's what I think it is, I don't want to see it. I'm already traumatized enough. Don't you all understand that?" I say.

I take my broken glasses off so I can't see.

Detective Dawson sets the file next to her on the cot. She looks at me, her mouth forming a tight line. It's the same look the optometrist gave me, only much graver this time.

"Why did you have an image of a dismembered body on a USB stick?" No reason to beat around the bush, eh, Dawson? It's not like I haven't answered this question ten times since I got here.

I regurgitate the same story, about finding the USB stick under my keyboard.

"Have you been in the woods recently?" Dawson asks. The question feels random.

"No." The lie comes instantly. If I tell the truth, about my stroll down to the creek, it will only cause more suspicion. And that's the last thing I need.

I didn't kill Rebel. There's no reason to try to explain my short-lived trek through the woods the other day.

"A few people have come forward to say they saw you on foot last week hobbling down the street and looking disheveled. Your lips were moving silently, almost like you were talking to someone, or hearing voices."

I bark with laughter, unable to hold it in.

"The people in this town need new hobbies. I didn't have my car that day, remember? After you all took me to the station to question me, yeah? When I left there, I walked all the way to work on injured feet, where I was promptly fired for being questioned by police and looking like a big, scary criminal. Being a criminal is bad for the nut-selling business, I suppose. I couldn't go back to my apartment, and I couldn't stay at my former place of employment, so I walked all the way to my mother's house, cutting through the woods to avoid gawkers. But apparently, I can't escape them, no matter how hard I try to hide."

"You should have just said that from the start. Lying doesn't do you any favors, Adrianna. When are you going to realize that?"

She's right. Lying hasn't gotten me anywhere. But neither has being honest.

"Why did you move out of your apartment recently?" Dawson asks, changing gears.

"Couldn't afford it. Didn't want to live somewhere where a killer was breaking in. Should I call my lawyer back in . . . ?"

I haven't done anything wrong, but somehow, every time I talk to the police, I feel like I have.

What am I guilty of?

Truth is, I can think of a million things I've done wrong in my life. For starters, I should have gone straight to the police when I saw the bruises on Rebel's face that day. A volleyball incident? That was probably bullshit. And I should have gone to the cops years and years ago about Mr. Hobbes. I should have turned around and went to the station the moment I saw those photos in Rebel's box . . . better yet, I should have called the police as soon as Candy handed me the backpack. I never should have opened it in the first place. I never should have agreed to help her in the first place with that contest . . . I never should have quit college and returned to this godforsaken town . . .

All those *coulda woulda shouldas*—what good do they do me now?

I feel like I'm a character in one of my books—but I'm not the hero this time, or even the villain. I'm just that unlucky person who never gets a happy ending. The one who gets killed off right before they reach the curtain call . . .

What's the point of writing anymore? My life has turned into its own story—only it's in the horror genre.

"Adrianna, a handwriting analyst is comparing the writing in Rebel's notebook and the loose pages we found, and comparing that to her schoolwork . . ."

I sat up straighter. Now she finally has my attention. "And?"

"That origami-folded letter was produced in the nineties, but Rebel's prints were all over it. The loose pages were written by Rebel, but the regular writing notebook definitely belongs to someone else."

My mouth falls open. "Wait. Seriously?" I knew about the letter—Saffron wrote it. But I still don't know how it came to be in Rebel's possession after all these years.

"That weird letter Rebel wrote, the one about pumpkin carving, I thought that might have been directed at me. I was pressuring her to work on the story for the contest, and she called me her writing 'teacher,'" I say.

"We're thinking that letter was actually written to another mentor. Maybe a real teacher at the school," Dawson says.

"Mr. Hobbes," I say, a sudden rush of certainty falling over me. Finally, they're listening.

"We also found some interesting things on Rebel's cell phone. We were finally able to bypass the code and get records from her cell phone carrier. You're right. She was working on a story. She had bits and pieces of it in the Notes app on her phone. I'm pretty sure the story was about you."

A story . . . about *me*?

I'm afraid to ask, but I do. "What is the story about?"

"About a girl who falls in love with her teacher. Unrequited young love. And you're not the only girl in the story who was enamored by this teacher. She didn't use his full name in the story, only called him 'Mr. H.'"

I roll my eyes. "So much for subtlety, Rebel," I say, trying to hold in a laugh. It's so ridiculous that I want to laugh. Or cry. "It's obviously Mr. Hobbes. Have you all spoken to him yet?" I ask.

Dawson ignores my question. "You had a best friend in high school who jumped into the lake and died correct? She left a suicide note behind. Was she also involved with this teacher before she ended her life?"

"Oh God." I cover my mouth with my hands. Is it possible that Mr. Hobbes was also messing around with Saffron? She was so sullen and secretive during those last few months leading up to her death. But . . . I thought I was the only one. I thought I was special. Remembering that now, I realize how ridiculous it was to believe that. But I was only a teenager. A child.

I stare at Dawson, flabbergasted.

Then I say, "Well, I knew there was a suicide letter. The cops back then forced me to read it over and over. Saffron loved folding letters into origami. She passed me notes like that all the time in class. The suicide letter wasn't actually addressed to me, though. It was given to her biological mother. And I have no clue how Rebel got her hands on the letter. Could it be a fake?"

"I know how," Dawson says, shaking her head. "Rebel went to Saffron's mother and paid her a couple hundred dollars for the letter."

"Excuse me?" I say, flabbergasted.

Saffron's biological mother—back then, she was in and out of rehab. Saffron paid the price for her mother's addiction, moving around from family member to family member and eventually being put into foster care.

"We spoke to Debra Mulvaney and showed her a picture of Rebel. She confirmed that Rebel was the one who came to her house, asking about Saffron's death and trying to get a copy of the suicide note that she still had in her possession," Dawson explains.

I close my eyes, imagining those words. This might explain why the letter was neatly folded in its original style. I can almost hear Saffron's sweet voice in my ear. *Origami. It's the one and only thing my mother ever taught me. Besides not to do drugs . . .*

The words she left behind:

> Goodbye Cruel World. I tried to make it work, but there's no place for me here. Every person who claimed to care about me broke my heart in two. I won't miss this place and no one will miss me either.

Those are the actual words she left behind, and they're burned into my brain.

Saffron was wrong—I missed her then, and I miss her now. I only wish she would have opened up with me, especially if she was also being groomed by Mr. Hobbes, like I was.

"Before you ask me again, the answer is yes. We have questioned Mr. Hobbes extensively. About his past relationships with students, and currently. He denies all of it, and the school is backing him up. They're essentially calling it a witch hunt," Dawson says.

"Of course they are," I say. No one is less surprised about this than me.

The wheels in my head are turning. Rebel was working on a story—about me, Saffron . . . She and someone else were both involved in writing it. But why? And most importantly, did someone try to stop them from telling it?

"I've spoken with Candy already as well. She assumed the backpack she gave you was Rebel's, but that's not a certainty. It's being processed for prints. Candy couldn't confirm whether the bag actually belonged to you, Rebel, or someone else in the shoppe. There is nothing with

Rebel's name inside the pack. Nothing to identify her as the owner. Did you ever see her carrying that pack?"

No, I didn't.

"We don't have time to wait for processing. If Rebel's still alive, we need to know who has her . . ." I say desperately.

I don't know what else I can say or do. All I know is that something deep and dark is forming inside me. I'm not a killer, but I suddenly feel angry enough to kill.

"I would never hurt Rebel. I cared about her. I was worried about her. I still am. Part of me is still hoping that body doesn't belong to her. When will you know that for sure?" I ask.

"It's complicated. We are missing some of the pieces."

"Missing some of the pieces?" I grimace.

But before Dawson can respond, there's a clink of metal against metal, the door of my cell sliding open.

McCabe stands in front of the door, hands on his hips like a cowboy from the Wild West.

"Did you ask her yet?" he says, directing his question at Detective Dawson.

"Ask me what?"

McCabe smiles widely. "Where is Rebel's head?"

Act Seven

She's Lost Her Head

Chapter Thirty-Nine

Where is Rebel's head? The question plays back, over and over, like a hideous, horrible soundtrack—it's like the worst song on the whole album, playing over and over, and over again.

This is the soundtrack of my life now, and I can't shut it off.

Flashes of the scene on the library computer—ripped-up leg and arm, a grisly torso. There was no head in that picture.

Detective McCabe wasn't lying—there wasn't a head. If there were one, why wouldn't it be included in that macabre display saved in the file?

I'm awake nearly all night in my cell—afraid to return to my dreams, afraid to return to my real life. There are no safe spaces anymore, no rabbit holes to slide down into.

My life is a nightmare.

◆ ◆ ◆

I wake up in my jail cell, again. This is my new life.

But Rita Ackerman's back, peering through the square again, almost like she's been watching me sleep. And they call me a creep . . .

"Another meeting?" I ask, blinking.

Rita is the sort of woman you might call *handsome*. She has thick black eyebrows. A chiseled jaw. She's wearing little to no makeup, but it's not like she needs it, anyway.

She nods at the guard, who looks half asleep himself.

"You're getting out," the guard announces, stirring me awake.

I'm on my feet within seconds.

"Out of my cell or out of this entire hellhole town?" I ask.

But if he hears me, he doesn't answer; simply, he unlocks the heavy metal door to my cell and leads me out of it.

This time, when the door clanks shut behind me, I don't look back. I can only hope it will be the last time I ever have to hear that sound or smell this place again.

◆ ◆ ◆

Reporters are clogging the stone steps of the police station. Rita moves me through the horde of zombies; they're hungry for answers.

"Keep your head down," she commands, and I listen.

The whir and click of cameras are all around me; questions flow from the zombies and buzz inside my ears.

"Were you Rebel's writing coach? What was your real relationship to the missing girl?"

"Did you kill Tamara Levy?"

"What is Tamara's connection to all this? Were you mentoring her too?"

"Why did you murder and dismember Rebel James?"

"Are you going to write about why you did it? A tell-all memoir?"

"Adrianna, where is her head?"

My breath freezes in my chest.

"Are you keeping her head as a souvenir?"

"Fuck you," I say, lifting my chin.

Cameras flash in my ghoulish face, blinding me.

By the time we make it out to the parking lot and get safely tucked away inside Rita's Camry, I'm sick. Stomach churning. Mouth burning. My own head feels like it might explode and vanish into a million particles, floating out into the atmosphere, never to be seen again . . .

There's a twist in my belly and a tickle in my throat. Promptly, I roll Rita's car window down and stick my head out of it. Vomit spews from my mouth, landing on the blacktop outside the window and dripping down the side of the passenger's side door. I hear more cameras clicking, but that sound could just be in my head. It's hard to tell the difference anymore.

"I'm adding a full car detail to your bill," Rita says flatly, popping open the glove box.

She hands me a fast-food napkin to wipe my mouth. The greasy smell of hamburgers and fries is all over it. I fight the urge to puke again.

"You going to be okay?" she asks.

"Absolutely not," I tell her.

Rita glances at me sadly as she puts the car in gear and backs out of the jail parking lot.

I stare out the passenger rearview, watching that cold building and reporters fade away, reducing all of it to a tiny buzz of ants.

"Where's my mom?" I ask.

"Waiting at home for you."

Home. I don't have one of those anymore.

No home. No job. No fucking alibi.

"Here is my advice, Adrianna, and I really hope you take it: Don't leave your mother's house once you get there. Don't answer the phone. Don't open the door. Don't talk to reporters. Don't get on the internet. If you have social media accounts, delete them."

"Okay . . ."

"Read a book, or write . . . no, *don't* write anything. We don't want any more of your words getting misconstrued or taken out of context . . ."

"I haven't written in a long time, anyway," I say dully.

"The good news is book sales are up."

"What? Really?" I stare at her, flabbergasted.

"The bad news is the internet is blowing up over this case. Amateur sleuths are analyzing everything you've ever written, discussing your mental state, your past . . . if you could be the killer, and what your motives are."

"I've written nearly a dozen books. I like how they think I have time to also go out and kill people," I say, with a dry laugh.

"Well, you've had writer's block. You haven't released a book in over a year, and they're claiming that's because you've been busy, planning and committing murder," Rita says.

She sounds so serious when she says it that I can't help but laugh.

"Maybe they should call my agent then and ask for their own book deal. Because it sounds like they have bigger imaginations than I do," I say.

Now it's Rita's turn to laugh.

The rest of the ride to my mother's house is quiet. I don't want to face my mother right now, but then again, anything is better than jail.

Chapter Forty

I know Rita told me not to write, but that's exactly what I'm doing.

Maybe this is all I needed—someone telling me I *couldn't* write—to get myself back into gear.

Three days shut inside my mother's house, with no fresh air or sunshine, has me feeling restless and uneasy.

Even when I used to go on outrageously long writing benders, I'd still sit on the porch or drive to the store for milk. But I've barely even opened the curtains.

Mom won't let me use her computer—she's acted overly protective of and slightly annoyed by me since I arrived. But I've been digging up old notebooks of mine, using blank white sheets as writing paper. I'm scribbling, my writing angry and bitter. My fingers are covered in blisters, but they feel good and well earned.

I'm writing about dark cages, injustice, repressed grief . . . everything that's been bottled up inside me. I could probably package it as fiction, but everything I'm writing is real. I need to get it all out, and I don't care if no one reads it—there are certain things that need to be written, simply for me.

My mom has been avoiding the news. And me.

Maybe it's better this way—if we go back to ignoring each other and fall into those old family patterns we're used to.

After three long days, my mother finally announces that she's going to the grocery store. "Spaghetti tonight," she warns me.

"Can I come to the store with you?" I'm regressing back to childhood, asking for permission to leave the house. Next up, I'll be asking her to bring me back a treat or a toy.

"Better not," she says, gathering up her list and purse, like she's dying to get away from me.

I get it. I do. These days, I want to get away from me too.

But then her face softens. "Is there anything you want me to get? Some more writing paper, or books? Something to pass the time until all this blows over . . . ? Because, honey, I promise it *will* blow over. I'm just worried for you. Your safety . . ."

"Some books would be nice." I force myself to smile.

"Don't go outside. Don't open the door or answer the phones . . ." she says. It's like I'm eight years old again, staying home alone for the first time.

I wait until I hear her car backing out of the driveway. Then I peer outside the bathroom window, watching until she disappears at the end of the street.

I have no plans of sneaking out. Reporters would jump me the second I stepped foot in town . . . but I do want to see what's going on in the world. And that involves internet access.

The grandfather clock in the hall starts chiming, followed by a bang on the front door.

"Adrianna, I only have one question for you!" someone shouts through the mail slot.

It's another pesky reporter trying to shout out questions I don't know the answers to. I can hear the screech of our letter box opening.

They're so desperate to get inside, to hear what I have to say . . . but the truth is, I have nothing to give them. I know only what they know, and like them, I desperately want the truth.

I slink by the front door, ignoring all of it.

The door to my mother's bedroom is closed, but luckily, it's unlocked.

I make sure her curtains are closed up tight, and then I sit down at her desk. The computer is off, so I turn it on, drumming my fingers while I wait.

The screen turns fuzzy, and then her screen saver pops up, along with a drop box, requesting her username and password. My mom has never password protected her computer before.

I punch in nearly a dozen possible username-and-password combinations, until I get locked out.

"Damn it, Mom!"

She has no right to shut me out, or to keep me from seeing the news.

Suddenly hit with another idea, I start digging through her drawers. When I don't find what I'm looking for, I slide around on the carpeted floor, looking beneath her bed and nightstand.

Jackpot.

A paper bag stapled shut is under the bed—it contains my wallet and cell phone, the ones that were on me when they hauled me down to the jail.

I remove my phone and wallet, stuff a roll of socks inside it for weight, then stuff the bag back under the bed where I found it.

Then I lock myself in my bedroom with my cell phone.

◆ ◆ ◆

I haven't looked at my phone since the morning before the library incident.

Mom and Rita don't want me to make calls or get on social media, but I don't care what anyone else wants anymore. Mom and Rita claimed that the police didn't return my belongings from when I was taken into custody, but I suspected it was all a lie from the get-go.

As soon as I turn the phone on, hundreds of missed calls and notifications buzz in.

The first thing I do is flip my phone on silent in case Mom comes home. I don't want her to know I have it back. At least not yet.

Slowly, I begin going through the missed calls and messages, one at a time.

I skip over anything that looks spammy, like it's from a journalist or reporter, which is about two-thirds of the notifications.

Aunt Gina has called more than twenty times. There are several texts from her too.

> Aunt Gina: God, I'm so worried. Your mom isn't answering her phone or keeping me updated. The jail wouldn't let me see you. Did the lawyer spring you yet?

Quickly, I text her back, telling her the situation—that Mom and Rita want me to avoid phones and news; they want me to live in a hole, basically. I tell her not to worry, although I know she will anyway.

There are other missed calls, too, some I recognize from friends or former classmates, people from college who saw the news. My agent. My editor. A few of my online writer friends.

Next, I skim through my email. There are messages there—a few from my editor, letting me know that my contract for my last two books has been terminated early.

There's the usual spam in my inbox, and then there are at least a dozen hateful messages from strangers. Calling me a murderer. A child killer. A pedophile.

I dread checking Facebook, but I click on the app anyway, watching hundreds of notifications and message alerts roll in. My wall is covered in hateful messages. Rot in hell, you evil bitch—and other variants of that same statement.

I click through private messages on Facebook and X; they are mostly just more hate mail from random strangers on the internet.

People who don't know me but who think they do. People who think they know what happened to Rebel and Tami, but they don't.

Then I log into Instagram last, nearly forgetting about it.

More hate messages.

But there's one message on Insta at the very top that stands out—a response from Christian Lorde. With the traumatic images, I forgot about the message I'd sent her.

There's a little bubble next to the message, filled with a round teenage face with a red bob inside it. It looks just like one of the photos of her I saw on the board at the memorial.

She responded to my message from last week!

> Christian: Hi! Thank you for reaching out to me. Listen, I don't really live in Baton Rouge. I just said that. Because my parents pulled me out of ND mid-way through my senior year and I've been finishing my classes online. Home schooling. I told my friends I was moving to LA because it sounded cooler, you know? I had to get away from that school. The only person who knew I was still in town was Rebel. We kept in touch. She was working on a big story. An exposé about one of our teachers who has a long history of taking advantage of young girls. Young Love, she called it. She was gathering information from me about why I left—my parents wanted to give me a fresh start, and I don't blame them. Rebel asked me questions. She was gathering info for her story. She was like that when she was focused on something. Determined af. She came to see me a few days before the murder. Tami and Carrie were helping with the project too, I think. They were working on it together and then someone must have found out and put a stop to it. I told her I didn't want to get involved, but now I'm really scared. Please don't tell anyone I'm still in town. Could we meet, possibly? Somewhere secret? The woods by Brickston Park? That's really close to my dad's

> house; I could walk there and meet you within ten minutes, or so. Just say when.

She sent more messages, asking me to respond as soon as possible.

I stare at the messages, absorbing her words.

Christian's replies seem to confirm what I already suspected. Rebel was working on something, and she pissed off the wrong people.

Meeting a young girl out in the woods by Brickston Park, after what I've been accused of, is a suicide mission. No fucking way am I doing that.

What would Rita do? She would notify the cops right away, that's what.

But I can't help myself from asking . . . from trying to get to the bottom of things . . . If Christian knows more than she's saying, she might be able to help me and the police find out who hurt Rebel and Tami. She could put an end to all this if she just comes forward . . .

I respond impulsively.

> Me: Hi Christian. Got your message on Insta. Sorry for the delay in my response. I appreciate your honesty, and I can understand why you are scared. Why do you want to meet? Can't you tell me over the phone or through messenger? I can't meet you; that's not a good idea right now. If you have information about Rebel's case, please just tell it to the police.

After it's sent, I sit and stare at the phone, willing her to write back.

I can't tell if she's read the message or if the message has even been delivered.

While I wait, I pull up the local news site, scanning through the headlines for my name.

I don't have to look long. News about the case is all over. In fact, it's all anyone is talking about in this town—which isn't surprising, considering the nature of the murders.

And then I do something really foolish. I google my name. The first hit is a blog post, dated for today.

Local Writer/Murder Suspect Released from Jail

Local writer, Adrianna McMahon, was arrested on Thursday after she made a bizarre scene in the Hornsey Public Library. When the head librarian tried to calm her down, she saw images of a dismembered corpse on the computer Adrianna had just been using in the children's section of the library. The police arrived and discovered a thumb drive containing gruesome photographs.

Police suspect that the image is of Rebel James, whose decomposing, dismembered body was recently discovered in the woods near Cooper's Canyon, not far from where Tamara Levy's body was discovered. The location of the murders is also not far from where the strange writer resides and the girls attend school. She's currently living back home with her mother.

McMahon denied that the thumb drive was hers or any knowledge of the murders, according to inside sources. All of this happened on the heels of another strange computer incident, also involving McMahon, where police found an image of Tamara Levy's dead body—that image was also found inside McMahon's former apartment.

The case against Adrianna McMahon is mounting. Sources say she was fixated on the pretty young girls, trying to be Rebel's writing coach and stalking her at the local high school and her home. She even went so far as to seek employment at the same nut shoppe where Rebel worked and imitate a police officer to get the young girl's address from the school's administrator.

Rebel's mother, Michelle James, and her father, Ronnie James, could not be reached for comment at this time. Currently, Adrianna is out on bond, pending a hearing.

McMahon moved back to Hornsey in 2020, but she isn't new here. McMahon grew up in this town and attended the same alternative, troubled high school as the girls.

In school, McMahon earned a fast reputation for fighting in school, promiscuity, skipping class, and shoplifting. She's written several strange books over the years, with mixed reviews from critics.

I have one thing to say to Adrianna—your books may have thrilled some people, but you haven't fooled the townspeople of Hornsey. There's no alternate universe in this world that could help you get away with murder, and no amount of "book smarts" will help you outsmart us—if you killed those kids, we will prove it!

If anyone has any information on the crimes or the suspected criminal McMahon, please contact Hornsey PD or reach out to my office at the Hornsey Star Tribune.

Disgusted by the article, I shut my phone off. I don't want to see any more.

Maybe Mom was right—looking at this stuff is a bad idea.

The sound of rocks shifting beneath wheels lets me know that Mom is back.

Quickly, I tuck the cell phone under my mattress in the guest room and hurry to the front door to let her in with the grocery bags.

Chapter Forty-One

My mom has always been a stickler for routines. At 11:30 sharp, I hear her brushing her teeth. Then, softly, she knocks on my bedroom door.

"You okay in there, Adrianna?"

I keep my eyes closed, pretending to be asleep.

Moments later, I hear the door to my room creak open and the swishing of Mom's house shoes. She creeps up to my bed. I feel the pressure of her body, leaning against the side of my mattress, and then a hand, soft and papery, stroking my forehead.

I wait, keeping my eyes closed and my breath even, until she goes back out. She closes the door to the guest room behind her, coating the entire room in darkness.

Hello, darkness, my old friend . . .

A sliver of moonlight sneaks its way in, casting a ghostly glow over half the room.

My mom will be asleep soon. She has always been an easy sleeper, falling straight to sleep like she doesn't have a care in the world. I can't even imagine what that must feel like. Although she did have alcohol to help soothe her into slumber over the years . . .

I've never been able to just lie down and go to bed. The second I close my eyes each night, my mind goes rampant. Every worry, every mistake racing through my mind, taunting me, doing the Sandman's bidding.

And then once I do fall asleep, I'm always prone to strange dreams. I often think that's where my writing comes from—stories created and cultivated during those darkest hours, when I'm lost within myself and can't get home.

Now home is the scariest place of all.

The cell phone is under my pillow now, gripped tightly in my hand. I take it out and turn it on. I wait for another shitstorm of messages to pour in.

But what I'm really looking for is a response from Christian.

I'm so sure there will be something, a notification of some kind . . . but there's nothing.

Clicking on Christian's Instagram page, I'm flooded with images of a happy young girl.

Christan looks younger than Rebel, and younger than some of the other girls she hangs around with.

I click on her photo album, flipping through it until I find a picture of Rebel. Rebel is with Tamara again; they're both flashing peace signs at the cameraperson, who, I assume, was Christian herself.

After that, I look up Christian Lorde on Facebook, finding nothing. I search for Rebel James and then Jane James, getting lucky when I try her birth name.

Jane (Rebel) has a profile picture that looks strange—smile forced and masklike. She's trying too hard, going through the motions of life . . .

But aren't we all?

Rebel didn't strike me as the kind of girl who hung out on Facebook, but then again, who doesn't have a Facebook account these days?

I click on her page. She hasn't posted anything in months. It's mostly memes and reposts, but there are some pictures of her and the other girls. There are pictures of her and her mom; her and her dad; and Uncle Rocky. A cute photo of her playing on the ground with Rocky's sweet pup, Sadie. And then there's an album labeled *S.S.S.* There it is again—proof that she has a connection to my former life, the same club Mr. Hobbes has always been in charge of.

What if he's the one who took those inappropriate photos?

The thought chills me, but it doesn't shock me.

For a while, I actually thought he was in love with me. I believed it back then, but now that I'm older, I realize he was a total creep, taking advantage of my youth and naivete. He was twenty-five and a teacher; I was a confused teen. He had all the authority in the world, and he took advantage of it.

As I click through the photos, I note the dates. Most of the photos of Rebel at school are nearly a year old. Something must have happened—something that broke the friend group apart.

I check my messages again, waiting for Christian Lorde to respond. Time passes, and I find myself stuck in that loop, doom scrolling, but this time it's my own life in the headlines . . .

Moving back to Facebook, I look through Rebel's oldest photos, and then all the way back to the new. Dark circles beneath her eyes, greasy hair, that forced smile . . . like there's something dark inside her, lurking just beneath the surface.

I look back and forth, dating the pictures. What happened during that year to make her change so much?

Rebel looks broken.

Teenagers evolve. Hormones get unruly. I know that better than anyone. But there was something in Rebel's life that happened and changed her.

According to Christian, she was working on an exposé—I can only assume that she was planning to expose Mr. Hobbes.

I stare at pictures of Tami and Carrie on Rebel's page. I find a few with Christian too. That's when I realize they're tagged in some of the photos. I click on their pages and hold my breath.

But then, to my surprise, my phone sends an alert. There's a new message on Instagram.

Christian: I think know who killed Rebel and Tami, but I'm too afraid to come forward. I don't know who I can trust. How do I know this is really you? Can you please just meet me so I can be sure?

My heart is pounding in my chest. It feels like thunder rolling through my body. I start typing, unsure how to answer her.

It's a bad idea. A terrible idea.

But I need to know the truth, and will I really be able to rest tonight if I don't see what she has to say? I've taken so many risks already—a full menu of bad decisions, in fact.

What could it hurt to make one more?

Me: When?

She responds within seconds.

Christian: I can be there in twenty minutes.

Minutes pass. I don't know how to respond.

But then after nearly ten minutes, I type out a final message.

Me: I'm on my way.

Chapter Forty-Two

Don't think it didn't cross my mind—that Christan might be the killer. That I'm walking right into a trap.

Lately, nothing seems too far fetched to consider, and I haven't had good luck when it comes to making decisions. At this point, I'm not sure which is worse—getting murdered or being stuck in this never-ending loop of uncertainty. So it's a risk I'm willing to take.

I creep around the guest room, finding the leggings I wore earlier and a crumpled old sweatshirt. I slip them on and yank my hair up into a tight ponytail.

After taking a deep breath, I peek out my bedroom door to make sure the house is still dark. It's been years—decades—since I snuck out of my mother's home. I tiptoe down the hallway, past Mom's door, and through the kitchen. I grab a knife from the kitchen, then tiptoe back to the guest room, locking the door behind me. The front door is too squeaky and I'm worried about the ring camera, so my old childhood habit of sneaking out the window will have to suffice.

Balancing on the window ledge, I lean my head over the side, straining to listen for any sounds outside . . . any sign that a killer is waiting by my open window or that reporters are somewhere, hovering in the dark. But all I can hear is the rhythmic croaking of tree frogs and wind blowing through the trees.

I have to do this.

For Rebel. For Tami. For all the other girls.

For me.

I take a deep breath, and then I jump out the window, hitting the ground with a hard thump.

The asphalt is wet and shiny, sparkling beneath the stars. It's a relief, being outside again. The chilly, wet air is invigorating, and much better than the stale, floral air I've been breathing inside Mom's all week. I try to suck in as much of it as possible. Who knows when she'll let me outside again?

I moved from my cage at the jail into my cage at Mom's. Being outside feels like a relief—the open air so intoxicating.

I move stealthily under the cover of night, unseen like a killer. I pass by nearly a dozen nearby houses; they are mostly dark and quiet.

Everyone in Hornsey is shut inside—afraid of reporters. Afraid of killers.

Afraid of me. I'll be the first to admit that walking around so late with a knife makes me look even more suspicious than I already am, but I promised Rocky I wouldn't give up on finding Rebel. And I won't.

Outside in the dark by myself, the walk to the park feels endless. Tree limbs look like bony claws, reaching out to snatch me up. Every rush of wind through the trees sounds like something dangerous slipping through the shadows.

The streetlights are glowing up ahead, like neon beacons of light.

Come. Come to us, they're calling. *You don't have much farther to go . . .*

There are a few porch lights on as I pass by a residential street. It's mid-October, and jack-o'-lanterns line porches and windowsills. Their mushy faces and glowing smiles remind me of the words Rebel wrote me—no, not to me. She wrote that letter to someone, but who? Mr. Hobbes?

I really hope Christian can give me the answers I need.

I'm careful as I pass by the houses, but no one seems to notice as I walk toward the shadowy mouth of the woods, edging up to the tree line.

I wonder if Christian has a car—will she drive to meet me at the park, or walk?

There are a million questions I should have asked but didn't. I just need her to tell me everything she knows . . . I need her to tell the truth and to explain those bizarre pictures, and then I need her to explain it to Dawson and McCabe.

Was she the one who took those half-naked photos of the other girls, or was it Mr. Hobbes? Or someone else . . . some other predator, preying on young girls?

Does Christian Lorde hold the answers we've all been looking for?

The park is eerie as I approach, taking my time and moving with caution. It's a poorly lit, run-down park, but it's all this town has ever had.

The old merry-go-round glistens and groans, shifting with the wind. There are monkey bars, a metal slide, and two swing sets.

The park is pretty in the daytime, with its concrete fountains and overgrown shrubbery. But at night, the angels on the fountains look dark and mysterious, their wings chipped and broken in places, their lips twisted in sinister sneers, as though they're holding secrets.

What secrets are you holding, Christian?

I enter the park, exposing myself from every angle.

Slowly, I spin around childishly, looking around the park. Maybe she isn't here yet.

My cell phone is low on battery, but I go ahead and open my Instagram. Service is shoddy, but I send off a message anyway. Hopefully, it went through.

Me: I'm here. At the park. Where are you?

Maybe this is some sort of prank . . .

I think of all those hateful messages I received online from strangers. And that hateful article written about me, authored by a member of my own community. That's what hurts the most—that my hometown thinks I'm a monster.

There are a lot of people who want to blame me for this. A lot of people who would probably like to hurt me, just like they think I hurt those girls . . .

What if someone set me up—a reporter or, worse, the killer . . . ?

But then I hear twigs snapping, see a shifting of shadows up ahead.

It looks like someone is peeking out at me from behind a fat oak tree, short and shadowy in the dark. But the shadow person is far away; with my poor eyesight and my one broken lens, I can't tell if it's a person, an animal, or a trick of light that I'm seeing.

"Christian? Is that you?" I shout-whisper, taking a few steps forward.

A twig snaps behind me. I whip around, but before I can see where the sound is coming from, someone—or something—slams into me. I fall forward fast, and hard, banging hands and knees on solid rock. My glasses get knocked off my face. Now they're somewhere on the ground, lost in the grass, and so is my knife. I scurry around frantically looking for both on the ground.

"Who's there?!" I crawl around, rolling over on my back and flailing my arms and legs in the air in defense.

There's a dark silhouette standing over me, but I can't see their face because it's covered in a thick, woolly mask.

There's a long metal object in their hand. It looks like a baseball bat.

"No, please . . ." I try to crab crawl backward to get away. Realization seeps in—that, this time, I might have made my final bad decision. One that I can't take back.

I don't want to die!

Mental note: This is what sheer terror feels like.

I flip to my stomach again and bounce onto my feet. I'm running . . . running with all my might . . .

But then I hear the bat before I feel it, a swoosh of metal by my head. The masked assailant swings it down, down, down, again and again. I'm back on the ground, face first in the grass, dirt in my mouth and nose.

I feel the shock of each and every blow, but there's no pain . . . none at all. And I'm helpless to stop the relentless violence.

The world is spinning, and the blackness consumes me, the sky falling over me like a warm blanket.

Mental note: This is what dying feels like.

Blackout

(Intermission)

Chapter Forty-Three

I keep waking up in strange places. Places I didn't create from scratch. Places I've never been.

I'm in a dark place, like a tunnel, but I can hear voices. There are many of them, and they are loud, but the words sound funny—like the warbled *wah wah wah* in a Charlie Brown movie, and they aren't getting any clearer.

Focus. Listen to what they're saying.

Slowly, pieces of sound form familiar syllables. Then tiny words; then big ones.

"She has to wake up soon. She has to, right? She's strong. A fighter . . ."

Just like piecing the sounds together, it takes a minute to connect the words, to string them together into full sentences.

My eyelids are heavy. Too heavy to open. I try lifting them, and it's like trying to move a brick with my pinky finger.

"She's stable," someone says.

"She's breathing on her own," says another.

"She'll wake up when she's ready. We must give her time," says a voice that sounds familiar.

That's the last bit I hear before I slip down the tunnel—or wait, I think it's a well. A dark and bottomless well where no one can reach down and save me.

◆ ◆ ◆

Time. It's a funny concept. You can't touch it—it's always one step ahead of you. It's like a zillion moments squeezed together.

If you take those moments and rearrange them, does time even really matter?

◆ ◆ ◆

"Does she even know we're here?"

Do you know that I'm *here?* That's what I want to say, but nobody can hear me when I'm screaming.

Someone is sobbing now, the sounds of their pain echoing through the tunnel shaft, or down the dark well—wherever this new version of hell is.

More sounds become words, and words become meanings.

And this time, the meaning belongs to a voice, one that I recognize with certainty.

The jerking sobs belong to Aunt Gina. I can tell by the way she sniffles and moans; it's almost like how I imagine a pig would sound when it snores. I used to tease her for the snorting when she laughed; apparently, she also does it when she cries.

She's whispering some sort of prayer. I didn't even know she was religious.

"It's okay. She knows you're with her. And she knows you love her. It's okay to go back . . . I'll call you as soon as she wakes up, I promise." Another voice I recognize—this one belongs to my mother.

"Call me the second she's awake." Gina's voice is stern. She never did like my mother.

Can't say I blame her.

There are paperweights on my eyes now . . . lighter than the bricks, but still too heavy to lift yet. I fight to open them. Fight to wake up.

But Gina is gone.

My mother is the only one in the room now. I expect her to talk to me. To comfort me.

But she just sits there. I can't see her, but I can hear her—she's breathing softly. If she's touching me, I can't feel it.

I hear her flipping pages—probably reading *Cosmo*.

◆ ◆ ◆

"Knock knock, anybody home?"

This is another voice I recognize—Detective Dawson.

I can feel her! She taps the side of my head. *Knock knock.* Then she squeezes my hand, gently.

Detective Dawson lets out a deep sigh. "Damn it, Adrianna. I really need you to wake up."

I focus every ounce of energy into the tips of my fingers, willing them to move.

Move, damn it!

"I wish I could say that I know who beat the holy hell out of you, but I don't. I'm struggling to make sense of it. All of it . . . the whole damn thing . . ." Detective Dawson's voice trails off, and I'm screaming inside, trying to force some kind of movement.

"What were you doing in those woods, huh? It was late—after midnight. Why on earth would you be out there alone after what happened to the others in that same area? With no flashlight, no car in sight. It doesn't make sense that you would be there unless someone put you there. I think you were moved to that location, but I don't know why. Did they want you to be found in the same spot as the others? Your pulse was faint . . . so faint . . . I think they assumed you were dead. But they were wrong, Adrianna. So wrong. They didn't finish the job. But I need you to do your job now, and that's waking up and telling me what I need to know so I can catch the fucker who did this to you, Tami, Rebel . . ." It sounds like Dawson is ranting less to me, and more to herself.

She's saying a lot of words, and this time, I understand every single one of them. Every single word.

I wasn't found in the park. I was found in the canyon, just like the others.

But I'm not dead . . . not yet at least.

Chapter Forty-Four

I can feel the tips of my toes and certain parts of my face. What I can feel, though, hurts. And my God, it hurts like hell.

I wiggle the end of my nose. Clench my teeth together.

I'm going to wake up from this.

Slowly, I focus back on my fingers. It feels like it's been weeks since Detective Dawson was here. Or maybe it's been hours. Minutes, even . . .

I can feel the flutter of my eyelashes, the pull of my eyebrows and chin . . .

Slowly, carefully, I open both my eyes.

Chapter Forty-Five

When my eyes pop open, the cool white lights above the hospital bed are blinding.

"Help." It comes out funny, like a strange animal call. But I keep moving my lips and pushing out noise, until I hear frazzled footsteps coming from down the hallway.

"You're awake!" A nurse stands at the foot of my bed, clapping. The clapping makes my skin crawl, and my head vibrates with pain.

My body is so stiff, I can't even move my neck.

"Dawson. Need to see Detective Dawson." It takes at least ten more tries before she can actually understand the words coming out of my mouth.

The nurse's eyes widen, and she nods. "First you see the doctor. Then the detective," she says firmly. It doesn't sound like I have a choice.

◆ ◆ ◆

It feels like days—weeks—of bright lights in my face, doctors, and nurses all around, poking and prodding. Asking questions.

"Holy shit, she's going to make it," one of the young medical students in the corner says, unable to help himself.

It's not Detective Dawson who shows up; rather, it's that prick McCabe. He's poised with his notebook in hand, sitting by my bedside.

"Your family wants to see you, Adrianna. But it's important that I talk to you first. If there's a chance you remember anything, I want to talk to you while it's as fresh as possible . . ."

"Where is Dawson?" My voice comes out in a whisper. My tongue feels like cotton, sticking to the roof of my mouth with every single syllable I try to push out.

"She's out in the field, doing police work. Did you get a good look at the guy who assaulted you? Tell me everything," McCabe says.

"No. It was dark, and he was wearing a mask."

The look of disappointment on McCabe's face is priceless. The most perfect example for future books.

"Why were you out there anyway? We had cops patrolling the crime scenes at the canyon. Why the hell would you choose to go out there? What was your purpose?" His questions sound like accusations, and they come so quickly, like bullets, that they make my head throb as I try to sort them out.

"I wasn't chopping up bodies if that's what you mean," I say. "I was meeting with a girl from Rebel's writing group. She said that she had information to share with me, that she knew something. I agreed to meet her at Brickston Park, but she never came. Did you find her? Did someone hurt her too?" This all feels like too much, too soon. I think about the man in the mask, swinging that metal bat, beating me again and again.

"We haven't found anyone else. Can you show me the messages?"

"Don't have my phone. Her name is Christian Lorde. We were messaging on Instagram. Look her up," I say.

"Okay. I will. But first, is there anything you can tell me about the masked attacker? Did you see what kind of car he drove?"

I try to shake my head, but it hurts too badly. "I was down on the ground, already hit from behind, when I turned over and saw him. Like I said, it was too dark to see eye color. He was wearing a mask. His hands . . ."

"Yes, keep going," McCabe encouraged.

"He was white. I could see his hands. That's all I know. And he was carrying a bat."

"Did the killer say anything to you? Anything at all."

I try to shake my head again, then wince. "No."

"I will talk to Christian Lorde and get back to you. Don't go anywhere," he says, and then his cheeks turn red.

"Sure thing, detective," I say, rolling my eyes. At least rolling my eyes doesn't hurt.

McCabe gets up and turns to leave, just as my mother comes into the room. She approaches the bed, looking pale and frail, like she's afraid to get near me.

"Hi, Mom."

She leans over the bed and awkwardly pats my leg.

"Wait, Detective. There's something else I need to tell you," I say.

McCabe looks irritated as he turns around. In fact, he's making "hurry up" motions with his hands. Still a prick.

"Rebel's story about me and the teacher. The one she was writing. It's true, all of it. Mr. Hobbes took advantage of me, but I never reported it."

My mother makes a small squeaking sound and looks away from me.

"I know I've brought this up, about you all needing to question him. But you need to do that now. He could be out there right this moment, hurting another girl. Please, lock him up until you finish investigating. Just to be sure."

I start choking, gasping for air. This has been too much and too fast.

My mother calls for the nurse, and she brings me a cup of ice chips. The nurse helps me lean up and rubs my back, telling me to take deep breaths.

"She needs a break from everybody right now," the nurse warns.

"But I just got here," my mother whines.

"Don't care, ma'am. You need to step out. You too," she tells Detective McCabe.

I don't even remember watching them go. The next thing I know is that my eyes are drooping, and it's back to Dreamland for me.

Chapter Forty-Six

Days later, they release me from the hospital.

The ride home is eerily normal. Mom listens to Elton John while I sulk in the back seat. It feels like old times.

There's this smell in the air at my mother's house—a familiar scent. I think it's been here all along, too, but it takes being away for a while to really notice it. It's this odd mixture of Mom's eucalyptus shampoo, cooking spray, and Dawn dish soap. It almost smells . . . safe.

But I don't feel safe anymore. Not with a masked attacker, who is also probably a killer, on the loose.

Before I can even talk to my mother, she's making a beeline for her bedroom. Again.

I've barely limped back to the guest room, carrying my own hospital bag, before her door slams shut.

I limp back out and stand outside her door, feeling hurt, confused . . . and angry.

"Can we talk about it? I'm sorry if I upset you by telling them about Mr. Hobbes, but I do think he could be involved in this. He was connected to those girls, Mom. He was a predator back then, and probably still is. I don't blame you for making me keep it to myself back then. Times were different, and I know you were worried about my future and my reputation . . ." I lean my head against her bedroom door.

"Your *reputation*?!" The door to her room flies open, and I stumble backward in surprise. It reminds me of those final moments, right before I went down face first in the park . . .

Shocked, I gaze at my mother, gripping the wall next to me for support.

"You were always a whore, Adrianna. Always. Screwing that teacher wouldn't have hurt your reputation. It was already damaged enough! You saw to that yourself, didn't you? That wasn't his doing. If anything, I felt sorry for that man. He was a baby himself, barely twenty-five, and a new teacher. It was *his* reputation at stake. And mine. I had lots of teaching friends back then, and how would that have looked for me? Even your father couldn't stand you. That's why he left us both," she snarls.

I gasp. My mother has always had a mean streak when she's stressed, but this takes the cake. "Let me get this straight. You're saying you felt sorry for . . . *him*? You are absolutely revolting, Mom."

I limp back to the guest room, wheezing for air. I can hear her following me.

"Adrianna, this whole ordeal has been so stressful for me. I thought I was going to lose you, and then those nurses were so awful to me . . . I don't mean to hurt your feelings. I'm just angry, and I don't know who to lash out at."

I whip around, and now it's her turn to stumble back and look shocked. I place both hands on her chest and shove her, as hard as I can muster with my limited strength.

"Never speak to me again, you self-centered, vile woman," I say.

Her face goes from shocked, to angry, to embarrassed in a matter of seconds.

I step into the guest room and slam the door, locking it behind me.

Chapter Forty-Seven

I crawl into the guest bed and sleep for hours.

Finally, I wake up to the sound of my phone ringing. It's Detective Dawson.

"How are you?" she says, her voice unusually soft.

"Someone tried to kill me, and I feel like shit. These pain meds aren't working, and my mother's a selfish bitch. How are you?"

"Sorry about that. All of it," Dawson says.

"Are you?" I don't mean to sound so skeptical, but I've lost my ability to trust in the people who are supposed to protect me.

"I am, actually. McCabe told me about the messages from Christian Lorde on Instagram. But here's the thing, Adrianna—there's no Christian Lorde at ND High School."

I sigh. "That's because her parents pulled her out midyear. She's doing homeschool now. She lied to her friends and said that she had moved to Baton Rouge, but she didn't. She's right here, still in town. Still in Hornsey. She lives with her dad near Brickston Park, apparently. At least that's the story she told me . . ."

"No, you don't understand," Dawson said. "There never was and has never been a Christian Lorde at ND High School. We did track down another Christian Johnson, though, who meets your description, and we're trying to reach her now. But we couldn't find any matching descriptions for that profile on Instagram either. The profile you alluded to is gone. It's completely vanished."

Great.

"So, what does that mean?" I say, pacing the room. It hurts to move, and I'm already out of breath, but I can feel the panic rising inside me. We aren't getting closer to finding out the truth about what happened to Rebel and Tami; we're getting farther away. "Are you saying she isn't a real person?"

"Oh, she's real all right. But I don't think you were talking to Christian. You were talking to someone who stole her photos off Facebook and used them to create a fake Instagram account. The person you were talking to is the person who attacked you; we're certain," Detective Dawson says.

"That reminds me . . ." I say, sitting down on the bed and panting heavily. "I remembered something earlier this evening. Something I forgot to mention to McCabe when he interviewed me at the hospital."

"What is it?"

"Right before I was pushed and the attacker started hitting me with the bat, I thought I saw someone else there, too . . . someone standing behind a tree in the park, watching me. But they were far away, and my glasses were half-broken. I think the attacker interrupted us and prevented us from meeting like we were supposed to."

Speaking of glasses, my lovely optometrist—who apparently doesn't think I'm a killer or doesn't care if I am—delivered me a new pair to the hospital.

I can finally see again, even if I do look Magoo-ish.

"Do you think there could have been two people involved? Two attackers?" she asks me.

"I don't know. Either that, or there's a witness who saw it all. Someone was standing there watching me get attacked . . . but there was only one person with a bat." I flinch at the memory of it.

Dawson asks nearly a dozen more questions that I don't have the answers to. While I try to answer as best I can, I grab my new iPad Aunt Gina brought me in the hospital, and I use it to log into my Facebook.

I scroll right past all the notifications—hate mail and well-wishes, what a weird combo—and go straight to Rebel's page that I was looking at the other day before Christian's messages interrupted me. I scroll and scroll until I find it—Carrie, Christian, Jane (Rebel), and Tamara are all tagged in one single photo on Rebel's profile. I click on each name, eyes widening as I look at them closer on Facebook. Dawson is right; I was mistaken.

Detective Dawson is still talking, but I'm not listening. She promises to "look into things," and I promise her I will stay safe and get some rest.

I'm getting better at lying.

◆ ◆ ◆

This time, I take the car. I won't risk getting attacked again on foot. And I wouldn't make it very far on foot, not in my state.

There's no time to waste.

I can remember where Mr. Hobbes lives by memory, only a few blocks from the school. Married. Or at least he used to be. I heard through the grapevine years and years ago, that his wife left him. I wonder why.

He never took me to his house, not even once. Most of our inappropriate encounters happened after school, in the park or down by the baseball field—or inside his classroom or car when we were alone.

Looking back, it is so clear to me now: He was grooming me from the very start.

Men like that don't get better with age; they get worse. Of course he's still doing it. Why would he quit after he got away with it—with me and with Saffron . . . and with God knows how many others since—all these years?

I think I've known all along that this is where I'm headed.

The monster in all my stories, the boogeyman hiding behind every single closed door . . . he has a face. And he's not just some piece of fiction . . . that face belongs to Mr. Hobbes.

As I drive to my destination, I can see Rebel in every single window I pass.

She's hiding in every yard . . . peeking around corners.

Rebel stretched out in the backyard, moon bathing. Half her head is gone.

Rebel wedged between a broken sprinkler and a dilapidated doghouse, watching me drive by.

I'm going to kill that fucker. I don't know how or when, but I will.

Before

It went on like that for months, the after-school one-on-ones with Mr. Hobbes in his classroom. It had started as touching in public, and then it escalated from there, his fingers reaching for me desperately in the halls when he thought nobody was watching and then keeping me after class, more and more. The other girls were jealous of the attention he gave me, but there were times when I was jealous, too, because he was nice to all the girls, not just me.

Saffron and I had become so close. She'd revealed things to me about her tough upbringing, and I'd talked to her about the problems with my parents too. But I never told her about Mr. Hobbes. It was too taboo—a student and a teacher—and I wasn't sure how she would react. But then, of course, she found out the hard way—catching us in the act one day after school, when he forgot to lock the classroom door.

"How could you?" she screamed. I wasn't sure if the question was directed at him or me, but the pain in her voice rocked me all the same.

"Saffron . . . wait." I yanked my T-shirt back on and shimmied into my gray wool skirt. I was just about to run after her when Hobbes grabbed me by the arm.

"Ow!" He was squeezing me hard. Too hard. "Let go, please," I said, struggling to get away from him.

"No." His face was so different from what I was used to; with his teeth mashed together and his eyes narrowed, he looked almost menacing.

"What do you mean by 'no'? She's my best friend. I have to explain . . ."

"There's nothing to explain. You showed up in my classroom, took your clothes off, and threw yourself at me. I know all about your history, Adrianna, and so do the school administrators."

"What?" My voice shook. Was he being serious? Last week, he'd told me that he wanted to leave his wife and move me into his house with him after high school. He said that I was the Juliet to his Romeo . . .

"Who do you think they'd believe—you and your slutty friend, or me? You'll be lucky if I don't turn you both in for this. After all, it's harassment."

"Harassment?" I said, stunned.

"I'm transferring you out of my class, and you're no longer welcome in the club."

"Wait. No, please . . . Why are you doing this?" I could hear the desperation in my own voice, and my throat was choked with tears.

"This can't go on, obviously. It's not worth the risk. We just got caught."

"But I love you," I said, my voice tiny and immature. I wanted to reel the words back in as soon as I'd said them, but it was too late.

I did love him. And I thought he loved me too.

"You're a child. You don't know the first thing about love, Adrianna. You said it yourself once—your own daddy doesn't even love you. I don't have time for you troubled girls with your goddamned daddy issues."

"Fuck you!" I shoved him in the chest, hard as I could, but he didn't budge. Instead, he laughed.

"Get the hell out of my classroom. And if you and your little bitch friend say anything about this, I'll make sure you both get expelled from ND for lewd behavior. Do you know what happens to kids who can't cut it in alternative school? They head to the next best place—juvenile hall. Do you really want that?"

I shook my head. Saffron definitely didn't want that—after all, she was already staying with foster parents who didn't like her much, and with her recent suicidal ideation, another transfer might send her over the edge.

"I won't say anything, I promise."

Hobbes's face softened. For a moment, I thought he might change his mind.

"That's a good girl. Now wipe the snot off your face and get out of my classroom."

I turned around and ran away, humiliated and heartbroken.

Chapter Forty-Eight

There's an old-timey swing on the front porch, swaying forward and back. Lonely ghosts in the wind. I recognize it as the same swing in the photograph that Rebel was sitting on.

So, she was definitely here at his, at some point.

I don't remember this swing from when I was younger. It looks like a new addition.

There were a few desperate moments when I rode by Mr. Hobbes's house as a teen, heartbroken and enraged, but I don't remember the swing. I'm filled with a sense of shame thinking about driving by his house.

I hate to admit it, but maybe that's the problem. I shouldn't be embarrassed or ashamed. I was a kid, yearning for a father's love (and a mother's), and my teacher seemed like the answer to all those things . . . all the missing pieces I needed.

My knocks on the front door sound hollow and lonely. My body aches from my recent injury and the long walk here, and I'm tempted to curl up on the porch swing and take a nap. But my anger drives me forward. It's too late to turn back now.

It's dark inside the house, and there aren't any cars parked out front. There's an attached garage, but no windows to look inside it.

I knock harder. Louder. I try to sound as angry as I feel.

But no one's home. Or they're not answering. And my body is throbbing with pain.

Leaves rustle behind me.

I whip around Mr. Hobbes's yard, seeing no one.

It was probably just a squirrel, but I have good reason to be paranoid, and afraid.

The remnants of an aboveground pool lie broken on the ground. A random water hose, twisted and bent, snakes its way around the yard, looking like a demented yet skinny python.

A snake in the grass. That's exactly what men like Mr. Hobbes are . . . They slither and prey, striking before the victim even knows they're bit.

I walk to the back of the property, slinking around the shadowy, moonlit edges of the house. The grass in the back is taller than the front; it's been months since someone took a lawnmower to it.

The screen on the back door is locked, and there doesn't seem to be a doorbell. I knock nearly a dozen times, wondering what I'd even say if Mr. Hobbes came and opened it.

If the cops won't confront him head-on, then I will. And I'll follow through on what Rebel initially intended—exposing him for his actions. His *crimes.*

Anxiously, I make a decision—to snoop. Isn't that what Nancy would do? Follow a hunch and plunge headfirst right into danger . . . ?

What's the worst he can do to me that hasn't already been done?

Call the cops? It's not like I haven't spent time in jail.

Take advantage of my mind and body? That's already been done too.

He might chop you up and leave you in pieces like me, dummy, Rebel says. Her ghost is standing by a broken birdbath, and then it disappears.

I step back and look at the backside of the house. Most of the windows are covered in blinds. I try to squint through the slats on two ground-floor windows, pressing my face against the glass.

Nothing but darkness inside.

I move to the right of the house. The side window is smaller and probably belongs to a bedroom. It might belong to that creepy bedroom with the dark bedspread where those inappropriate photos of the girls were taken.

I can't see inside through the side window either. But there's a ceramic pot full of weeds nearby, so I pull it over, grunting, and turn it over to use as a stepping stool.

It's unsteady, wobbling back and forth beneath my feet, but I clutch onto the ledge of the low, first-story window and try to get a look inside.

Little pig. Little pig. Let. Me. In.

This window offers a small glimpse into a large bedroom. A large queen-size bed sits in the middle of it. There's no comforter on the bed, but there's something lying over top of it. Is that plastic?

What if it's some sort of kill room?

There are other large pieces of furniture in the room, but they're draped in heavy white sheets.

Why? Is he moving somewhere?

That just adds to my suspicions that he's guilty.

After I climb down from the pot-stool, I make my way around the rest of the house, walking the full perimeter. The roof is sloped and skewed at the top. There's a tiny window at the very top, probably a bedroom or bonus room.

I stop in front of the garage, noticing that the garage door is slightly bent. There's a narrow gap between the door and the ground.

If I squat down and push up on it, I can probably get inside.

I have nothing to lose at this point.

After doing a quick look around to make sure no one sees me, I drop to the ground, peering through the crack under the garage door. The garage is full of tools and everyday household supplies, like brooms and rakes. A tool bench. Cleaning supplies. *Probably a saw for cutting up bodies,* I think, lastly, with a grimace.

Most importantly, there are no vehicles inside. He's definitely gone.

I'm tempted to leave now; after all, I've seen all there is to see. I can't confront someone who isn't home.

But I have more questions than answers, and I want to hear him admit it. I want solid proof. A confession. Who better to get it out of him than me?

I pull myself up to my haunches. Gripping the bottom of the garage door with both hands, I pull up as hard as I can. It slides up easier than I anticipated, the door springing up with a loud, metallic groan. I scurry inside, pulling it back down behind me before any of the neighbors notice.

There's nothing much to see inside the garage, but sure enough, there's a plain white door. I can only assume it leads inside the house.

I turn the knob, not shocked to find it locked as well. Unlocked would be too easy—something that would happen to Nancy, not Adrianna fucking McMahon.

But there's a welcome mat in front of the door. And sure enough, when I lift the mat, there's a shiny gold key beneath it.

My mother was the same way. She never liked leaving keys outside, especially inside those silly fake-rock things. But she'd always stick a spare key inside the garage, and our garage was often left unlocked, which made no sense.

Okay. Maybe I'm a little lucky after all.

Just to be safe, I knock on the internal door again, fist heavy. I make myself count to one hundred, baiting my breath, before sliding the key into the lock. Then I enter Mr. Hobbes's home, uninvited.

Chapter Forty-Nine

I'm too afraid to turn on the lights, and I don't have a flashlight either.

The side door opens into a laundry room. It's seen better days; the walls look beat to hell, black scuff marks and piles of shoes. Empty cardboard boxes and bags. There's a pale light shining from somewhere else, deeper in the house. There's a large piece of furniture in the laundry room, covered up by a sheet.

He definitely has plans of leaving town—where does he think he's going?

I lift up the corner of the sheet, just to make sure nobody's hiding under it. My heart freezes in my chest—under two layers of sheets, there is a bike. Not a child's bike, but a larger one with a small motor on the back.

Oh my God. Please don't let this be Rebel's bike. No . . .

There's no reason for the bike to be pulled all the way into the laundry room. Why not leave it inside the garage? After all, there was plenty of extra space for it, and a bike like that doesn't usually belong indoors.

I want to scream, but I can't. I swallow it down and cover up the bike, moving forward.

From the laundry room, I enter a long and narrow hallway. Moving slowly over the carpet, I try to ignore the rocking pain in my still bandaged head, the ache in my side, and the growing terror in my chest.

In the dark, I feel along the walls, using them to guide me, but also to hold me up. I'm panting, unable to subdue my labored breathing no matter how hard I try.

The hallway opens into a sunken living room with a TV and two well-worn recliners.

My eyes are finally adjusting to the dark; there are marks in the carpet, from where a couch or other long piece of furniture once sat.

He's been moving things around. Boxing up.

What are you running from, Mr. Hobbes?

I peek my head inside a tiny bathroom off the living room, then move on to the kitchen. It smells clean, like disinfectants. The counters are mostly clear, except for a few empty food containers and a dozen canned goods in a box.

He's definitely going somewhere; there isn't even a kitchen table in here. But he's been here recently, the food in the containers not yet rotten.

It suddenly occurs to me that I might be too late—that he's already gone and skipped town within the last twenty-four hours.

I look in the kitchen drawers, one by one. There's still some silverware, a few odds and ends. Match books and fast-food napkins.

I open up the refrigerator and freezer, surprised to find them still crammed with food. Frozen dinners and pizzas. Smelly leftovers in containers, a thick layer of mold on top of some of them.

I peek inside the main bedroom—the same one I saw when I was looking in from outside. The dresser is covered, but the drawers still contain some underwear, socks, and T-shirts.

Nervously, I tiptoe over to the closet. With a deep breath, I fling it open.

Like the fridge, it's full.

So he plans to go, but he hasn't yet. He must still live here.

Where did he go, though? Out hunting more girls, perhaps?

The bed in the master bedroom is wrapped in plastic—not like a kill sheet, but a clearly wrapped, brand-new mattress, with the price tag still taped on it.

Why did you replace your mattress if you were planning to leave soon? Did it contain evidence that you wanted to hide, Mr. Hobbes?

There are some suits in the closet that definitely belong to Mr. Hobbes. I don't know why, but I lean in and take a whiff of one of his sleeves.

I thought I'd forgotten his sweaty, fruity smell, but it all comes back to me in an instant: His grimy fingers twisted up in my hair. His inappropriate touches in the hallway when he thought no one else was watching. The stale coffee on his breath.

"Be a good girl, won't you?" I'm the one mouthing the words this time, but I can still hear his scratchy voice in my ear, saying them, plain as day. That creep!

Shuddering, I exit his bedroom. I never want to smell him again. Unless it's the rotting aroma of his dead body.

From the outside looking in, nothing here is unusual in the house besides the bike. Could the bike possibly belong to him instead of Rebel? After all, I never saw the one she was riding before; she was saving up for a new motorized one, according to her Uncle Rocky.

It seems like a normal person lives here, albeit one in the process of moving. And who could blame anyone for leaving this town, with the scary shit going on and the national headlines?

I'm sure he's not the only one leaving Hornsey, but I'm certain he's the only one with secrets like these to hide.

Beneath the surface, hidden beyond the average-looking house and all its normal fixings, there's a monster.

Inside this house. Inside this town. And he's been here all along, right under our noses. Just like that disgusting rat in my apartment.

There are all these different versions of Mr. Hobbes:

Teacher. Writer. Husband. Neighbor.

Rapist. Killer.

A thump from above brings me back to life. My whole body halts.

One by one, the hairs on the back of my neck stand up straight.

I'm not alone in the house.

Chapter Fifty

I should run straight out the back door. Or hide in one of the closets . . .

But I can't.

I can't hide from the truth anymore.

I'm propelled by Rebel's courage. I wear it like my own version of war paint. She is my prehistoric whale, carrying me along the rough currents of the Whispering Sea . . .

She pushes me toward victory . . . vindication.

Justice.

She was trying to tell our story. Not just hers and her classmates', but those of the girls who came before. Me. Saffron. Other victims . . .

I thought Rebel was like me, but the truth is, she's way braver than I ever was.

She was trying to ask for help, but in a way that nobody could hear. I should have been listening better.

Slowly, I make my way back toward the kitchen and through the living room.

I pass by a set of stairs leading downward into what I presume is a basement. The thump came from above . . .

A crooked set of stairs leads up to the second floor. That is where the thump was coming from earlier, I'm almost certain of it.

The staircase leading up is steep, each individual step uneven under my feet.

I grip the handrail, limping up the steps, one by one.

There are funky purple squiggles on the bar, almost like they've been drawn there with a marker. Like something a child would do.

On the second floor, I make my way toward the closed bedroom door on my left, the one with the little port window facing the road. I turn the knob and push the door open.

I didn't come well prepared, but I didn't come without a weapon either. The kitchen knife feels good pressed against my back, cold and heavy where I secured it.

I take it out now, grateful that I decided to bring it. My mother might be a terrible cook, but at least she has good cutlery.

The blade feels strange in my hand, like it doesn't belong there in the first place.

"Who's there?" My voice is shaky and unfamiliar. And it's layered with truth—I'm scared shitless in this moment. I thought that the worst thing was not knowing the truth, but right now, my heart is pounding and sweat drips down my back, and I'm more vulnerable than ever due to my recent injuries. Coming here was probably a big mistake . . .

Mental note: This is what pure terror feels like.

But this is what bravery feels like too—moving forward in spite of the terror. And that's exactly what I plan to do. Whatever happens now, I have to know the truth—if he's in this house, then I must face him, once and for all.

The knife wobbles in my hand, so much so that I'm afraid I'll accidentally drop it and cut myself, or trip over my own two feet, plunging face first into its sharp edge.

I turn the knob and thrust the next bedroom door open, jumping back in preparation.

But no one lunges out at me. No boogeyman in the dark.

I reach my free hand inside, feeling around for a light switch. When the light pops on and I see there's no one in the room, I breathe out a sigh of relief.

I wanted a showdown, but am I really ready for one? I'm not so sure anymore.

There's a small bed placed in front of the port window. It's neatly made and completely covered in porcelain dolls. Hobbes and his wife split up years ago. Did this collection once belong to her or someone else?

I walk over to the creepy doll collection, holding the knife out in front of me, as though one of the dolls might lunge from the bed and bite my face off, Chucky-style.

The dolls look less like a display and more like someone's spooky little shrine.

My heart beats like a hammer in my chest.

I look around the room, taking it all in. There's a pile of girlish lingerie stacked in one corner. The makeup and clothes look like they belong to a teenage girl. Mr. Hobbes doesn't have any children, so why are these here? It's almost like someone else has been staying here . . . The dolls . . .

The dolls are just uncanny.

I feel like they're watching me, with their beady, glass eyes . . .

I creep even closer to them, wondering why anyone would have so many . . . Did Mr. Hobbes buy these for the young girls he invited over? Or is this what he thinks of girls—that we're part of his pretty little doll collection . . . ?

There's a larger doll in the middle, a large porcelain face with its eyes closed, its mouth parted. I move in closer, suddenly hit by a tangy, rotten smell that reminds me of my former kitchen.

"Oh, shit." I cover my mouth with one hand. The knife in my other falls to the floor with a loud clank.

"No. Please no . . ." I sink to the floor on my knees, crawling toward the bed.

There's a face in the middle of the doll shrine. Lips shaped like a tiny little Christmas bow, the head too large to fit on a doll's body . . .

"No, no, no . . ." I start throwing glass dolls off the bed, but I already know.

One by one, dolls smash against the hardwood floor.

Vomit springs from my mouth and nose, but I keep digging.

I know that face—that pretty little smile.

I've finally found what the cops have been looking for—here lies Rebel's head.

Act Eight

Curtain Call

Chapter Fifty-One

There's the sound of a door opening from behind me, one of the other rooms on the second floor. But I'm too stunned to move, too in shock to do anything.

A young girl walks into my field of vision and squats in front of me, clapping like she's reached the end of her favorite play.

"You going to be okay?" she asks, holding her hands together now, prayer style.

I stare at her, my mouth and eyes wide open, struggling to make some sort of sound.

Mental note: This is what shell shock looks like.

I recognize this girl—after all, I just saw her photo an hour ago.

"You dropped this," she says, picking up my knife. She studies the blade, turning it side to side, almost like she's admiring its power.

"Please give me back the knife, Carrie," I say. But everything sounds slow and funny, and my ears are tingling.

I steal another glance at Rebel's face before retching on the floor right next to Carrie.

She reaches over and rubs me on the back. "Now, now . . . it's going to be all right," she coos.

I can't help but recall the photo I found in Rebel's room. With that big adoring grin as she stood arm in arm with the other members of the SSS writing group. Their eyes were filled with laughter, posing for the photographer, but Carrie's weren't. She was staring at the teacher behind the lens with a look of pure adoration. A twisted version of love. I recognize it—that worship in her eyes for Mr. Hobbes. I used to worship him too. But over time, I realized what he truly was—a monster.

"Shhh. You're okay," Carrie says, continuing to soothe me.

"Where is Mr. Hobbes? We have to get out of here! He has Rebel's head! He killed her . . ."

"Rebel looks prettier this way, don't you think? No longer a plain Jane, like we used to call her. Truthfully, when she's not whoring around or running that pretty mouth of hers, she actually looks kind of . . . sweet. Don't you think so?" she says, ignoring my questions.

"How long has Mr. Hobbes been hurting you too?" I ask, wiping vomit from my chin. "I saw the photos Rebel was collecting. I know he groomed you too, Carrie."

Carries throws her head back and laughs. It's a weird chuckle, loud and unhinged, and it sends chills up and down my spine.

"He hurt your friends. And when I was your age, he hurt me too," I tell her.

The smile on Carrie's face doesn't fade. Like one of those painted doll faces, she looks unaffected by all this.

Hobbes is a monster. Did he turn her into a monster too? I don't want to believe it . . .

"He never hurt me. Never." Suddenly, Carrie springs forward, lunging at me. She swings the knife, slicing my cheek with the blade.

I press my hand to the cut, ears ringing. It feels like a bomb's gone off in my brain.

My face stings, and I can feel the rushing heat of blood, but it's numb and I'm too scared to care.

"So, did he kill them, or did you?" I ask, holding my arms out in front of me defensively, in case she decides to swing the knife again.

Carrie grins, watching my blood run down the tip of the blade, mesmerized by it.

I remember those final moments in the park . . . right before I hit the ground. The shadow I saw by the oak tree, watching. It was tall. The person with the bat was short.

"You were there at the park. You attacked me, didn't you? Why did you pretend to be Christian Lorde?" I ask.

Carrie walks over to the makeup vanity and places the knife on its mirrored glass top. I use the opportunity to look around the room. This room seems to belong to her. She's been here—playing some sick and twisted version of "house" in his home.

Carrie opens a drawer and takes out something else.

The bat.

"Yes, it was me. How foolish could you be, agreeing to come there? And all I had to do was wait for you to leave the police station and plant that silly name in your head. Christian's last name wasn't even Lorde, dummy. It's Johnson. And she left school months ago. But by later that day, you'd already fallen right into my trap. There you were, messaging my fake account on Insta. I couldn't believe my luck when you agreed to meet me. You almost made it too easy. That's not very fun."

"Why didn't you kill me in the park, like you did the others?"

"Oh, I tried to. But, of course, he wanted no part in the murders. He's too good a man for that. And too squeamish. But he provided me with whatever I needed to get the job done. I was going to bring you back here and keep you. Have a little fun with you and maybe do a little photo shoot . . . but when we got to the woods, there were officers patrolling, and you looked half dead anyway. I had hopes you wouldn't make it, but I guess you're stronger than you look," Carrie says.

The photos I saw flash through my head. Girls on the bed while sleeping . . . or dead, possibly.

"You're stronger than you look too, Carrie," I say, scooting across the floor and trying to get back on my feet. My head spins like a Tilt-A-Whirl, and I can taste the blood flowing from my cheek and dripping inside my mouth.

"I saw the photos Rebel had locked in her box. You were in them too. I can't imagine what he's done to you. You've probably received the worst of it."

Once again, Carrie laughs—the sound of it an awful, high-pitched ringing in my ears.

"Now that he has me, he no longer has any use for those photos anyway. And no need for you either. When I saw you there at the school, following him around the memorial and sniffing around his classroom, I knew that I had two choices—to get rid of you like the others or pin the crimes on you. That's why I broke into your apartment and I planted Rebel's little backpack of stolen goodies at the shoppe. But you just wouldn't play along with it, would you? You interrupted me in your apartment, but I got away. You nearly messed up my master plan."

"For such a genius, Carrie, you sure made a lot of mistakes. Rebel was onto him, and you couldn't stand it, could you? She gave me the notebook she found for safekeeping. You were planning all along to follow Hobbes and Tami, and then to take her life! Rebel knew you were a victim, and she wanted to help you. She wanted to save you . . ."

"I'm not a victim! He loves me!" Carrie lunges at me again, this time swinging with the bat. She's aiming for my head.

I lift my forearm over my head and let it take the blow instead of my face.

Carrie screams in frustration and swings again, but I grab hold of the bat, and we fall to the floor, wrestling for it.

As soon as I have it, I'm struggling back on my feet, still gripping the bat in my hands.

I can't believe this small hunk of metal is what caused me so much pain, all those days in thc hospital . . .

Carrie's off the floor too, opening more of her drawers. Looking for another weapon?

I don't wait to find out, running for the bedroom door . . . but then I hear the unmistakable sound of a gun slide.

"You're not going anywhere. Now drop the bat and get over there on the bed," Carrie says through clenched teeth. When I turn around, I see that she's pointing the gun right at my head.

I do as I'm told, letting the bat hit the floor. She grins, motioning for me to take a seat right next to Rebel's head.

"It's time to join her. Although you're a little old and worn out for my collection, I guess you'll do."

Grimacing, I hold my hands up in a "don't shoot" gesture as I walk toward the bed. I try to keep my eyes focused on Carrie, instead of that horrible head on the bed.

Rebel's dead . . . Oh God.

"Why are you protecting him? He's a molester and a murderer. You think he loves you, but he really doesn't. The only person he loves is himself," I cry.

"You really think he's capable of killing those girls? Give me a break! He might be a pervert, and he's got a thing for little sluts like you, and that's what was going to get him caught in the end. They used me, all of them! They pretended to be my friends, but then they didn't want to play with me. They just wanted to seduce him and steal him away from me, but that was never going to happen. I invited them over for a party. One fun night. Lots of photos for his collection. I thought if he could just get it out of his system and realize that I'm his biggest supporter and they're just playthings, it would be okay. But afterward, they wanted their revenge on him. Just like you. Rebel stole his box of photos and told Tami, too, and they started digging up old stories and doing interviews to gather information. They even blamed him for that one girl's suicide! He doesn't deserve to have his whole life ruined! I was never going to let them expose him like that." She points the gun again, gesturing toward Rebel on the bed.

"So, what? You followed Rebel and Tami to the canyon and ran them down with your car? The police have the photos and the notebook now, Carrie. You can't get away with this. They know Rebel didn't take those photos and they know it's not her handwriting. It's only a matter of time. They're on to him." I'm trying to stall the inevitable, but I have to get on the bed . . .

"Exactly. That's why we're packing up and leaving town. He's already submitted the paperwork for a transfer. I knew it was only a matter of time before you'd come here, looking to steal him away."

"No, Carrie. You're wrong about that. I came here to confront him and find out the truth once and for all," I explain.

"Well, it doesn't matter. This works out perfectly, really. I didn't succeed in pinning it on you or killing you, but third time's a charm. And this time I'm going to do both—I'll make it look like a suicide. You were forced to off yourself after giving a confession."

"What confession?"

"The one you're about to write. Your final piece of fiction. It's brilliant, truly. He's going to love me for solving this problem, once and for all. We might even be able to stay in Hornsey together when it's all said and done, now that I've cleaned up his mess!"

Carrie walks over to the desk, digging for paper in a drawer with one hand while pointing the gun at me with the other. I look around, desperately searching for a way out and avoiding Rebel's head on the bed.

"But Tami was your best friend. You said it yourself . . ."

"She left me no other choice. But Tami wasn't the only one who betrayed me. Christian came here from Baton Rouge to try to expose him and ruin our relationship. She was going to help the others with their little project, but returning to Hornsey was a huge mistake," Carrie says.

"And Rebel? What did you do to her, exactly?"

"Well, she was the ringleader. That's why I've been keeping her, having a little fun with her . . ."

Keeping her.

I start digging through the doll heads now, clearing them away from Rebel's face. What Carrie said just now didn't add up . . .

Keeping her . . . *alive*?

The more I dig, the source of the stench I smelled earlier becomes obvious—there are small animals mixed in with the dolls. Small plastic toys with real rodent heads sewed to the top of them. Puke rises in my throat.

"Where is Christian's body anyway?" I ask.

I have to keep Carrie talking. Keep her going for as long as I can . . . But I can hear the sound of pages turning. She found what she was looking for . . .

But I keep digging.

There's a neck attached to Rebel's head. A torso too.

Underneath the pile of dolls, I've uncovered an arm. A leg . . .

Tears are streaming down my face.

I press my finger to Rebel's neck, feeling for a pulse. She's alive, but barely.

"The cops already found her. Well, most of her. She fell to pieces, head over heels, and even though she claimed that she wanted to expose him, I think it's just because she was jealous. They all were!" Carrie says, still ranting. "So I broke her into little parts . . . so she could look as broken on the outside as she made me feel on the inside . . ."

I reach for Rebel's hand and squeeze it as hard as I can.

Wake up, Rebel. Please.

"But why? I thought they were your friends . . ." I'm trying to keep Carrie talking as I finish uncovering Rebel's body, but when I turn back to look at her, I realize my mistake.

She's moved in closer. Much closer.

Now I'm staring down the barrel of a gun, wondering if it's the last thing I'll ever see.

I can't change her mind. She's going to kill me. And if she kills me, I can't save Rebel.

"I know he hurt you, Carrie. You might not understand that now, but someday you will. He hurt me too. He used me, just like he used you! I thought I was the only one, but he was seeing my friend Saffron too. He drove her to kill herself! Listen, you don't have to kill me. I'll tell the police that Mr. Hobbes killed those girls . . . I'll tell them whatever you want. We can blame every single bit of it on him if you just let me leave and take Rebel with me. No one would ever believe you're capable of doing all that . . . and I'll back you up, I promise," I beg desperately. It sounds pathetic, even to me.

Carrie stands there with the gun, smiling.

I can't get through to her. And she hasn't lowered the gun.

"Actually, I just had another genius idea! I should write the suicide letter for you—that way they'll match your suicide letter to my notebook. I'm so clever. Isn't he lucky to have me?" Carrie grins.

"That won't work. It won't! The cops will figure it out. And what about your mom and dad, Carrie? Won't they miss you if you go to prison? Because those detectives are on their way. They're coming here. I didn't make the same mistake as last time. This time I told someone I was coming . . . I texted Detective Dawson, just in case . . ."

"Well, then we better get this over with quickly then," Carrie says, smile widening.

She presses the gun to my forehead. It feels so cold on my skin that it almost feels hot . . .

Is this what acceptance feels like?

"My mom and dad didn't raise me. My uncle did, and he hates my guts. He won't miss me when I'm gone. Mr. Hobbes is the closest thing I've ever had to a real father," Carrie says.

My heart aches. Carrie so desperately wanted to be loved by the adults in her life . . . Just like Saffron. Just like me. Mr. Hobbes might not be a killer, but he's a master manipulator . . . a groomer who targeted troubled young girls who he knew would worship him. Girls who thought they needed his love and acceptance to be considered "good."

"That's not true. My friend Saffron thought the same thing. That no one would miss her! But I do. I miss her every day. And I saw you with all your friends at school. I bet they would miss you too."

Carries shrugs. "Maybe. But they won't have to miss me because I'm not the one who's leaving. That's you."

I close my eyes as she steadies the gun on my head.

I found Rebel. I almost saved her. But I'm not going to make it out of here alive today . . . not this time. I came so close. So close . . .

And just like that, Carrie pulls the trigger.

Chapter Fifty-Two

I close my eyes, but nothing happens.

When I open them, I see that Carrie's pulling the trigger over and over again in frustration, but there's only a tiny clicking noise.

"Is there a safety on this thing . . . ?"

I lunge from the bed with all my might. The gun falls from her hand.

Grabbing a fistful of her hair, I yank her from behind, knocking her off her feet.

She lands hard on her back. My hand still wrapped up in her hair, I fall to the floor right beside her.

I take Carrie's head in both my hands and slam it down again and again, screaming wildly. She wiggles like a worm, trying to get away, but I won't stop. Can't stop.

Not until I know she's out cold.

With one final blow, she lies there. Still. Unmoving.

I check for a pulse. She's alive, but unconscious.

Slowly, my knees shaky, I stand up from the floor. Carrie's not dead, but at least she's incapacitated for now.

I race toward the bed and grab Rebel by the shoulders. "Wake up, Rebel!" Her cheeks look hollow and drawn, her face so white that she almost looks as pale as the dolls that surround her.

"Please, Rebel. Wake up . . ." I beg.

Her eyelids flutter. Oh, thank God . . .

"Adrianna, is that you?" a voice says behind me.

It's him—the rat—standing in the doorway of Carrie's room.

Has he been here all along? Watching Carrie? Watching the monster he created . . . ?

Mr. Hobbes looks down at Carrie's unconscious body on the floor. But if he cares about her well-being, he doesn't show it. Instead, his face is pale with fear.

"It wasn't my fault. Carrie was out of control! You know how these young girls are. I was trying to stop her. To help her! But I was frightened of what she might do to me too . . ."

That's when I remember the gun. It got flung off the bed, and it's way closer to me than him . . .

He sees it at the same time as I do.

I dive for it, groping my fingers across the floor, wriggling like a snake to reach it in time. My fingers barely graze the butt of it when I feel him taking hold of both my ankles.

"I can't let you nasty bitches ruin my life . . . it's not worth it . . ." he mutters.

He yanks me across the floor; all the while, I dig my nails into the hardwood, clawing and screaming as he pulls.

He pulls me from the bedroom on my belly, dragging me all the way down the hallway toward the stairs.

I grab at the rug, the baseboards . . . anything to slow down the inevitable.

But then he's moving down the stairs, pulling me along with him . . .

My chin bangs hard against the top wooden step. I try to hang on to each single step as he pulls me down, down, down, but the blood from my face—as it connects with the wood, again and again—makes my hands slippery.

My head meets the floor at the bottom of the steps with a final, painful thump, and I feel some of my teeth knocked loose.

I moan, spitting blood from my mouth. But he keeps on, grunting as he drags me farther, all the way back the same way I came inside, through the laundry room, and eventually out into the garage.

The concrete floor feels like ice against my raging hot skin. For a moment, Mr. Hobbes disappears from view, but then he's back again.

With another grunt, he tries to lift me off the ground. His car is parked right outside of the garage with the trunk open. He's going to put me inside it!

But he's no longer spry, and I've grown tougher with age.

Hit with a new rush of liquid fear, I fling my arms and legs around, screaming as loud as I can. I'm off the ground, his arms tucked underneath my armpits.

But I won't go in that trunk easily . . . not for him.

I buck wildly, swinging my full body weight back and forth in his arms.

"Ah!" My body slams against the concrete as he lets go, dropping me back on the ground.

I pop up to my feet, oblivious to the pain, ready to fight him once and for all, despite the way the world is spinning.

The walls closing wildly around me . . . and I see Mr. Hobbes—the real-life boogeyman—standing with his legs and feet apart, like he's primed and ready to block me from running out. But he's wheezing, his face so red that it's almost purple.

He's not a criminal mastermind; he's a man-child, pathetic, taking advantage of young girls because he's too scared and weak to make things work with someone his own age.

"You're a sad little monster. And you created another monster in Carrie. I should have turned you in years ago for what you did to me. That was my only mistake. But I won't let you walk away scot-free again, not this time!" I scream, blood spurting from my mouth.

Mr. Hobbes is bent over, still gasping for breath, but he's staring at me. He looks terrified, as he should be.

"I'm surprised you didn't try to rape me. Or am I too old for you now?" I yank a screwdriver off the tool bench and hold it out in front of me as a weapon in case he tries to take a step toward me.

"Carrie might have killed them, but you murdered their souls first. You tore us down piece by piece . . . but not anymore. Everyone will know the real story now. We're no longer the keepers of your secrets," I say.

Mr. Hobbes falls to his knees, weeping like a baby.

"Please, Adrianna. This isn't you. I remember. You're a good girl. A good woman! And you know me. You know I'm not a killer. It's not my fault she became so obsessed with me! She had problems. Serious problems! We can get her some help. I've missed you after all these years. Please, let's talk about this . . ."

I imagine what it would feel like, to jab the screwdriver in the side of his neck. To yank it back out and watch his blood cascade out the sides like a water hose, spraying my face and everything around us . . .

But a quick death is more than he deserves, and I won't let him make a monster out of me.

Mental note—this is what vindication feels like.

Chapter Fifty-Three

Detective Dawson runs in, gun drawn.

"Are you okay?" she asks, eyes widening as she takes in the blood pouring from my mouth and Mr. Hobbes sobbing like a small child on the garage floor.

"I'm okay, but he's not. He was molesting those girls, just like he did me and Saffron when we were younger. He knew about the murders and did nothing."

I know I must look frightening, like someone walking out of a horror movie.

That's what I feel like. Like some sort of final girl. But, thankfully, I'm not alone.

"Rebel is upstairs. She needs paramedics. And Carrie is in there too, knocked out on the floor. She'll also need an ambulance. She kidnapped Rebel. She killed Christian and Tami too."

Dawson is already squawking into her radio. She yanks Mr. Hobbes to his feet and starts placing him in handcuffs.

By the time I make it back inside the house, I can already hear the sirens. They're coming. Help is coming.

I follow the blood—my own trail—up to the second floor. My entire body roars with pain, but I keep going . . . stumbling up the stairs in tears. I can't stop now. I'm so close.

I have to get back to Rebel.

I don't know if she's going to make it, but either way, I won't leave her alone.

I stumble and fall, landing on the floor with a cry. But I can't stop. Won't stop.

I crawl over Carrie's unconscious body on the floor and pull myself onto the bed with a grunt. I lie on the bed next to Rebel. Her eyes are closed, but she's still breathing. Her pulse is weak, but it's there.

I close my eyes, too, and let the darkness consume us both.

Finale

Chapter Fifty-Four

There are all these versions of me walking around this town. But this one is my favorite: the one I become when I know I have to. The one who feels weak sometimes but knows she must be strong—because other girls are watching.

"I told you already. I don't want to be a writer." Rebel rolls her eyes at me and picks up the college application.

"Journalism school. That's kind of the same thing, though, isn't it?" I ask playfully.

"Nah. Writers lie. Journalists tell the truth."

I can't help it; I laugh. She's right, sort of.

Rebel hasn't been the same since her abduction. There's a haunted look in her eyes, darker and more mysterious than ever before. But there's something else there too—a new kind of strength. Determination. She's grown up overnight.

"It's true, I guess. But fiction is its own sort of truth, don't you think? The truth is in the margins . . ." I say.

Rebel grabs a pillow off the couch and hurls it at my face. "See? That's exactly what I'm talking about. Why do writers talk like that?"

"Like what?" I say, still laughing.

"In riddles. It's annoying."

My phone chimes, interrupting our usual banter.

Since getting out of the hospital and turning eighteen, Rebel has chosen to come stay with me at Aunt Gina's quite frequently.

"It's my agent," I say in a hushed whisper while reading the text.

"So? Spill it," Rebel demands.

"I got an offer on the new book!" I squeal.

Rebel comes over and sits beside me. I'm expecting another playful jab, but she reaches out and hugs me instead.

My eyes fill with tears. My instinct is to wipe them away, but I let them fall.

"I'm so proud of you," she tells me.

Before I can respond, she asks, "What's this book about anyway? Please don't tell me it's a memoir."

"Nope. Not a memoir. It's not even about the murders. I'm writing something light and fluffy, a small-town space-themed romance, believe it or not. And it's not exactly a book. It's a play, like a story performed in acts," I explain.

Rebel raises her eyebrows. "So that's why you've been keeping it a secret from me. Your secret project. Please tell me it's not based on your experiences with my uncle." Rebel makes a fake gagging sound, and I roll my eyes.

"It's not that serious," I say, nudging her.

But it is. Rocky and I have been on several dates now, and for the first time, I actually enjoy having someone's company, someone who isn't a book character.

"Maybe it's about the other new love in my life," I tease, reaching over to pick up Gizmo, my adorable hairless cat.

"Double yuck." Rebel scrunches up her nose at the cat but reaches out to pet him. I know she loves him too.

"I'm going to miss you when you go away to journalism school, but I'll be rooting for you every step of the way," I say.

Rebel smiles. "Don't worry. I'll write some stories about you in the funny papers."

I think about the last time I saw my name in print. "God, I hope not," I say, shaking my head.

She must be thinking about it, too—not my name in the headlines, but her own. In the months that have followed the murders and her abduction, she's read every story and every post that occurred while she was missing. I thought she would want to keep it to herself—all the trauma and pain—but Rebel's generation isn't like the ones that came before it. She's talked about her abuse by Mr. Hobbes, the abduction, and the murder of her two school friends, both in print and publicly, on social media.

Christian Johnson and Tamara Levy were not only victims of abuse and murder; they were failed by the troubled-teen school system and every adult who didn't protect them along the way. There are days when I wonder if I should include myself in that list of failures. If I had only come forward about Mr. Hobbes, all those years ago . . . but then I remind myself that I was a child too. It was my own mother who should have taken me more seriously and come forward back then.

Christian Johnson's head was located in the basement of the Hobbes's House of Horrors, as the papers have dubbed it. It was found among another collection of dolls that had been tossed away in a pile of dirt downstairs, like they were yesterday's garbage. The pieces of her body were brought back together, and she received a proper burial by her family. Her own parents, who thought she'd gone away to start early college-course credits in Baton Rouge, were never even aware that she'd gone missing.

There was another memorial service for both the girls, Tamara and Christian. This one was held at a local community center instead of the school.

Rumor is, the school is under investigation and might be closing soon, as it's been unable to hold up in the eye of public scrutiny and is going bankrupt due to the cost of legal fees, fighting all its subsequent pending lawsuits by female students.

Carrie pled guilty to the murders. Even though she's a minor, she'll be tried as an adult and will probably receive the maximum sentence for her crimes. She's currently being held in Hornsey Jail, awaiting transport to Logansport Juvenile Correctional Facility. I know what the inside of that jail looks (and smells) like, and I can't help imagining what she's thinking, and feeling, in there.

Is she too far gone to realize the truth—that ultimately, she is a victim too? A victim who became a monster . . . ?

I don't know which prison Mr. Hobbes will be going to, and I don't care. His trial will be held next year, but there's overwhelming evidence that will put him away for good so that he'll never groom and destroy another young person again.

Aunt Gina joins us in the living room with a platter of crackers. She's elevated her platter game from when I was a kid, including weird new things as toppers—fish eggs, fancy cheeses, and spicy mustard.

She places the tray on the coffee table, returns to the kitchen, and comes back holding a binder. It's my book. When I was little, I used to share my stories with her. As an adult, I never did. But this time, I decided to let her read it before submission.

The only problem is that I'm super impulsive, and I went ahead and turned it in anyway.

"The story is good, but I do have some notes for you before you submit it," Aunt Gina says, sitting down with the book in her lap and popping a whole cheese cracker into her mouth.

Rebel looks at me, like, *Should we tell her the book's already sold?*

I shake my head and try not to smile.

"Yes, please! I'd love to hear your feedback, Gina," I say.

"Well, first off, plays typically only have three acts, with a maximum of five. So you made a critical structural error, right from the start."

Oops. I hope my readers forgive me.

I listen as she goes on, sharing a mixture of compliments and criticism, all while I'm eating and trying not to look at Rebel. I know that if I do, I'll laugh.

As excited as I am to be back in the world of writing fiction, my real life is turning out to be okay. Better than okay.

I like this version of me—the healing one.

If I say it enough, maybe I'll even start to believe it.

Acknowledgments

Of all the books I've written over the years, there is no single book that has given me a bigger headache than this one. Please let me explain—there are all these versions of this book, walking around this town. You just experienced some of them, but most of them you didn't. I came up with the plot for this book in 2015 as a new baby writer and got to work on it. I was so certain it would be "the one"—the one book that would get me signed by a literary agent and, ultimately, lead to a good publishing deal. Although I'm normally a fast writer, I spent years writing and rewriting this one and making little progress. It felt like it was missing something, but I couldn't put my finger on what that "something" was.

Ultimately, I decided to set the novel aside (it was then loosely named *Pretty Little Dead Girls*), and I got to work on my next project. My next book was written with a fair amount of ease compared to this one, and as it turns out, it was "the one"—a thriller some of you may have read called *My Sister Is Missing*. It was, in many ways, my "breakout novel" and it was the story that led to me signing with my agent and securing my first major book deal. After *My Sister Is Missing*, I went on to write nearly a dozen more books, but THIS story—the story of a struggling writer who connected with a troubled teen—just wouldn't go away. In between projects and deadlines, I would pull this story out and read it, again and again, thinking of ways I could do it better.

Finally, in 2024, I decided the book could be used as inspiration, but it was nowhere near where it needed to be. Therefore, I tucked it away in a drawer for good and completely rewrote it from scratch, from the bottom to the top. I discovered what was missing in the story along the way—ME. I needed those years of struggle in both the writing industry and life in general, and years of finding my VOICE, before I could pull off the voice behind the characters of both Adrianna and Rebel. I finished the rewrite in a few short months, and I've never enjoyed writing any book as much as this version of it. The story is so, so different from the original—but it's finally the story I needed and wanted to share.

Dear readers, I truly hope you enjoy this dark and quirky little story even half as much as I enjoyed writing it. If you don't, that's okay too—there have been plenty of days when it pissed me off too. No matter what, I appreciate you taking the time to read it and giving me a chance when I know there are so many incredible books and authors out there to choose from.

Now let me step down from my soapbox and thank some people, the REAL ones—my incredible literary agent, Katie Shea Boutillier, who scooped me out of her slush pile and changed my life in 2018 when she signed me. Katie has stood by my side through some of my best writing moments, and also my worst, and I appreciate her more than I could ever put into words; and that's saying a lot because I do LOVE words!

To Jessica Tribble Wells, my absolute DREAM EDITOR (!!!) for believing in me and this story and giving me a chance to join the Thomas & Mercer family. Jessica is the editor for some of my favorite authors, including Jess Lourey, Minka Kent, and Rachel Howzell Hall. Having an opportunity to collaborate with her on this story felt very surreal, and I will never stop feeling grateful for her support.

Thank you to Manu and the entire team at Thomas & Mercer for your help in making this story the BEST possible version of itself. Thank you to all my editors I've worked with in the past, who have helped shape me into the writer I am today: Toni Rakestraw, Charlotte Ledger, and Jennie Rothwell. Thank you to all the amazing authors, especially those in the crime thriller and mystery genres, who have inspired me along the way and kept me entertained over the years with your brilliant stories.

Thank you to my beautiful family: Shannon, Tristian, Dexter, and Violet! Thank you all for loving me, believing in me, and putting up with my grumpy and distracted writing days. In another version of my life, I work as the team lead for a group of crisis counselors. I would like to thank each and every single one of my coworkers, for inspiring me with your empathy and strength every single day.

Most importantly, thank YOU, dear reader. To all my readers, old and new, you are the reason I get to do this job every day, and being able to entertain and distract you from your daily lives with my stories is a privilege I will never take for granted. THANK YOU.

Direct Services for Crime Victims

988 Suicide & Crisis Lifeline

- Call or Text*: 988
- Chat: https://988lifeline.org/chat

Childhelp National Child Abuse Hotline

- Call or Text*: 800-4-A-CHILD (800-422-4453)
- Chat: https://childhelphotline.org

Courage First Athlete Helpline

- Call or Text*: 888-279-1026
- Chat: www.athletehelpline.org

Cyber Civil Rights Initiative Intimate Image Abuse Helpline

- Call: 844-878-2274

Defined Monetary Assistance Victims Reserve, US Department of Justice (restitution for victims of child pornography)

- Call: 844-487-2282
- Email: DMAVictimsReserve@usdoj.gov

Disaster Distress Helpline

- Call or Text*: 800-985-5990

Female Genital Mutilation/Cutting Survivor Support Line

- Call: 877-751-0880

Love is Respect (dating abuse)

- Call: 866-331-9474
- Text*: LOVEIS to 22522
- Chat: https://loveisrespect.org

Mothers Against Drunk Driving

- Call: 877-MADD-HELP (877-623-3435)

National Domestic Violence Hotline

- Call: 800-799-7233
- Text*: START to 88788
- Chat: https://thehotline.org

National Elder Fraud Hotline

- Call: 833-FRAUD-11 (833-372-8311)

National Human Trafficking Hotline

- Call: 888-373-7888
- Text*: 233733
- Chat: https://humantraffickinghotline.org/chat

National Organization of Parents of Murdered Children

- Call: 513-721-5683

National Runaway Safeline

- Call: 800-RUNAWAY (800-786-2929)
- Chat: www.1800runaway.org

National Sexual Assault Hotline

- Call: 800-656-HOPE (800-656-4673)
- Text: HOPE to 64673
- Chat: https://hotline.rainn.org/online
- Español: https://hotline.rainn.org/es

Safe Helpline (sexual assault support for the DoD community)

- Call: 877-995-5247
- Chat: online.safehelpline.org

StrongHearts Native Helpline (domestic, dating, and sexual violence support for Native Americans)

- Call or Text*: 844-7NATIVE (844-762-8483)
- Chat: https://strongheartshelpline.org

Connect with the Author

- Amazon author page: http://amzn.to/2bKQCyz
- Twitter/X: https://x.com/carissaannlynch
- TikTok: https://www.tiktok.com/@carissaannlynch
- Facebook: https://www.facebook.com/CarissaAnnLynchauthor
- Instagram: https://www.instagram.com/carissaannlynch_thrillers/

About the Author

Photo © 2019 by Danté Cooper

Carissa Ann Lynch is the *USA Today* and *Wall Street Journal* best-selling author of *The Bachelorette Party*; *The Traitors*; *The Summer She Disappeared*; *My Sister Is Missing*; *Without a Trace*; *Like, Follow, Kill*; *The One Night Stand*; *She Lied She Died*; *Whisper Island*; *The Secrets of Cedar Farm*; and more. She lives in a small town on the border of Indiana and Kentucky with her partner, children, cats, and a growing collection of books. She has a degree in psychology and has always been a little obsessed with the darker areas of the human mind. When she's not writing, she works as a suicide and crisis intervention counselor and coaches a team of emergency service workers on how to assess risk and respond to community mental health crises and disasters.